# Love and Sportsball

# LOVE *and* SPORTSBALL

## MEKA JAMES

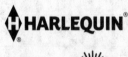

Recycling programs for this product may not exist in your area.

ISBN-13: 978-1-335-57483-1

Love and Sportsball

Copyright © 2024 by Meka James

For questions and comments about the quality of this book, please contact us at CustomerService@Harlequin.com.

Harlequin Enterprises ULC
22 Adelaide St. West, 41st Floor
Toronto, Ontario M5H 4E3, Canada
www.Harlequin.com

Printed in U.S.A.

# One

## Khadijah

*This is going to be fine. I'm going to have fun.*

I repeated the mantra in my head as I sat in my sister's luxury crossover vehicle, with what she deemed "sultry makeup" and a casual but 'sexy-adjacent' outfit headed to parts unknown.

Since I'd told my family I'd landed the job with the Atlanta Cannons as the athletic trainer and would be moving back, Jah had been on me to go out and have a girls' night. I'd had to delay for a while since first I had to deal with organizing the cross-country move. Then I'd needed to get settled. It'd been at the top of my priority list to have my house in order before work. I couldn't think otherwise.

I trusted my sister…mostly, but it was killing me she'd refused to tell me where we were going for the night. Her behavior at my house, coercing me to change clothes, sprucing up my makeup, had me thinking some sort of setup was in my future.

*This is going to be fine. I'm going to have fun.*

It wasn't as if I didn't want to have a good time. Go with the flow and let my hair down as the saying went, but relaxing didn't come easy. However, after the stress of the last year—two if I really wanted to be honest—I did need a night out.

She easily maneuvered her Mercedes through the streets of Midtown until she got to Atlantic Station. The area had a good mix of restaurants and bars to choose from. After circling the parking deck a few times, she snagged a space surprisingly close to the elevator.

"Now will you tell me where we're going?" I asked as we exited the car.

Still she said nothing as we walked toward the elevators. The doors opened with a soft swish, and we stepped to the side to let the current passengers off before we entered.

"Jah?" Impatience colored my tone. "I've caved and given in to your demands, the least you can do is finally let me in on the destination."

She rolled her eyes and pressed the button for the ground level. "It's a bar/lounge place that opened maybe a year or so ago. I thought you'd like it." Her answer sounded like an exasperated sigh.

Again, I narrowed my eyes at her.

She was my ride, and once I gave my word, I didn't go back, so there was no escaping. Plus, I really had missed hanging out with her. It'd been too long, and life would be shifting once she gave birth. Letting her vagueness go, I followed her off the elevator and across the street to another sleek-looking building.

*This is going to be fine. I'm going to have fun.*

The area was upscale—surely the atmosphere wherever we

were headed would be more comfy couches, glass of wine vibes rather than cheap drinks, loud thumping music and too many bodies gyrating on a too-small dance floor. Jah pushed the button in the second elevator for a place called Lucky Lady.

I scrunched my face in confusion. "An Irish bar?"

The grin she displayed was not comforting. "Not quite." She proceeded to check her reflection in the mirrored doors, adjusting her breasts to maximize her cleavage in a cowl-neck halter top that dipped so dangerously low it could cause a wardrobe malfunction if she moved the wrong way. Coupled with the faux-leather maternity pants, her outfit was the perfect combination of cute and sexy. Her thick black waves had been brushed and gelled into submission close to her head for a tight ponytail, but they reigned free at the end. Large gold hoop earrings, bangle bracelets, silver eyeshadow, and deep red lips completed her look.

"What?" she asked in response to my frown. "I haven't always had these. Hopefully they stick around after I've squeezed this kid out because my boobs have never looked better."

I laughed at her answer, though she wasn't wrong. In the genetic lottery she got the height, standing nearly five-nine, taking after our father. A fact she liked to tease me about since I stopped at five-five—on a good day, with heels—but I did get the chest, so I called us even. We'd both inherited our mother's rich ebony complexion and thick black curls from our father.

When the elevator stopped, the insulated car gave way to a current R&B radio hit, but remixed. Lucky Lady was nowhere near an Irish pub, but instead was an upscale, ritzy nightclub.

*Okay, I could work with this.*

After showing our IDs to the bouncer at the entrance, Jah

immediately danced her way into the place, quickly and easily picking up the rhythm.

She turned to face me, grin wide, wiggling her fingers in a come-hither motion. "Whaddya think?"

It was nice. The music was audible without being overbearing or forcing you to shout. There was a large main bar along the mirrored wall to the right. The leather-bound counter spanned the entire length, allowing for generous seating and strategic openings for walk-ups to order. It was hard to get a good idea of the color scheme due to the purple-and-fuchsia lighting cast throughout the entire place. However, the rotating spotlights sometimes landed on one of the matching leather sofas. White, maybe.

What really stood out was from the patrons to the waitresses to the bartenders, hell, even the security at the elevator, there wasn't a man in sight. I snapped my gaze back to Jah, who was still dancing, and cheesing like the Cheshire Cat.

With quick steps, I closed the small distance between us. "Really, Jah? Really?"

Not as bad as the blind date I was sure she was trying to set me up on, but still, a setup nonetheless.

"What?" She linked her arm in mine and directed us toward the massive bar. "I think it's great. I'll have you know I make an excellent wing-woman. And I'm a built-in DD, this way you can have a few, because this is a celebration, and I can drive you home. Maybe."

I narrowed my eyes. "What do you mean maybe?"

She lifted a shoulder. "Well, I'm hoping you might find some hottie and…" She let her comment die off but the conspiratorial smile on her lips was plenty.

*Fucking hell. I knew better. I fucking knew better.* I should have stood my ground and pushed to know what the plans were because I could have nipped this in the bud.

I took in a calming breath. "So…let me get this straight, my sister has brought me to a lesbian bar in hopes of getting me liquored up and sending me off with some rando for a one-nighter?"

She paused and tapped her chin. "Yup! Now let's get those drinks." There was not a hint of shame to be found in her.

Arching her back to make her stomach look bigger than it was, she maneuvered us through the not-so-thick crowd and managed to secure us two seats near the end of the bar. I worked to stamp down my annoyance at her, and frankly at myself for not pushing like I should have. It'd be fine though. Not like her plan would work anyway, because random hook-ups were a no-go for me. I needed timelines, projections of where the future was headed. How soon we should move in together. When marriage talks should start. Like with my career, I had a checkpoint in my head for each of those steps and more, which always eventually became a point of contention with whoever I was dating.

I pressed my lips together and again repeated my night's mantra in my head.

*This is going to be fine. I'm going to have fun.*

I could salvage the night by keeping the focus on spending time with my sister despite her less-than-honest intentions. From where we sat, we had a decent view of the entire place. My attention drifted, taking it all in, before zeroing in on the back corner where heavy black velvet curtains were drawn partially closed. A woman sat on a stool next to the red ropes, the word *Security* emblazoned on her T-shirt.

"You know, I thought this night was supposed to be about us. Catching up, hanging out like old times. Why are you trying to pawn me off?"

"Because you need to unwind a little. You've been more uptight than usual with the move and everything," she answered while signaling for service. Once she got acknowledgment from the bartender, Jah gave me her full attention. "Seriously, I've been in my house for four years and still have boxes I haven't unpacked. But you, you had your place put together in a weekend. That's not natural."

I laughed at her comment. "So, because I like order and organization, you think I'm too uptight and need to get laid?"

She nodded. "Something like that. Not to mention how those assholes did you dirty in LA. You came out on top like the boss bitch you are. But that doesn't mean you don't need and, more importantly, deserve all the stress relief."

I didn't want to think about my old job; however the mention of it burned sour in my stomach. But I wouldn't let the memory ruin the night. And I would never admit to Jah she was right. I would have loved nothing better than a night of mind-blowing, no-strings sex. But given my propensities, I didn't trust myself.

"You know a spa day works just as well as sex."

A woman who appeared out of nowhere to Jah's left laughed with my sister. When I made eye contact with the stranger, my breath caught. Even though she was slightly leaning, her impressive height was the first thing I noticed, though being a tad vertically challenged, it was something I *always* noticed.

She was stunning.

Golden-bronze braids done half up in a topknot highlighted her face like a beautiful work of art. A sculpture I wanted to gaze upon for hours. Full lips on her wide mouth stood out against her smooth light brown complexion. Thick, shapely eyebrows and long lashes set off dark eyes that sparkled in a mesmerizing chestnut color. With thoughts of sex already running through my head, my body scrambled to hopeful attention.

I glanced away, but not before I noticed a smirk on Jah's lips. Luckily, the bartender arrived, which stopped any sort of comment from my sister.

The bartender's brows knit together when she laid eyes on the woman I was trying not to stare at. "Are they not taking care of you back there?"

"No, they are. But since I'm already out here I figured…"

*Jesus, even her voice was sexy. Smooth and a little husky.*

"Alright, just needed to make sure I don't have to get in somebody's ass. Whatcha need?"

Tall-and-sexy inclined her head toward us. "Them first."

How often did she come here, because their exchange made it seem like she was a regular. I shook off the thought—it was no business of mine. I was here to have a little fun—I cast another glance at the beautiful woman—maybe some flirting, but nothing more despite Jah's suggestions.

The bartender nodded then rested her tattoo-covered forearms on the wood top. "What can I get y'all?"

"What mocktails do you have?" Jah asked.

The young woman straightened, tilted her head, and shrugged. "I can make you whatever you want."

"A martini, extra dirty," Jah added, with a full-on flirtatious smile.

She was shameless and I couldn't help but laugh. She wanted a night out and in truth I wanted—no, needed—the same. Buying a house, then organizing a cross-country move, and getting settled before my first day of work had me extra stressed. But I'd made a plan and had executed it near flawlessly.

"You got it. And for you?"

I shot Jah a side eye, then looked back at the bartender. "Um, do y'all have a signature drink?" She gave a curt nod. "Okay. I'll take that."

Jah clapped her hands. "See, that's the spirit. Seriously, I want you to have a good time tonight. You are all business all the time. Take a breather and enjoy the moment." She squeezed my hand, and her dark eyes softened.

I knew she was right, and even though sometimes unconventional, she wanted the best for me.

"One Virgintini, extra dirty, and a Lucky Lady comin' right up." The bartender set her attention back on the distractingly beautiful woman I was trying to not drool over. "And you?"

"Macallan on the rocks. And I'll take care of theirs." The corner of her mouth lifted into a half smile as the bartender nodded and walked off.

"Oh, you don't have to," I said.

Jah turned her stool so she fully faced the woman. "What my sister meant was thank you." She stuck out her hand. "I'm Jahzara, but most folks call me Jah."

"Nice to meet you. Shae." She shook Jah's hand.

The silver watch on Shae's wrist caught the light and brought attention to the intricate, colorful ink covering her right arm.

The design disappeared beneath her button-down top and I instantly wanted to run my fingers along the artwork and see where it led.

She fixed her gaze on me. "And you are?"

"Single," Jah blurted out.

"Jah!"

"What? You are." She shrugged as if her comment wasn't massively embarrassing.

I closed my eyes and shook my head, trying not to go off on my sister. Good intentions or not.

*Have fun. Have fun. Have fun.*

Mentally I reminded myself of the goal for the night. No pressure. No expectations of what needed to come next. Just good ol'-fashioned fun. When I opened my eyes, Shae had an amused expression on her face as she patiently waited for me to answer. I stretched my hand out and Shae wrapped her warm fingers around mine.

I swear a jolt shot through me, zinging all the way to my toes. Dating was off the table for me, and I'd dismissed Jah's lewd and ludicrous suggestion from earlier, but if ever there was a person who could make me say "what the hell" and simply live my best life for a single night, it would be the tatted goddess Shae.

I relaxed my shoulders and put a smile on my face. "You can call me Dijah."

# Two

## Shae

Dijah…the sound of her name was a soft caress to my ears. When I'd agreed to go out with my teammates one last time before preseason training started, I'd told myself I'd keep it low-key, be more reserved and avoid temptation. Sasha's increasing inappropriateness had me fleeing the VIP area, leaving my teammate Courtney to deal with her wife. I'd been ready to scoop up my other teammate Tina and call it a night when I'd spotted Dijah.

The first thing I'd noticed was her hair. It was hard to miss. Thick and beautiful, the fullness framed her face almost like a halo. She was even more beautiful up close with dark smooth skin so flawless it damn near glowed. Warm deep brown eyes sucked me in. They were like orbs of onyx, and the eyeshadow and liner she'd applied amplified their almost mystical appearance. Her cheekbones were dramatic and the dimple that appeared when she smiled made her lethal. The moment I spotted her, my legs had me moving in her direction before my brain seemed to process what I was doing.

Paying for their drinks had been risky because if they were a couple, it could have caused an issue, especially with the large ring on Jah's finger, but her enthusiastic acceptance had deleted that worry.

Mai returned with our drinks, nodding at me before walking off to take care of the other waiting patrons.

"A toast," Jah said. "To new acquaintances and good times."

Jah winked at her sister who in turn rolled her eyes. But after we clinked glasses, I noticed the slight grin Dijah hid behind her drink before taking a sip.

I waited for some spark of recognition. Not to be cocky—because admittedly we didn't have the same level of fame as NBA stars—but since me and a couple of the other players had gotten some endorsements, including TV commercials, we got recognized more often than we used to. But neither of them seemed to have any clue. Which could work in my favor. Because recognition was a double-edged sword; on one hand, it was great to be gaining fans for the league, but on the other, some forgot the "don't kiss and tell" idea when faced with their fifteen minutes of fame.

"I'm going to run to the ladies' room. Shae, can you keep my seat warm for me?" Jah asked.

"I have a better option, if you two are up for it?"

"Couches instead?" Dijah asked.

"Close," I replied. "Come with me."

Jah slid from her stool first, and with more of my focus being on her sister, I'd totally missed the protruding belly. Both ladies grabbed their drinks, and I led them to the VIP area.

"Oh. You fancy," Dijah said, a hint of humor coloring her tone.

"Sometimes." I laughed.

I expected the "what do you do" question, but it never came. I used to think doing VIP was pretentious, but I was learning it had its perks. Sometimes I wanted to chill and not be bothered; other times I wanted to be in the thick of things, and the lounge provided me with those options. Luckily, since we'd been here before, tonight had been pretty low-key with only a few people taking pictures when we'd first arrived.

The bouncer kept an impartial face as she unlatched the ropes to let me and my new guests back. I had a moment's hesitation as I'd left Courtney and Sasha in the beginning stages of an argument. Sasha was about three sheets to the wind and had started to get overly flirty with me. Though Sasha's drunken inappropriateness had been a blessing. If I hadn't needed to escape, I might have missed the beautiful woman following behind me.

Luckily, the tides had turned for the couple as they were in the middle of a make-out session, but they came up for air long enough to give me a quizzical look. I waved them off as I showed Jahzara the door to the private bathroom, which she got very excited about. I knew what Courtney would say—not that she had much room to talk—but after my last few encounters, I was supposed to be keeping my head down, focusing on the season, and not being drawn in by a pretty face and a killer body.

The talking points toward the end of last season still pissed me off: *Shae Harris, she's got game, just not the right kind. Maybe if she spent less time trying to rack up notches on her bedpost, she could focus on racking up points on the court.* There wasn't a damn thing wrong with my game on or off the court. But that didn't stop sports anchors or gossip sites from using any trash-talking they could to discount us because we dared to think we should be paid more. One of the bastards had even gone so far as to coin the term "Harris Honeys," which had really fucking pissed me off.

Maybe it'd been a little naïve on my part to think my private life would remain private, but I'd learned with more fame came more prying eyes, and loose lips. Though I hadn't given a shit about what folks said until it'd started overshadowing the team and was used as a reason we were struggling. All bullshit, but it was easier to focus there than on shitty management and constant turnover due to said shitty management. Either way, I was supposed to be starting fresh. A simple night out with friends, then going home, alone. But I was also bad about denying myself, so while I probably should have walked away from Dijah, I couldn't, and she was receptive, which to me said it was meant to be.

Courtney kept a smirk on her face as I made introductions and Dijah apologized for crashing our party. I settled beside her on the couch, close, but not too close. Dijah cut her eyes over at me before she drained the remainder of her drink in one go.

"You want another?" I was already signaling to one of the waitresses.

While I ordered her another cocktail, Dijah sat at the edge of the couch, back uncomfortably straight, and swirled the straw around in her glass, clearly having an internal battle. By the time the server left, Dijah had relaxed her shoulders, seemingly having resolved whatever issue she'd been mentally wrestling with.

She slid back to lean closer to me. "I should warn you, my

sister is one hundred percent trying to get me to hook up with you."

The tail end of the conversation I'd overheard between the two of them replayed in my head. I laughed and took a sip of my whiskey. "I'm down."

"Normally, I would have been rationalizing all the reasons not to entertain the possibility...but they call it liquid courage for a reason, right?"

My reply was cut off when Jah plopped down on the other side of Dijah.

"That was a much better option than waiting in line."

Dijah was forced to scoot closer to me. Her leg brushed against mine and although I would have rather stayed pressed against her, I moved over to make room. The waitress returned and Dijah thanked her as she swapped out her empty glass for the new one.

The previously somewhat spacious private room suddenly felt smaller. I wanted to talk with Dijah, find a plausible excuse to touch her, to find out if the spark I'd felt when we shook hands had been all in my head. I wanted some privacy without Courtney silently questioning me. Despite the gossip, I didn't consider myself the "love 'em-and-leave 'em" type. More like, let's have fun while it's fun and stop when it's not. Though the stopping came sooner and sooner these days.

Sasha started grilling Jah on her pregnancy, with Courtney giving me the evil eye. Kids were one of the latest rounds of disagreements between them.

Dijah took another long sip from her glass then turned to smile while leaning closer and whispered, "You...are...so fine."

"That's the best compliment I've gotten in a long time."

She raked her gaze over me again, slower than when she'd checked me out while at the bar. I momentarily braced for the hint of recognition and the possible "hey aren't you…" question to follow.

But all she gave was a sultry smile. "I find that hard to believe."

I shrugged. "Speaking my truth."

Her stunning grin widened as she stood, setting her drink down to remove her blazer, revealing toned arms and an amazing set of breasts barely contained beneath a thin cami, and held her hand out for me. "Would you like to dance?"

I briefly contemplated saying no, but I'd already shot laying low to hell by approaching Dijah. It was a club—dancing was expected. And it's not like this had to go anywhere beyond the dance floor. Besides, how in the hell could I be expected to pass up an opportunity with a built-in excuse to have my hands on her? I took another pull from my own glass then set it down next to hers. The moment our skin connected, another current surged through me, transforming the glimmer of attraction into a tangible thing.

"Jah, you good?" Dijah asked.

Her sister picked up her drink, settled back against the couch and nodded. "Comfortable seating and a private bathroom. I'm golden."

"If you want anything else from the bar, there's a waitress, she'll take care of you. It'll go on my tab."

Courtney arched a brow at me, and she slowly shook her head. I wasn't sure if it was a warning about being with Dijah or leaving her sister behind. When Sasha untangled herself from Courtney, moving to occupy the seat Dijah had vacated,

I got my answer. I felt kind of bad leaving Jah to deal with a slightly inebriated Sasha, who lost what little filter she had the more she drank, but that guilt slowly faded as I watched the easy sway of Dijah's hips and ass, which got more pronounced the closer we got to the dance floor.

The DJ played a throwback Aaliyah song that got everyone on the floor hype, including Tina, who always managed to find herself the center of attention but always went home solo. Dijah and I settled into a spot and easily fell into sync. The way she moved her body made me want to stop and simply watch. She swayed and rocked to the beat, eyes closed and mouth slightly open as she gave herself over to the music. I put my hands on her hips as she gyrated her ass against me.

As one song ended, we adjusted pace to move into the next. Changing with the different beats as one. Through it all we kept connected. She held my hand, or I wrapped an arm around her waist. It didn't matter—we both seemed to have the need to physically touch.

Time melted away and my sole awareness was of the woman who'd stopped me in my tracks the moment I'd spotted her. When the DJ spoke, hyping up the next song, Dijah linked our fingers with one hand and placed her other on my shoulder, stretching up to her tiptoes.

"I need another water break."

I nodded and placed my hand on the small of her back as we weaved our way to the VIP area.

"I haven't had this good a time in a minute," she said, collapsing onto the couch still trying to catch her breath. After a moment, she looked around then set her attention on Tina, who sat scrolling through her phone. "Hey, where did Jah go? Bathroom again?"

Tina frowned and shook her head, her short black dreads swishing with the motion. "Nah, she said she was tired and was heading home. She left not long after Courtney had to damn near carry Sasha's drunk ass out of here."

Dijah jumped up from the couch. "She what? I know she didn't up and leave me here." She pulled out her phone and called her sister.

"I... I thought she told you," Tina stammered.

I knew Dijah and I had been occupied for a while, but we'd taken other breaks for water and to make sure her sister was still doing okay, so, it wasn't like Dijah had totally ignored her. I shot Tina a look and she held her hands up and shook her head.

"How was I supposed to know she'd ditch her sister?" Tina asked. "I thought she'd find y'all on the floor to say bye, or whatever."

Throughout the night the siblings had been doing little jabs at each other, but it seemed to all be in good fun. Even if Jahzara thought her sister might want to hook up with me, leaving her without some sort of heads-up was a bitch move. Though I didn't really know the woman, so I wouldn't express that out loud. However, lesbian bar or not, Girl Code 101 stated you never left a friend or sibling behind. At least not without it being known to the other party.

The fun, carefree woman had been replaced with a pissed-off pacing individual while Tina and I sat exchanging glances, saying nothing.

"I am going to kick your ass when I see you. I can't believe you left me. And then send my call to voicemail."

Dijah pressed the end button on her phone so hard I thought she'd crack the screen. She ran her hands down her face and took a few breaths. When she realized where she was, again her entire demeanor changed.

"Oh shit. I'm sorry. Um, Shae, it's been fun, but I'm gonna call a ride service and head out."

I didn't agree with what her sister had done, and I felt bad, but internally I did cheer a little. It gave me an excuse to prolong my time with her. The universe clearly wanted us together and who was I to turn my nose up at that?

I stood and stepped to her, resting my hands loosely on her waist. "Let me drive you."

She shook her head. "No. You don't have to, I can find my way. And then try not to murder a pregnant woman tomorrow."

"Look, I totally get it if you don't want to get in the car with a person you just met, but…that is what you'll be doing with a service. And I won't even charge you."

That last part brought a smile to her beautiful face. "I don't want you to cut your night short if you aren't ready to go, plus you're here with your friends."

I glanced at Tina, who sipped quietly on a bottle of water. I did make the offer forgetting I was Tina's ride for the night.

"Shit, I'm good," Tina said, pushing off the couch.

Dijah picked up her discarded blazer and slid it on. "Thank you both. I'm so sorry."

"Nah. Don't even worry about it. Let me close out my tab and we can go."

# Three

## Khadijah

I silently fumed, but as I sat in Shae's spacious Wagoneer, stealing glances at her as the lights from the street highlighted her beautiful features, the anger lessened a bit. I was still plenty pissed and Jah's text of you'll thank me later did nothing to help my annoyance with her. But I'd deal with her at family brunch.

Shae's friend Tina had hopped in the backseat before I could even offer to do so. I slid the passenger-side up as much as possible to give her and her long legs plenty of room. When we'd gotten on the way, Shae didn't ask for my address or directions, and I'd been slow to offer them up.

I might have been beyond pissed at Jah for her desertion, but I couldn't deny I'd had a hell of a good time with Shae. I'd gotten out of my head and simply enjoyed the moment instead of trying to figure out how compatible we could be. And the part of me that had committed to enjoying the night wasn't

ready to call it done. My suspicion Shae felt the same was solidified when she pulled up to the curb of a condo building
in Midtown, not far from Lucky Lady.

"Have a good night, y'all. Dijah, it was a pleasure meeting
you. And we got you for an alibi with your sister." Tina's light
brown eyes sparkled, and a playful grin spread across her face.

I laughed and nodded. "Thank you."

She tapped the door twice before heading inside. Shae waited
until her friend disappeared behind the tinted glass doors before driving off. I pulled up the Maps app on my phone and hit
the "home" button. The robotic voice filled the cabin, and I
sat back against the plush leather seat hoping it would take her
longer than the indicated twenty minutes to get to my Grant
Park neighborhood.

The quiet started to engulf me, and I had to resist the urge
to begin rattling off questions. "Thank you for driving me
home," I said, trying to fill the silence.

"It's all good." She flashed me a half smile and it was like
having a crash cart send a lifesaving jolt to my neglected libido.

Shae gave off a laid-back energy, which helped keep me
simply enjoying the moment. As we drove through the quiet
streets of Atlanta, mentally I went through my options. One,
say goodbye at the door and end the night. I'd enjoyed myself,
but technically it was a new day so I'd fulfilled my promise to
let loose for one evening.

Two, I could see things all the way through, scratch the itch,
as it were, and go all in. Because half-assed wasn't my style,
and if I was living for only one night…

My spiraling thoughts were cut off when Shae pulled into
the short driveway of my townhome and killed the engine. A

small building-up of jitters intensified with each passing second. I had a choice to make. I could let Jah's stunt totally fuck up what was otherwise a great night. Or I could keep to my promise. It didn't have to be anything more.

I leaned as close as I could with the large console separating us and ran my tongue along the bottom of my teeth. "Thank you again."

Shae rested her forearm next to mine, and the minor contact sent the sizzling current of excitement through me as it had all night.

"You're welcome."

I lowered my gaze to the lips I wanted to taste. Full and tempting. *I deserved one night. I could have it be only one night. And I always saw things through to the end.* "Can I at least tip you with a kiss?"

I internally cringed at my comment. I was really out of practice with flirting, but when she cupped my cheek, I figured my line wasn't too off the mark. Her mouth connected with mine, soft and warm. She didn't rush—the kiss was more a series of light touches and tentative gestures rather than the full-on devouring I wanted. I tangled my fingers in her hair, taking control. She acquiesced, allowing my tongue to slip between her lips and deepen our connection.

Her fingers teased at the nape of my neck, but her touch remained light. Her reserved behavior only made me want her more. She tasted of a hint of sweetness mixed with spice. Light yet complex, and all intoxicating. My nipples ached and the dull throb between my legs increased.

I pulled back but kept my forehead resting against hers. "Come in with me."

"When I drove you home, this wasn't what I was after."

I stared deep into her eyes. "It was when I said yes." I wanted this. I wanted her. I could allow myself one night to just be, with no thoughts of what came next. Embrace the moment.

Her playful and dazzling smile made another appearance, and she gave the slightest nod, which sent my stomach into a free fall.

Shae stood close behind me, hands resting on my hips, and the warmth of her body cocooning me. I hoped she didn't notice the tremor in my fingers as I punched in the code on the keypad to open my front door. Over the course of the night, each touch, each glance, each time she leaned in and brushed her lips against my cheek or neck had been a form of foreplay.

The pendant lights over my island illuminated the space in a soft glow. No sooner than the click of the lock sounded between us, Shae had me against the wall, kissing me in the way I'd wanted in the truck. I wrestled with the buttons of her shirt as she simultaneously tried to push my blazer off.

I gripped her waist, relishing in the feel of her skin beneath my palm, and she wedged one of her long legs between my thighs. A low moan escaped my lips when she trailed kisses down the side of my jaw. I rocked my hips forward, grinding against her thigh. The pressure added to the pulsating need growing with each passing second.

I didn't think. I didn't worry. I just felt.

And her hands and mouth on me felt damn good. I had to have more, and too many layers separated us. We became a flurry of frantic limbs as we worked to get our clothes off while trying to maintain any connection we could.

"Two weeks ago," she breathed. "Last health check."

The thought hadn't even crossed my mind. I was really out of practice. "A year," I offered up. "But it's been me, myself, and I so—" I was hit with a tiny wave of self-consciousness realizing how long it'd been due to my self-imposed relationship time-out.

If Shae was bothered by my admission, she didn't let it show. We made our way farther into my house and tumbled onto my sofa. I shoved the back cushions onto the floor to give us more space. A burning need to take in every inch of her that I could consumed me. Settling beside her, I dove in for another kiss. Her lips were sinful and had tempted me all night. Shae thrust her tongue forward and tangled her fingers in my hair. There was something almost possessive in her hold that sent my already amped-up desire into overdrive.

Skin-to-skin, we were a tangled mass moving and touching. A give-and-take of exploration and I freely sank into the wonder of it. Shae palmed my ass, squeezing it as she pressed me tighter against her as our mouths continued the frenzied dance. Somehow, I managed to feel lightweight and anchored at the same time.

I finally broke from the kiss and pulled in a deep inhale. Slowly, my gaze drifted down from Shae's face to truly admire and appreciate her. Her body was a work of art. Statuesque in its perfection. Being close to her sensual form had my nipples hard and my pussy throbbing with wanton need. It'd been too long since I'd let myself give in to pure carnal desires and tonight, just for tonight, I was all in on the pleasure possibilities laid out in the exquisite woman before me.

A burning need to hear her moan and whimper sparked. Cupping her firm breast, I circled my thumb around her dark taut nipple as I kissed and nipped at her neck. She groaned when I moved lower and sucked one of her tight buds. I rolled my tongue around it, enjoying the sounds she made and the grip of her hand in my hair.

Shae arched her back, as I continued to lavish attention on her chest. My body tingled. Tiny pricks of awareness radiated beneath my skin. I trailed my hand down the contoured planes of her stomach and a small gasp broke free when my fingers journeyed south, making contact with her pussy. She was as wet and turned on as I was. Her arousal coated my digits as I easily glided them down, then up before applying slight pressure with my thumb.

Shae sucked in a sharp breath, which brought a smile to my face.

"You like that?" I whispered against her heated flesh.

I did the action again, watching as she sank her teeth into her plump bottom lip. I fought against everything in me not to rush this. Watching the way she squirmed, hearing each of the escaping tiny moans, made me continue to take my time. Edging her closer and closer to the end with my slow teasing strokes.

She draped a leg over the back of the couch, opening herself up to me. I pressed my lips to her neck, groaning from the warm silkiness of her body as I eased my fingers in and out, delighting in her small contractions. My own need for release cranked higher. I shifted, pressing myself harder against her muscled thigh. Shae gripped my leg in response, helping to add to the friction I was so desperately chasing to relieve my mounting pressure.

"Almost," she whispered.

The single word was all I needed. I flicked my tongue across her puckered nipple and applied more pressure to her stiff clit. Her grip on my thigh tightened as she arched her back, overcome with tiny spasms. But I was greedy and wanted more.

I cupped her pussy, loving the wetness that covered my palm. With the heel of my hand, I applied more pressure while grinding against her firm thigh.

"Oh, fuck, yes!" she cried out, gasping for air.

With aching nipples, and a heaviness between my legs, my own release shot through me, stealing my breath as the tiny prickles of satisfaction rained down on me. After a few moments, Shae tugged me on top of her and instantly locked her lips to mine. When she pulled away, a lazy grin spread across her face and my already racing heart kicked up another notch.

She trailed her fingers up and down my spine, the action causing a wave of goose bumps to break out. Chest to chest, I wasn't sure if I was feeling her rapidly beating heart or my own, but I knew it thumped in time with the still pulsing desire heavy between my legs.

Shae smoothed back the stray hairs stuck to my face. "On your knees." Her voice was slightly breathless, which added another level of seduction.

"What?"

She pushed against my waist to guide me into the requested position. After she wiggled her long form down, the flick of her tongue against my needy clit made me gasp.

"Oh shit!"

She wrapped her fingers around my thighs and pulled me down onto her face. I fell forward and gripped the arm of the sofa. She closed her lips around me, the gentle suction making my mouth go dry. I squeezed my eyes shut as I gave my-self over to the sensations. With my body already primed I wouldn't last long.

My foot slipped to the floor, but it gave me leverage as I started grinding against her face. Each swipe of her tongue beckoned me closer and closer. Gripping my ass, she tilted her head and fucked me with her skillful tongue. Moving it in and out of my body as far as it'd go.

My breath quickened. "That's…oh, yes, right there—"

The normally soft fabric of my couch scraped against my sensitive nipples, adding another level of sweet torment. A glo-rious knot formed in my stomach right before I rode a second tidal wave of bliss.

"Fuck! Oh my god, yes."

Shae didn't stop. She kept licking and sucking—lapping up everything my body had to offer. Her continued attention had another smaller orgasm running through me that made my stomach clench and locked any words I wanted to scream in my throat. I clawed at my couch, needing some tether to keep me grounded as I was consumed with pleasure. Drunk on the euphoria, I was barely aware of Shae kissing her way up my body, stopping to tease my nipples briefly before mov-ing us both into a seated position.

My heart continued to race, as did my thoughts. Work started on Monday, so I was determined to make the most of the free pass I'd given myself. I rested my head on her shoulder and linked my fingers with hers. "Give me a minute, then we can go upstairs. I need way more space with you."

"Say less."

# Four

## Shae

"Would you like something to drink?" Dijah asked as she placed soft kisses on my shoulder.

I licked my lips, enjoying the lingering taste of her. "Water please."

She nodded before untangling her fingers from mine. I tracked her movements, noticing how the dim lights highlighted her curves. The roundness of her hips. The fullness of her ass. The slight pudge on her waist. I wanted to lick and explore every dip and curve of her body.

She washed her hands before moving over to her fridge. There was a promise of more time to be had. A chance to enjoy her company awhile longer. And I couldn't have been happier.

She smiled as she set a bottle of water on the island. Pushing off the couch, I glanced around the space on my way into the kitchen. The downstairs area was one large room with the living room separated by a six-person dining table centered beneath an oversized light fixture.

Dijah stood sipping on her water, her rich ebony skin acting as a beacon against the light tones of her gray cabinets. She slid the bottle closer, not bothering to mask the lust in her eyes.

"Thank you."

"You're welcome."

I slowly ran my fingers along the marble countertop, keeping my eyes on hers, until our tips touched.

Again, it was there. The pull. The spark.

She tilted her head up to look at me, eyes hooded, hair disheveled. Neither of us spoke, but we continued the tepid caress of our fingers dancing with each other.

"Would you like something to eat?" She sank her teeth into her bottom lip to stop her grin when I quietly chuckled at her question.

I locked our fingers together and stepped closer. "I'm down for seconds."

"I meant food."

I lifted a shoulder. No more words were said but her deep dimples went on full display. Dijah led us from the kitchen, up the stairs, and down a carpeted hallway into her double-door master suite. We stopped at the foot of a queen-sized bed with an upholstered headboard and way too many decorative pillows. The room was as neat and orderly as the downstairs had been.

Refocusing on the angel in front of me, I cupped her face and leaned in for a kiss. Dijah parted her lips, allowing my tongue access. She moaned and dug her fingers into my hips, pulling our bodies closer.

"I taste good on you," she murmured.

The simmering arousal cranked up as the kiss transitioned from leisurely to intense. I walked us backward, continuing to explore her mouth. Balance lost, we fell onto the bed in a fit of giggles over our clumsiness.

The laughter died out when Dijah ran the back of her hand along my face. "You really are amazingly beautiful."

I glided my thumb across her lips. "You're one to talk. You literally stopped me in my tracks tonight."

Dijah shifted so she straddled me. I tilted my head, enjoying the view. Neatly trimmed black coils with a hint of darker flesh peeking out with the slight glossy sheen of her arousal. The weight of her body felt right. The heat of her sex. The dampness. I licked my lips, mouth watering for another taste of her.

She spread her hands out on my stomach, her touch as soft as the satin bedding beneath me. I ran mine up her thighs, watching her watch me. My thumbs met at the apex of her legs at the same time she palmed my breasts. I arched into her touch, sighing from the combined sensations of the silkiness of her pussy under my caress and the tease of her fingertips as she pinched and toyed with my nipples.

She was bold and sure in each touch and that confidence added another level of sexy. I was weak for a woman who knew what she wanted. The scent of sex lingered in the air. Heady and intoxicating.

Like Dijah.

Intoxicating. Beautiful. Intriguing.

Slowly, she rocked her hips against my thumbs. Her wetness slickened my skin, making her movements easier. Dijah released a low moan. The action, the sound, both urging me on. Something in my belly coiled tight and I knew I'd want to see her again. This couldn't be a one-night-only deal. The season was starting, and yes, I'd be busy, and had promised Coach I'd work on having my on-court game be the only thing that got tongues wagging, but there was something about Dijah—plus the fact she didn't know who I was—that made wanting to see where this could go an attractive endeavor.

"Kiss me," I whispered.

She wrapped her fingers around my wrists, pulling my hands away from her body to gently force my arms down onto the pillows as she complied with my request. Her hard nipples pressed against my own as our mouths worked in sync. Our tongues moved in a tango, a give-and-take. Exploring. Dominating. Submitting.

The hold she had on my wrists wasn't tight, but the bit of control she displayed sent a thrill through me. When she pulled back, our faces hovered inches apart. I resisted the urge to flip us and bury my face between her legs again. Instead, I waited, drinking in the sight of her, to see what move she'd make next.

"Are you okay with toys?" she asked between soft kisses down my neck.

I craned to the side, giving her more access and nodded. The most glorious grin spread across her face before she sat up to retrieve a black-and-silver case from the top drawer.

"I'm meticulous about cleaning them. I promise."

From what I'd seen of her house, I had no doubt. She unlatched the lid and pulled out a thin pink vibe resembling a tongue but with wings, then put the case back on the nightstand.

"What's that?"

A sexy, lazy grin spread across her face, which got closer as she moved in to kiss me again. I jumped and started laughing when I felt the subtle vibrations against my hard nipple. When she tried to pull away, I grasped the back of her head, keeping her lips molded to mine. I couldn't get enough of her.

Dijah nipped my bottom lip between her teeth as we finally came up for air. I trailed my hands down the smooth skin of her back as she circled the vibrating stimulator around my nipple, following the action with her tongue. The warm, wet heat of her mouth, coupled with the tickling from the silicone wings made me shudder. Everywhere she touched me set my body alight.

Slowly, she worked her way down, kissing every place the toy made contact with my skin. When she got to the top of my pussy, I held my breath, clenching and unclenching, the wetness coating my thighs and trickling beneath me. Dijah glanced up at me, a coy smile on her lips. She kept her eyes on me as she moved the small silicone device lower. My clit throbbed in time with my erratic pulse, eager for what came next.

My legs seemed to spread open on their own when the vibrations touched the neediest part of me. I gripped the silky bedding as Dijah slid the thin toy between my sex. It glided easily, up and down, spreading me a little more with each pass. The buzzing sensation, along with the soft kisses and light nips to my inner thighs primed my already sensitive body. The tightening in my belly intensified as the descent into bliss neared. The need for it to be a shared experience hit me out of nowhere. I wanted to look into her beautiful face as we hit the peak together.

"Wait," I gasped.

She immediately removed the toy, dropping it onto the

bed as she looked up at me. "Everything okay?" Her brows pulled together.

I licked my lips and nodded as I slid into a sitting position. She did the same and I reached for her, maneuvering us so we sat with our legs intertwined, face-to-face and pussy-to-pussy. The worry on her face transformed to understanding. Dijah tilted her neck up when I leaned to kiss her. I couldn't get enough. Her full breasts were the perfect weight in my hands and the soft whimpers she released when I brushed across her nipples sounded glorious. We gyrated our hips in small, deliberate circles, finding a rhythm in the movements. The low buzz of the toy continued.

"Put that between us."

She felt around until she found the silicone disc. Dijah wrapped her warm fingers around the back of my neck, giving a soft tug until our mouths connected again. With her other hand, she worked the toy into place. The subtle vibrations drew a simultaneous moan from both of us.

Being with her, touching, tasting, feeling, had me lightheaded in the best possible ways. It was more than the euphoria from the endorphin rush of sex. When we broke from the kiss, I pulled in a deep inhale and shuddered from the building of sensations. Dijah looked at me, her eyes heavy with lust, was damn near enough to make me come.

She rested back on her hands, the move pushing her breasts upward against my palms. I closed my lips around one of the hard buds, her skin hot and salty against my tongue.

"Mmmm, yes," she moaned.

We moved faster, rocking, panting, and groaning. Dijah

gripped my thigh, the added closeness of our bodies with the vibrator between us made my belly tighten.

Her nipple popped free from my mouth when I let out a low "fuck."

Gripping her waist, I arched my back and dug my fingers into her side as my release crashed through me. The blissful oblivion. Dijah's own strangled cry rang out and she shivered, falling forward in my arms. We both collapsed onto the covers in a mess of tangled limbs breathing heavily, creating a symphony of pants in the otherwise quiet night.

"Bathroom?" I managed to croak out the question after a few minutes.

"Um, through there," she replied through a yawn and a lazy finger point toward the second door across from the room.

I rolled out of bed and headed toward where she'd indicated. When I returned, I found her curled on her side. Hair a frizzy mess but sleeping peacefully. I eased in beside her and she immediately flipped, draped a leg across mine and an arm over my waist, wiggling as close as she could. Once she was comfortable, she sighed ever so slightly. Her hold wasn't tight, but it was secure.

I stared up in the darkness. The heat from her body I'd enjoyed earlier now raised my own in a less appealing way. I wasn't much of a snuggler, but I couldn't bring myself to disentangle her. Instead, I moved the covers off as much as I could and let myself relax into her big spoon treatment before finally drifting off to sleep.

# Five

## Khadijah

I rolled over and nuzzled closer to the warm body. My eyes flew open. *Body?*

A person was in my bed.

As the sleep fog cleared, the events from the night before flew through my mind like one of those flip books that came to life as the pages picked up speed. All good, and hot, and… shit I shot up, whipping my head to the side.

"Wha? What's wrong?" Shae asked, voice heavy with sleep mixed with alarm.

"Shit! Shit! Shit!" I threw the covers back and jumped out of bed. "I'm late."

I glanced around the room in search of my phone, but it was in my pants, which were downstairs. Fuck. This…this was why I didn't let loose. This was why I had to remain focused because the first time I give in again I get all thrown off.

Shae scrubbed her hands down her face. "For what? It's Sunday. You got church or something?"

I stopped to look at the woman in my bed. The blanket and sheet were pooled at her waist leaving her naked on the top and she didn't seem to care one bit. *Why would she? We'd been all over each other last night.* Her small dark brown nipples had tightened from exposure to the air, flooding me with more memories. The sight of her was almost enough to tempt me... almost. She glanced at me with a hunger that drew awareness of my own nakedness. Covering up would be ridiculous at this point so I focused on the issue at hand.

"No. Family brunch that is in—" I paused to look at the clock on my nightstand again "—twenty-minutes and my parents live thirty minutes away." I took a breath and brought my hands to my mouth in prayer position. "I, um, hate to..."

She held up her hand while climbing out of my bed. I drank in the sight of her long, lean nude body once again. She'd been an absolute bad-timing distraction, but damn she was a sexy as hell one.

"I get it. I'll get dressed and head out." Instead of heading downstairs to gather her clothes, she strolled over to me. I had to crane my neck up to meet her eyes. I didn't resist when she wrapped her hands around my waist and pulled me to her. God, she was soft and warm, and...

"If I leave you my number, will you call?"

I pinched my tongue between my back teeth as the light of day brought back all the reasons why this should be a one-and-done. Hell, if not for Jah, it wouldn't have even been a one. I wanted to say yes. I wanted to say we could meet up for lunch, maybe get to know each other better. But I pushed those wants down. I wouldn't and couldn't let myself fall into old patterns. One night. That's all.

My goals now were to focus on my new job, and the five-year plan I had, which didn't include even the possibility of anything hinting at a relationship. Though I was getting way, way ahead of myself. Like always.

I shook my head. "I'm starting a new job tomorrow and I… The timing wouldn't be…"

Shae didn't say anything. Instead, she leaned and placed a quick peck on my lips. My body craved more, but I forced myself to step away.

"I need to shower. You can let yourself out, right?" I bit back the *unless you want to join me* that threatened to pop out as she stretched her languid form.

"Yeah, I can manage."

I wouldn't let myself get caught up in the lack of sparkle in her eye and the general flatness of her tone. We both knew what this was. The worry over my tardiness kept me from walking her out. Plus, it provided a clean break. No prolonged or drawn-out goodbyes. However, the idea she'd be unsupervised in my space prickled beneath my skin, but I didn't have a choice. Before I lingered on watching her long, graceful body, I darted into my bathroom. As the water heated up, I groaned at the sight of my hair. A rat's nest for sure, between the sex and the fact I'd been too worn out to even braid it and tie it up for the night.

I quickly gathered it up into a haphazard bun, forgoing the shower cap in hopes the steam would loosen it up a bit, and took the quickest shower of my life. By the time I was dressed and my hair was reasonably tamed, I was beyond officially late and surprised my family wasn't beating down my door. Once downstairs, I snatched my jeans from the floor and retrieved my phone.

No surprise I had a series of missed calls and text messages. I was the punctual one. As I settled in my car another text chimed through.

Jah: okay kinda getting worried now

"Serves you right," I muttered to the device. I still couldn't believe she'd left me last night.

I briefly considered making her sweat by not responding, but that would also inadvertently worry my parents, so I shot off a reply before hitting the road.

"Baby, are you sick?" Mom asked as way of greeting when I entered the house through the garage, which dropped me right in her kitchen.

"No, ma'am. Forgot to set my alarm." I gave her a quick hug and kiss on the cheek.

"Uh-huh. Help me carry these to the dining room."

I grabbed oven mitts from the drawer then picked up one of the casserole dishes she'd pulled from the warming tray. The sweet scent of her baked French toast hit my senses hard, and my stomach growled in response. In the dining room sat my father, who got up to greet me. As well as Vance and his traitorous wife, who at least had the decency to look somewhat guilty. I set my dish on the buffet with the other items.

"Alright, now that we're all here, we can eat," Momma announced. The pointed look she gave me made me squirm and amped up my annoyance at Jah.

I grabbed a plate but stepped out of the way to allow my parents to fix theirs first despite my protesting hunger.

Jah bumped me with her hip and whispered, "So…any special reason you happened to be late for the first time ever?"

I narrowed my eyes at her. "You are never. Ever. Never. Going to be in charge of my transportation again. Ev-er." I stressed the last word.

"Oh come on, Dijah. I was tryin' to help a sista out."

I set my plate on the table and glared at her as she proceeded to do an exaggerated waddle back to her seat.

"No. What you did was abandon me and leave me stranded. So, thanks, but no thanks. No more help from you."

Vance's light brown eyes went wide as he looked at my sister. "You left her?" Surprise and shock colored his tone. Clearly, she'd given him a different set of events, which wasn't surprising. I liked my brother-in-law. In contrast to my sister's personal brand of semi-controlled chaos, Vance was calm and logical. I used to think he might be too buttoned-up and strait-laced for her, but somehow, they made it work.

"What y'all fussin' about already?" Dad questioned.

Jah put on her sweetest smile. "Nothin', Daddy. Khadijah is being her usual uptight self."

"Wrong," I defended, jabbing my fork into my pile of eggs. "Your youngest daughter had zero concerns for my safety and left me at the club *she* took me to." I shoved the bite into my mouth while I continued to glare at my sister.

"Jahzara!" Both my parents called out her name.

"You know folks don't got sense these days," Dad started with his attention fully on Jah. "We have always told y'all you have to look out for each other. Because nobody got ya back like family. Just 'cuz you two are grown doesn't mean that's changed." His bushy brows were knit together tightly and again she at least had the decency to look ashamed of her behavior.

"I was doing a good thing though," she rebutted with a small whine to her voice.

I shot her a "shut up" look because I knew where she was going.

"I got tired, but she was having a good time." I didn't miss the slick grin she gave before the next sentence tumbled out of her mouth. "She met someone, and I didn't want to be the Debbie Downer that ruined her night."

I took a long pull of my OJ while mentally sending her "I'm going to kick your ass" thoughts. I wasn't purposefully not being open about my dating life—or lack thereof—with my parents, but I'd learned to stop talking about every woman who seemed to sweep me off my feet only to be broken up two months later. It was a merry-go-round I'd had to get off.

After the last disastrous end, I'd put dating on the indefinite backburner to focus on my career. Matters of the heart were not my friend because they wouldn't conform like I wanted them to, but my parents remained hopeful. Jah's pregnancy had taken the focus off my singledom.

For a while.

The short reprieve had been nice, but Jah's comment catapulted me right back onto the figurative ride.

I bit into one of the crispy strips of bacon and chewed slowly. I knew more commentary was coming—though more from Mom than Dad, he only ever wanted to know if we were happy and requested no additional details—but in true parental fashion, the two of them ate with no rush, leaving me to squirm internally, waiting for the inquiry. It didn't matter how old we got, silence from Josephine Upton always made us feel like we were in trouble.

Shooting Jah another death glare, I decided to cut off whatever thoughts they might have before questions started coming. "She's overselling. It was a nightclub, by nature of the place you meet and talk to people. I hung out with a woman whose last name I didn't even get, nor did we exchange numbers. I won't be seeing her again."

That confession seemed to satisfy most everyone. I didn't really care my sister appeared shocked by my statement. Her heart might have been in the right place, but what she'd done was still shitty even if it had led to an amazing night. Regardless, I wouldn't be seeing Shae again.

I debated changing one more time, but decided against it. I'd been torn between completely dressing down in a pair of joggers and a T-shirt, but it was way too casual for a first impression. The navy slacks and white blouse paired with low pumps said professional yet relaxed. This was my first day on the job, even if it was basically a meet-and-greet.

I went over the short speech I'd prepared and memorized. I wanted the words to sound natural, like I'd made them up on the spot instead of rehearsing. It was important for me to not come off as stiff and unapproachable, but at the same time, I wanted to present as professional, confident, like I belonged. The accompanying well-practiced smiles appeared genuine and hid the battering ram of nerves knocking around in my gut.

This was my first *official* head position, and I was ready. I knew my worth and my abilities. No more being used as an interim lead only to have someone from the outside be brought in to take over. Unlike in LA, I'd have no more empty platitudes about how I was an asset to the team, but… There was always a but.

I laughed to myself at the irony of it all. Me, someone who couldn't care less about sports, had stumbled into a career surrounded by them. But once I was in, I'd gone all in—career wise at least—and now I was *the* athletic trainer for a WNBA team. And my five-year plan was still on track.

Hold a position of prestige.

Make connections and build a solid reputation.

Pad my portfolio to show I was worth the economic risk.

Have an ironclad business plan.

Open my own physical therapy business.

That was my endgame and I would not lose sight.

With a final glance, I headed out of my room and down to the kitchen. I tried to ignore the writing on the magnetic whiteboard on my fridge. In my rush to get to brunch, I'd not paid attention, but Shae had left her number anyway, scrawled neatly next to my grocery list. I'd started to erase it countless times, but couldn't quite bring myself to do it.

Later. I'd deal with that later.

Grabbing my bag and travel coffee mug, I headed out to the arena. There was a moment of panic worrying my key card wouldn't work to get me into the staff parking, but the light turned green, and the iron gate jumped then creaked as the mechanisms cranked it open. I whipped into a spot and stared at the basic gray building.

Squeezing my hands on the steering wheel, I closed my eyes and counted to ten.

*You can do this. You earned this.*

I repeated the affirmations in my head in an attempt to beat down the first-day jitters. I knew my stuff and knew I was damn good at my job, but years of being passed over had started to chip away at some of my confidence. Roadblocks, a detour, but I'd landed on something bigger and better.

When I was ready, I exited my Fiat and headed toward the steel double doors. Again, the light turned green when I held my pass up to the scanner and a click sounded, releasing the lock. My shoes echoed on the tile floor as I made my way down the hall trying to recall the layout from when I'd done my final interview and had been given a quick tour.

After getting turned around twice, I managed to find my way to the training room where my modest office was located. Standing in the space, I inhaled the scent of…empty. Not even a faint odor of cleaning supplies. Most of the room was made up of exercise equipment, which was expected, but there were also three physical therapy tables and storage racks—slightly disorganized—with elastic bands, towels, and other supplies I'd use. I made a mental note to get those arranged to better suit my needs and to do a complete inventory so I could order any additional items I required.

I made my way to the two closed doors and ran my hand over one of the nameplates: Khadijah Upton, Athletic Trainer. Inside, my office was bare-bones. A basic metal desk, three chairs, shelving. The walls and flooring sported the team colors. But it was all mine. After years of being the assistant at first the high school level, then in college sports, I was finally the one calling the shots.

"You're early." The voice behind me made me jump.

I turned to find Dillyn Smith, the head coach, in a much more casual outfit consisting of dark blue nylon athletic pants that made a soft swooshing noise as she walked and a team T-shirt. She had several file folders and a tablet tucked under her arm. We'd met briefly during my second interview, and she'd come off as an easygoing woman. Down-to-earth, logical, a personality I felt I would easily work well with.

And again, I was slightly envious of the shaved head she pulled off. Without thinking, I reached up to pat my own hair, imagining the time I'd save. If I had to guess, I would have said she was probably five to seven years older than my thirty-two, but her smooth, medium-brown complexion gave nothing away. I could only go by the seemingly strategic gray patch in the front of her low buzz cut and the few spatterings around her temple.

"Good morning, Coach Smith. I wanted a chance to get in and get a bit oriented before meeting the team."

Her dark brown eyes crinkled at the side when she smiled. "Good. Good. I was just dropping these off. Player's medical records so you can get up to speed." She set the items on the desk. "But later, come meet the rest of the coaching staff."

Digging into the team files was something I desperately needed to do. They wouldn't release them to me until after my background check cleared, and the paperwork had hit some strange snag that had taken longer to settle. I'd had to rely on basic internet research to get an idea of where the team stood physically, but I knew those reports were lacking at best. Putting my desire aside, I nodded and followed her down the corridor to a smaller room that held a few folding chairs, a long table, and a large whiteboard with a premade basketball court on one side.

I met the assistant coaches, Jason Vickers, a tall light-skinned guy with a full beard and a friendly smile, and Tyler Adams, a pale, slender guy with dark hair. Marni Wilson was the strength and conditioning coach. Like Coach Smith, the brunette was a retired player who'd spent her game time overseas then turned coach. She had the office next to mine and would be the one I'd work the closest with. They filled me in on the challenges they'd faced with turnover in the coaching staff, especially with keeping someone in my position. And they all hoped I'd be around for more than a season.

My anxiousness went into overdrive at the news. I was curious as to what the issue was there. Had the previous trainers quit or were they let go? But I didn't voice the question. I didn't want to come across as a gossip. However, a new determination kicked in. I'd never been fired from a job, and I didn't plan to start now.

Work was the one aspect of my life I always managed to wrangle into success. I'd hit some snags, some roadblocks, but I persevered, ending up in better places than where I'd left. I belonged here, and would prove I would be an asset to the team.

After about an hour, voices carried down the hall prompting Coach Smith to direct us all to the locker room.

"Knock, knock, ladies. Everybody decent?" Coach asked as she walked in.

After they all gave the okay, Jason and Tyler crossed the threshold, and I followed behind them, staying close to the door.

"Welcome back, ladies. I hope you're all ready to put in the work for a kick-ass season." There were a few cheers and agreement. Coach clapped her hands to get everyone's attention. "Alright, alright. Okay, since most of y'all are here, I'll go ahead and introduce our newest Cannon, athletic trainer Khadijah Upton."

There were a few murmurs and claps. I pulled in a breath and put a smile on my face. My introduction speech was memorized and ready to be spoken. I stepped between Jason and Tyler and the audience of tall people looked in my direction, but it was one set of eyes on me that made my breath catch in my throat and my mind go blank. Every practiced word lost.

# Six

## Shae

$W$hat a small world. I'd been kicking myself for not getting her number and now she was here. Looking as beautiful as ever.

Tina tapped my arm. "Yo, what the hell? Isn't that ol' girl from Saturday?"

I nodded. "Yes, yes it is."

"Did you know she'd be here?"

"Hadn't a clue. But I'm liking the turn of events."

She leaned in closer and dropped her voice lower. "Did you two hook up?"

I ignored her whispered question and kept my eyes on the woman who captured my attention just as she'd done at the club. Khadijah, however, avoided looking in my direction as she made her way to the center of the room. She seemed almost like a different person than the one I'd spent the night with.

Her beautiful hair had been tamed into a single thick braid

wrapped around her head like a crown. The sexy cleavage-revealing cami had been replaced with a dress shirt buttoned to the neck. And the wide-leg pants managed to somewhat camouflage the curve of her hips, but nothing could hide her generous ass.

Shoving her hands into her pockets, she shot a glance around the room, not lingering on Tina, Courtney, or me for too long. "I'll keep this short. I just want you all to know I'm excited to be here and be part of this great organization. I'll be reviewing everyone's record and finding time to meet with each of you one-on-one to find out how I can help make sure you're in the best shape for peak performance."

She stepped back so she was partially hidden behind the coaches. As Coach Smith talked about a few more housekeeping issues, Marni made her way to Khadijah. I kept my attention on them as they whispered among themselves.

I hadn't imagined the spark between me and Dijah, and I'd been thinking about her ever since being unceremoniously kicked out of her place. I'd spent Sunday hoping she'd call or at least text, but she'd done neither. However, the universe was working in my favor. Once Coach dismissed us to finish getting ready for practice, some of the others went to introduce themselves to our new trainer.

Courtney walked up to me. "So, what's up with that?" Her brows were drawn together as she played with one of her mini twists.

"What?"

"That's her, right? The one with the sister from the club. Why is she giving off 'I don't know them' vibes? What'd you do?"

Tina crossed her arms and stared at me. "Yeah, Shae. What happened after you took her home?"

"You took her home? What? Sasha's drunk ass had me missing everything."

I whipped my sweatshirt over my head. "It was no big deal. Her sister left her so I dropped her off."

"You know what's funny?" Courtney and I both shook our heads. "Not long before the sister dipped out, she'd made a comment about our height and whatnot, and I told her what we did. She didn't say shit. She had to know about her sister's job, right?"

I stared at Tina trying to process her statement. "Serious?"

"Yeah."

That was interesting information. There was no way her sister didn't know about the job, which really made me wonder. Once again, my attention drifted to where Khadijah stood. This time she was looking at me, watching me.

Courtney let out a cackle. "Oh, I know what you did. Or better yet, who."

I swung my shirt at her, which only made both her and Tina laugh harder. When I glanced back in Khadijah's direction she'd disappeared. After I finished changing, I headed to the training room to see her before hitting the floor.

*She was a good actress, pretending not to know who we…who I was.*

"Not gonna speak?"

She glanced up from the file she'd been looking over and folded her hands on top of the desk. "I was. I just… It didn't seem like the appropriate time." She massaged her temple. "I don't know why I didn't put it together. The height and all."

"Not every tall woman plays."

"True. But considering what I do, I should have at least suspected."

"You really didn't know?"

She shook her head. "If I had, I wouldn't… No, I didn't know."

The vibe was definitely off with her. Maybe it was surprise over seeing me again, which I guess made sense. We hadn't even exchanged last names, let alone discussed jobs—other than her saying she was starting a new one as a reason for us not to see each other again. And apparently, she hadn't researched the team she was going to be working with if she didn't recognize any of us. Not to mention, if what Tina said was true, her sister hadn't spoken a word to her about it.

"I hope you weren't too late to your family brunch."

She bit the corner of her lip and dropped her gaze down for a moment. "Not too bad." A slight grin graced her mouth and all I could think about was how soft her lips had been when we'd kissed.

"Good. Well, I'll see you out there."

"Yeah. Looking forward to getting my hands on you." Her eyes widened almost instantly.

"That makes two of us." I spun and exited before she could say anything else.

"Nice of you to join us, Harris," Coach Adams said, staring at me, unimpressed with my tardiness.

"Sorry."

I trotted onto the court and easily fell into step with the rest of the team, who were in the midst of doing suicides. From there we moved on to dribbles, layup drills, and free throws. At some point I noticed Khadijah in the bleachers watching and taking notes. I tried to keep my focus on practice, but she was proving to be a distraction. And the fact my head wasn't fully in it wasn't missed by my coaches.

"Harris! I know this is the first day back, but what's up?" Coach Smith asked. "Off-season is over, it's time to work."

"My bad, Coach. Just shakin' off the rust."

"Shake faster."

I briefly sent my attention to where Khadijah was now near the sidelines talking with Marni. I barely turned back in time to catch the ball being passed my way and sank a three.

Coach clapped then yelled, "That's what I'm talkin' 'bout. More of that."

For the remainder of practice, I kept my focus on what I needed to do, though I did note each time a teammate went to our new trainer. Once practice was over, we all filed back to the training room. I plopped down onto one of the benches and rotated my shoulder, attempting to work out a kink while Coach Smith did wrap-up.

Khadijah walked over and applied pressure to the space between my neck and shoulder with one hand while encouraging me to lift my arm with her other. I had to bite back the moan threatening to escape when she applied gentle pressure, massaging the tightness. Her deft fingers worked magically, hitting all the right spots and conjuring up all the memories of our night together. Reminding me how those same fingers worked me over in very different ways.

She leaned closer, and the soft smell of her perfume, a light floral-and-jasmine combination, tickled my nose. I had to stop myself from pulling in a deeper than necessary inhale.

"Lean your head to the right," she whispered.

The desire to turn and connect our lips was strong, but this was not the place. Instead, I closed my eyes and did as she asked. Tuning out whatever Coach was saying and focusing in only on how Dijah's hands moved over my skin. The soft brush of her body as she stood close to me. I was a firm believer that things happened when you needed them to. The universe didn't want me to just have one night with Khadijah Upton. No, it put her directly in my path, in my life, and who was I to ignore that?

The stiffness that had been trying to creep into my joints lessened as she continued her work. When I looked around the room, I didn't miss the smirks on Courtney's and Tina's faces. Coach dismissed us and Khadijah gave my neck one last squeeze.

"How's that?"

I did a few rotations. "Better. Thanks."

"That's what I'm here for. If it keeps giving you trouble, let me know and I'll provide you with a few extra stretches you can do before you start practice."

I swiveled on the bench to face her. Watching and waiting for the room to thin out. Only it didn't, at least not fast enough for my liking. My teammates needed attention and she had a job to do. I ducked out to the locker room for a quick shower in hopes that I could catch her alone after I was done.

The carefree sound of her laugh followed by Tina's carried down the hall as I neared the training room. When I walked in, Tina was getting her ankle worked on as they easily chatted away. I wasn't sure how I felt about the easiness Khadijah seemed to have with my friend in contrast to the standoffishness she'd had with me. The conversation wavered when they saw me. Tina thanked Khadijah and slid off the table.

"Is there something else I can do for you?"

"All business."

She busied herself with wiping down the table Tina had occupied. "I'm at work."

"For how much longer?"

"For a while. I want to finish going over y'all's records so I can be even better prepared for tomorrow." She tossed the paper towel in the nearby trashcan.

I moved closer, getting in her orbit, but stamping down the urge to touch her. "Can you help me understand what's happening here? Because I thought we left things on good, although hurried terms."

The comment Courtney had said earlier ran through my head. Although I would catch her stealing random glances in my direction, she'd spent most of the time trying to not be near me, or acknowledge me much at all outside of the massage. I would be lying if I said that subtle rejection, or dismissal, whatever was going on with her, wasn't plaguing me.

She ran her hand along the side of her head, smoothing hairs that weren't out of place, then tilted up to stare at me, exposing her tempting neck. "You're right. I wasn't expecting to see you again. Today. I wasn't expecting to see you again, so quickly. Today." She clamped her lips together and forced air out through her nose.

"I wasn't expecting you either. But I guess we didn't really have time to talk about, well, anything really, considering you practically shoved me out the door Sunday morning." I rolled my tongue along my bottom lip. An action she followed then mirrored. "But maybe we can grab something to eat. My treat. A 'welcome to the team' celebration."

She started shaking her head. "First, I didn't shove you out the door. You let yourself out. And second, I don't think that's a good idea. I have a rule about not mixing work with… It's not a good idea."

"So, this whole 'pretend you don't know me' thing is because of a workplace romance gone bad?" If she'd been somehow burned before, I could almost understand her behavior. No one wanted to repeat bad history. But at the same time, not all experiences would end the same.

She lowered her gaze for a moment, then rolled her shoulders back before shaking her head. "I've never been involved with anyone I've worked with. In fact, I've learned to keep everything business-friendly." Her answer was strange, like she'd deliberately chosen to word it in a certain way, but it left an opening of possibility.

I stepped closer, resting my hand on the table next to hers, and just like the night in her kitchen, she stretched her fingers out until they barely brushed against mine. *Possibility indeed.*

"So, this rule that you have isn't borne from a bad experience?" I didn't bother to hide the tiniest bit of hope laced through my question.

It may have been one night, but I honestly felt there was something more worth exploring. That we'd clicked in a deeper way. I mean, it could have just been the sexual chemistry, but we wouldn't know until we tried to figure it out.

Khadijah released a barely audible sigh. "Shae—"

"Hey, Shae, you wanna… Oh, my bad." Renee, one of last year's rookies, darted her eyes between me and Khadijah,

who'd quickly shoved her hands into her pockets at the interruption. "Um, Courtney sent me to see if you wanted to grab
a bite with us. But I'll let them know—"

"I'll be there in a sec."

She gave a parting glance before ducking out of the room.
I set my attention back on the woman in front of me. Part of
me wanted to hear what she'd been about to say, but it would
be a conversation for another day.

"You have files to go through, so I'll leave you to it." I
made it to the door then looked back. "Welcome to the team."

# Seven

## Khadijah

I dropped my Cannons duffel bag filled with all my new team apparel on the bench next to the garage entrance before moving farther into my kitchen. I'd planned on eating one of the meals I'd prepped for the week, but after the day I'd had, I stopped to pick up my comfort nachos from Olé Olé.

It was supposed to have been an easy first day. My list included meeting the team, reviewing their medical histories, and making note of any current treatment plans in place. It helped that Marni talked with me for a while to give me Cliffs-Notes of things I'd find in the records. It allowed me to figure out what I would keep doing, or possibly talk with them about changing it up if things weren't effective.

It was not supposed to include the woman I'd continued to think about, despite how I'd downplayed things to Jah.

*Shae.*

Seeing her had been enough of a surprise. But the clear disappointment on her face, well, that had hit me harder than expected. Of all the training rooms in all the cities, she had to walk into mine. We'd had one night. No promises had been made. Yet an inkling of guilt gnawed at me. I couldn't shake the parting look on her face.

My mind wouldn't settle even in the quiet of my house because Shae's number mocked me as I yanked open the door of my fridge to retrieve my favorite flavored water. My eyes drifted over to the couch as the memories from Saturday night rushed back. Normally, I'd kick off my shoes and curl up on that very sofa to watch TV while I enjoyed my meal. But now I couldn't look at it without remembering the seemingly hurt feelings of the woman who'd been sprawled out on it less than forty-eight hours ago.

I carried my drink and food over to my bistro kitchen table, picking the chair that would have my back to the living room. The first bite of the loaded chip pulled a contented sigh from my lips. The mixture of the spicy ground beef and chicken topped with their house salsa, lettuce, sour cream, black beans, and jalapenos for the added kick, was the indulgence I needed and hit way better than the grilled salmon with Caesar salad and raw veggies sitting in the plastic portion containers stacked neatly in my refrigerator.

All would be okay. We were both adults. We could deal with the situation as such. Behaving as and being seen as nothing but the utmost professional was an aspect of my life I'd never strayed from. Being a woman made things hard enough. Being a Black woman meant I had to put in the extra effort to be taken seriously and prove I was capable of doing my job. Beyond capable in most cases. *Yet still not good enough for some.*

I couldn't jeopardize my future, not after I'd made it this far. Shae had to understand that getting involved with someone you worked with was ill-advised. Relationships came with emotions, feelings, and conflicts that could get real complicated real fast when they turned south. Dealing with a breakup was hard enough. But dealing with one where you still had to see the person on a regular basis, that was trouble in the making.

*Relationships.*

I shoved another nacho into my mouth and forced an annoyed breath out through my nose. There I was getting ahead of myself again. It'd been sex. A great night of sex, but still just sex. Pushing back from the table, I stomped over to the magnetic whiteboard and before I could overthink it, I grabbed the little eraser and swiped it across, ridding the surface of the loopy handwriting she'd left behind. I stared at the newly empty space until the buzzing of my phone vibrating on the granite pulled my attention.

A text from my sister. I wouldn't be in this weird predicament if not for her. Though sleeping with Shae was one hundred percent on me. I'd convinced myself that one night, just one fucking night, I could let loose. Have some fun. That it wouldn't be a big deal. What was the worst that could happen? And it was all coming back to take a big bite out of my ass. I picked up my cell and carried it back to my table.

**Jah: Just checking to see how day 1 went**

I laughed sardonically at her message and was tempted to respond back that I had to face the woman whose face I'd ridden and act like I didn't know her. But I wouldn't. I consumed another loaded chip then wiped my hands before answering.

Me: Great. Everyone was nice and welcoming

Jah: That's it???

The question included the arched brow emoji. I frowned at her message and hit the call button next to her name. It rang longer than it should have, considering I knew she had to be close to her phone.

"What more are you expecting?" I asked as soon as she answered.

"Nothing. I just thought you'd have something a bit more exciting to say." The high pitch of the nothing was enough to know she was up to something. That was always her tell, even when we were kids, and she'd never grown out of it.

"Jahzara Nicole Jones."

"Damn. Why you calling my whole name like you my momma?"

"Because. Now what's up? What did you do this time?"

"I didn't do anything. I'm being a loving sister and inquiring about your day."

I pinched the bridge of my nose then rolled my neck trying to work out the tension creeping into my shoulders. I wanted to unload on her about Shae and the unfortunate situation, but I stayed quiet. It wasn't worth getting into it with her, especially since I had a good idea of what she'd say. *Don't be so uptight. Live a little. Every step doesn't need to be planned out to exhaustion.*

"Jah, seriously. I know you, and your not-so-innocent questions."

She sighed heavily. "First you have to promise not to get mad. And to not snitch again. You know Vance still randomly comments about the whole club mishap?"

"Mishap? You know what you did was fucked up. And for you to be setting up whatever with a preface of me not getting mad means you've done something else shady. So, let's have it."

"Okay. Not my finest moment, but seriously, I honestly thought I was doing you a favor. You were having a really, really good time with Shae."

The mention of Shae had my eyes shifting back to the now-clean whiteboard. And she wasn't wrong, I had enjoyed my time with Shae at the club and—my gaze went to my sofa—later.

"So, how is she?"

Her question brought me out of my reverie. "Who?"

She paused for a beat. "Shae."

My earlier suspicion came roaring back. I pushed my plate of food away and rested my elbows on the table. "Why would you think I'd know that?"

"'Cuz she plays for the team you work for now." Her words came out in such a quick rush that I almost missed what she'd said.

Or maybe I wanted to pretend she hadn't said what I thought she'd said. "How...did you... Wait."

"Look, I didn't know at first. But since you left me in the VIP lounge with her exceptionally tall friends, the topic came up when I commented on their height with the not married one. The couple had left because the one chick, whew, she was 'white girl wasted.'" She chuckled to herself while my mind still reeled over the fact my sister knew the woman I was hanging out with was someone I was going to be working with.

And she hadn't given me a heads-up. Instead, she'd left me with her. Her shocked look at brunch, when I'd mentioned not seeing Shae again to shut her up, now made sense. I blew out a slow breath and tried to keep a rein on my pissed-off state. "Are you fucking kidding me?" *Okay, attempt failed.*

"You said you wouldn't get mad."

I shook my head. "I never agreed to that. You made the statement, that's all. How could you find out this information and, instead of doing what a good sister should have, which was let me know, you leave me with Shae so I'd end up in bed with her?"

"Did you?" Her voice hitched with excitement.

"Not the point right now, Jahzara. You know—" I blew out another breath. "This is a worse setup than you taking me there in hopes of me hooking up with someone. You know I don't mix work with personal. I… I need to go."

"Come on, Dijah. First off, it's not really my fault if you didn't research the team you were going to be working for."

I sighed, knowing I'd had the same thought earlier. I'd only looked up stats of the injured players to have talking points for how I could help and what my experience was with their different injuries. "I researched what I needed, Jah. And that doesn't negate the fact you did know, or found out, and didn't say shit."

"Look, if there's no rule or 'strong suggestion' against fraternization then what's the big deal? You were into her. Like hard-core—if your ass was lighter we would have seen you blushing—into her."

"Not the point. Look, it's been a day. I'll talk to you later."

"Love you," she said right before I ended the call.

I set my phone down and dropped my head into my hands. It was a series of events that might have started with the best intentions but had quickly devolved. Though Jah hadn't forced me to invite Shae in. I could have called it a night in the drive-way.

But man, I'd wanted her. Her general presence. Her smile. The smooth melody of her voice. I had been enraptured with everything about Shae Harris. We'd had one glorious night and I'd forever have that memory. But that's what it had to remain. A fond memory.

# Eight

## Shae

When my phone started ringing at 7:15 a.m. on the dot, I knew who it was before I even looked at the screen.

"Mornin', Ma."

"Happy birthday, baby. Wait, your dad is still here. Charles..."

"Happy birthday, Shae," my dad said, sounding like he was hollering from down the hall. Probably halfway out the door on the way to work.

Their call brought a smile to my face. My mother made a point to give us her birthday wish at the exact time we entered the world. My oldest brother had the short end of the stick there since he wasn't born until 11:33 at night. But it was her thing, so I always answered it, even if it meant the call woke me two hours before I needed to get up for the day.

I scrubbed a hand down my face then rolled the kinks from my neck. As I crawled out of bed, I pulled the loc sock free from my head, letting my braids hang free.

"You have any big plans today? It is your final year in the twenties," she said with a slight chuckle.

"You trying to imply I'm getting old, Ma?"

"I mean, I didn't want to say it, baby, but—"

I laughed and gave my body a good stretch before picking up the remote for my blinds and pressing the button to allow the early-morning sunlight in. Another beautiful day in Atlanta. At least for now. All my years here proved the weather could turn on a dime in this fair city. Though I didn't mind too much; the milder winters compared to Michigan were enough of a trade-off for me.

"No big plans. I have practice in a few hours, and I'll be doing dinner with some of the players from the team."

The mention of the team instantly took my thoughts to Khadijah as I stared out my twelfth-floor window at the private courtyard below. It would be just my luck that the first woman in a long while who didn't care who I was, and had been into me for me, had already put the brakes on because we now worked together.

"Oh, that'll be nice." Mom's voice brought me back to the conversation. "And next time you come visit I'll bake you your favorite cake like always."

My stomach grumbled at the thought of her homemade German chocolate cake. "Thanks, Ma. Or you and Dad can come out to visit me."

She released a heavy sigh. "You know your daddy don't like getting on a plane."

The conversation wasn't a new one. They'd been happy for me when I'd gotten drafted right out of college, though less so because of where I'd be going. They'd one hundred percent supported all my choices and passions. But they were also pretty set in their ways. Dad didn't think there was anything he needed to see that wasn't in a fifty-mile radius of the home they'd raised me and my siblings in.

Mom, she did have a more adventurous spirit, to a degree. However, she didn't like traveling alone and didn't feel right leaving Dad "unattended," in her words, as if the grown man wouldn't be able to function without her for a few days. The attitude resulted in them coming to visit me exactly twice in the eight years I'd been here. Once for my first professional game, and a second time when I'd bought my condo. I'd deliberately chosen a floorplan with a second bedroom hoping it'd entice them to come more often. It hadn't. And I'd resigned myself to having to be the one to travel to see my family.

Though my brothers had rotated through a few times over the years. I was grateful that my parents would always make the drive to Indiana to see me play whenever I had a game there. I was the one to move away, the only one of my siblings to do so, so it was a compromise—or better yet, a fact of life I'd learned to live with.

Initially, I'd second-guessed the condo purchase since it'd failed to do what I'd hoped, but my place had grown to be my sanctuary. My quiet escape that I protected fiercely. So much so, my address was on a need-to-know basis because I didn't want pop-up visitors, even if the 24/7 doorman kept that from happening. If you weren't on the list of expected visitors for the day, they called to get approval before buzzing you into the elevator bank. That was worth the exorbitant condo fees alone.

"I won't hold you, baby. You have a good day. Love you."

"Love you too, Ma."

I ended the call and tossed the device onto my bed before heading into the bathroom. Once I finished up, it was off to the kitchen. I pulled out eggs, spinach, tomatoes, and mushrooms. A nice birthday omelet was exactly what I needed, with a side of chorizo sausage patties. My mind wandered back to Khadijah. For the past week, Courtney and Tina had been itching to figure out what was up with us. Meanwhile Renee had kept her head down, and said nothing about what she'd walked in on, though she paid extra attention anytime Khadijah and I were in the same room.

It was getting harder to assure them all was cool, especially when she would pull the standoffish attitude, by avoiding eye contact and overcorrecting when we'd get too close. She said it was an issue about us working together, but I couldn't shake the feeling it was more, almost as if she was embarrassed. Like she'd rather pretend things had never happened.

I shook off the thought as I plated my food, then poured myself a generous glass of OJ before settling at my small table overlooking the city. More thoughts of the beautiful distraction floated through my head. Did Jah know about her sister's no dating coworkers rule? If so—I laughed as I cut into my omelet—she was quite the sneaky matchmaker.

As I finished off my breakfast, I decided I'd see how the day went with Khadijah and how she behaved. If she continued to try to pretend as if we didn't know each other, I'd find a way to ignore the attraction we both knew was there and keep it strictly professional.

Tina dribbled the ball between her legs twice then chest passed it to me as we did drills down the court. "Have you talked to her today?"

I repeated the action, swapping balls with her to continue the warmup exercise. I glanced to the sidelines where the "she" in question stood talking with Marni. There was something about seeing her in the team apparel. The joggers hugged her hips and ass and the T-shirt sat snug across her large breasts. Ones I remembered all too fondly. I barely caught the ball next time Tina passed one back to me.

"No need."

Coach hollered for us to switch up to the next drill and we broke off into two sets to do rotations of free throws and re-bounds. The change may have cut off Tina's reply, but that didn't mean her face hadn't said it all beforehand. But I couldn't worry about what she thought right now.

I focused on the place I loved being. On the court. The squeak of the shoes on the wood floor. The thump of the ball and swish of it in the net. They all worked together to cre-ate the soundtrack of my happy zone. I'd taken to the sport from the moment my parents forced my brothers to let me play with them.

I'd gotten wise to their attempts to get rid of me after a few dirty plays. Be extra rough and the annoying little sister will go away. But it hadn't been long before I went from being a nuisance to them fighting over whose team I'd be on. Basket-ball had been my love well before I'd grown into the height that served to help my passion.

We transitioned into fast break shooting and the constant physical activity kept me engaged and my mind occupied.

"Harris," Coach Smith yelled. "You keep rubbing that knee. Go see Upton."

"I'm good, Coach."

"It wasn't a request. We have thirty-six games ahead of us this season. I need each of my players to start in peak condition. If it's a little thing now, it could get worse later and we're not doing that."

I dropped my head and held back a groan. Coach had only been with us for three seasons, but we'd quickly realized she wasn't a woman to be trifled with. But for as tough as she was, pushing us to be the best on and off the court, she also held a big sister quality—because she was maybe only ten years older—making sure we were getting what we needed.

Since the change of ownership five years prior, the team had been in a near-constant state of flux, at least where the coaching staff had been concerned. It had gotten so bad, I'd been in talks with my agent to possibly look for a trade. Things had been too uncertain for too long and as a team we'd been trying to muddle through as best we could, but it had started to wear on me. Then Coach joined and we started finding our stride, and I had to believe we were on the upswing and were coming out the other side of some tumultuous times. This team had been my home, these women my sisters for the last eight years. My heart was here, and I truly didn't want to leave.

"Add a limp to really sell it," Courtney whispered as I walked past her.

I shoved her playfully, which only made her laugh more. Picking up my water bottle and towel from the bench, I made my way through the tunnel back toward the training room. With the way my thoughts had been lately, I counted it as some sort of victory that I'd managed to get my focus solely on practice instead of tracking Dijah's movements. I hadn't noticed she'd left the court.

Music trickled out of the open doorway, and as I got closer, I realized that mixed in with the song playing was Khadijah's voice as she sang along. She was a little off-key, but I could tell she was completely into it. An unease weaved its way through me, but I pushed it aside. I wasn't one to dwell. People flowed in and out of your life. But that didn't stop the subtle rejection from stinging all the same.

Not wanting to scare her, I knocked on the frame before stepping into the room. She'd been busy rearranging the area, putting most stuff on the middle and lower shelves. "Coach wants you to take a look at my knee."

Khadijah blinked at me a few times before pulling her phone free from her pocket, pushing a few buttons to kill the music that had been coming from a small red Bluetooth speaker. "Um, sure. Take your brace off and hop up on a table."

I did as she instructed, resting back on the incline. She disappeared into the office and returned with a tablet.

She flipped the cover to the back and did a few swipes across the screen. "I was reviewing the files, and saw that you had an ACL tear sophomore year of college."

"Yeah, that was minor."

She looked up at me. Her large, dark eyes searched my face. "I've been meaning to speak with you about it." She dragged the corner of her lip between her teeth as the unspoken reason for the delay danced around us. "Does it cause you pain often?" Khadijah set the device on the empty table behind her before laying her warm hands on my leg. They were soft. And efficient. And I remembered the way they'd explored my body.

I cleared my throat and shook my head. "No. It's really working out the 'getting back at it' kinks. I stay active in the off-season, but not at the same level."

She applied pressure above my knee and slowly worked her way up. "Does any of this hurt?"

"No. Feels good."

She lifted her gaze to mine. Sliding one hand beneath my leg, she guided it so that I bent it. "How about now?"

"There's a little discomfort. But nothing I've not dealt with before." I sighed against the pressure she applied. "In another life you could have been a masseuse."

A smile spread across her face as she lowered my leg then moved to adjust the incline on the table so I laid flat. "There will be no full-body massages." Khadijah rested my calf on her shoulder and went back to giving my knee a gentle massage.

I shifted my head so I had a better view of her. Like always, she worked diligently, gliding her hands over my skin to relax the stressed muscles.

"Not even on my birthday?"

She stopped her actions and tilted her head. "Is it your birthday?"

"You've read my file. You tell me."

A shadow crossed her face as she started back with her task. "Happy birthday, Shae."

"Thank you, Dijah."

Her gaze fluttered back toward me when I used the name she'd given me that night. Saying it felt like a familiarity despite the weird behavior.

"Are we really going to do it like this?"

She continued to let her hands glide over my skin, abandoning my knee and drifting farther and farther up my thigh. "Do what?"

"Pretend there isn't something between us. Because your hands seem to have a mind of their own."

Her eyes went wide, and she quickly yanked her hands away. I eased my leg off her shoulder in fear she was about to bolt.

"Shit! I'm sorry. That was highly inappropriate."

I pushed up to sitting. "I wasn't complaining."

She shoved her hands into her pockets. "Still, I shouldn't have. I'm a professional. I'm not supposed to be wanting to feel up the players. Let alone do it."

I couldn't stop the laugh that escaped. "I'm pretty sure that ship has sailed."

A small smile graced her face at my statement. "I'm sorry, about how I acted, how I'm acting. Yes, I was thrown off by seeing you, but that's no excuse. I want you to know it's one hundred percent a me thing though."

Hearing the last part eased some of the doubt I'd had. At least before she spoke again.

"I don't want the team—or you—to get the wrong impression of me."

I slid off the table and I expected her to step back, but she didn't. Like the night at the club, or any time we'd been around each other in the last week, the draw for us to be close was strong. She kept her hands in her pockets and I fought the urge to pull her into my arms.

"And what impression would that be?"

"That I'm reckless. That I'm the kind of woman who goes to clubs and has one-night stands. It's not me. I don't do those things."

I mulled her words over in my head and tried to figure out

the best way to approach them. "But you did. I did. Are you saying you somehow have a negative impression of me?"

"What? No! Damn it." She huffed out a breath. "I had a plan. I knew what I needed to say to you, but nothing is coming out right."

She covered her face with her hands for a moment, seemingly to compose herself. "I've never been in this situation before. So, I'm trying to do the best I can to just…put it out of my mind and move forward." She peered up at me with her dark eyes pleading.

I scrubbed my hand over my face and tried to ignore the low whooshing of the blood pounding in my ears. "I get it. You don't like mixing personal and professional. I understand, I do. But I can't simply forget what you taste like. Or the sounds you make when you come. How am I supposed to forget the way you draped your leg over mine and pressed against me as you fell asleep? You held me like you never wanted to let go." I stepped a bit closer. "Am I forgettable?"

I searched her face, and I could almost see the wheels turning as the memories played. She swallowed and ran her tongue along her bottom lip. Voices carried down the hallway, getting louder by the second. I moved back, putting more space between us. The random chatter changed from talking to singing as the team came into view singing "Happy Birthday" complete with a cake and balloons. They circled around us as the song came to an end with them all cheering and clapping as I blew out the candles, with my attention on Khadijah rather than the burning sticks of wax.

# Nine

## Khadijah

It was just dinner. With the team. Yet I hadn't stopped kicking myself for saying yes. I had stuck my foot in my mouth with Shae, and I needed a way to make it better, so I'd accepted. We were adults, or so I kept telling myself, yet I was the one making things weird where they didn't have to be. I needed to turn things around, and dinner in a group setting would help. *I hoped.*

I'd stressed over what to wear, and even as I pulled into the parking lot of the upscale steakhouse on Piedmont, I worried my choice of outfit was wrong. I'd thought about pants and immediately heard Jah's voice mocking me in my head. It'd taken me longer than it should have to finally settle on my calf-length, high-waisted yellow skirt. It was flowy with a vintage look and the best feature was the deep pockets. Paired with a simple black fitted, off-the-shoulder top and my favorite floral-print wedges, I pulled off a casual enough look. And it fit within the restaurant's dress code.

I glanced at my reflection in the rearview mirror. I understood where Shae was coming from. Regardless of what I'd tried to tell myself, I would have called her again. She was anything but forgettable. A pang hit me again when the pained look in her eyes flashed in my mind. I grabbed the gift bag and took one more calming breath then exited my car. As I got closer to the entry, I noticed a small crowd surrounding a few of the players.

They posed for pictures and seemed to not be bothered in the least about the attention. *How did that not happen at the club?* I tried to recall any incident of people watching us or women approaching Shae or Tina, but I couldn't. Tina had gone through her share of dance partners, but that wasn't unusual given the environment. Maybe Jah and I had come late and missed the initial uproar.

One of the players, whose name flew right out of my mind, noticed me first. She released a catcall whistle as I approached. "You're turning heads."

"I could say the same thing about you."

The blond hair that I'd only seen up in a messy bun during practice now hung free around her shoulders in soft waves that rivaled any shampoo commercial. She wore a deep royal blue bodycon dress that showed off her amazing figure.

Tina looked me up and down, smiling and nodding. "Alright. I see you." She was also dressed up in white fitted ankle-length pants and a loose-fitting shirt decorated with large red roses. A much different look than the jeans and polo she'd had on at the club.

I rolled my eyes and laughed. One of the kids who'd been snapping pictures walked over to me.

"Can I get one with you?"

I shook my head. "Oh, I'm not a player."

"Whatever," Tina said, moving to stand beside me. "You're a Cannon now." She smiled wide as the other ladies all grouped around me for one last picture.

I noticed that the woman of honor wasn't among the group. As I was about to ask about her, Shae popped her head out the door.

"Our table is ready." When she saw me, she broke out in the brightest grin.

Why did she have to be so disarmingly beautiful? Her braids were done in a similar style as the night we met. Lips that I remembered the feel of far too vividly held a tiny hint of gloss. But it was the dress that really made my mouth go dry. It was a simple black sheath design with capped sleeves that showed off the intricate design of her tattoo, and a thin red belt. Shae wasn't an overly curvy woman with her athletic build, but the added accessory gave her waist more definition and an illusion of roundness to her hips.

*How was I supposed to make it through dinner without staring at her all night?*

I trailed behind the rest of the group, trying to put as much distance between myself and Shae as I possibly could. A move that backfired as I was the last to step into the room. The seat that remained open was the one next to temptation herself.

After easing into my chair, I handed her the gift bag. "Happy birthday."

Shae's fingers brushed against mine. An innocent enough

move, but one that somehow seemed more forbidden. Especially given how we'd left things earlier in the day.

"Thank you. You didn't have to get me anything."

"I wanted to." A simple and true statement. I'd left work and knew deciding on a gift for her was a priority before I went home. When I managed to tear my attention away, my body immediately warmed from the interest the rest of the table had in our exchange.

"So, what'ya get?" Courtney asked, breaking up the prolonged seconds of awkward silence.

Shae removed the blue and white tissue paper, setting it on the table, then pulled the bottle free. "Oh nice. An eighteen-year-old single malt whiskey." She twisted her lips into another heart-skipping smile. "Very thoughtful. Thank you."

The blonde, whose name I finally remembered to be Claire, held her hands out toward Shae, wiggling her fingers in a give-me motion. "I didn't know you were into whiskey."

Renee, who sat next to her, leaned in closer for a look. "Yeah, I didn't know either."

They both darted their eyes between the two of us. Shit. I'd debated over what to get and went with whiskey because I'd remembered her drink from the Lucky Lady. I'd wanted to get her something she'd hopefully enjoy, but now hearing that not everyone had that knowledge... Fuck. Why didn't I go with a generic bottle of wine? This would either be the time to disclose our prior connection or lie.

"What y'all should be focused on is that Khadijah has been here a week and got me a present. The rest of you bums are empty-handed," she joked and stuck her hand out, silently asking for her bottle back.

They all playfully mumbled and looked around the room as if she weren't talking to any of them, and I willed my nervous heartbeat to slow. Being witness to the team dynamic off the court was new for me. Sure, we'd likely dine as a complete team during away games and things like that, but that was different. This dinner was more a private, friends hanging out to celebrate situation, and as I glanced around the table, I realized I was the only nonplayer. Courtney's wife wasn't even in attendance.

*What was I supposed to make of that? Was I supposed to make anything from it?*

"Where are the other coaches?"

Courtney picked up a roll and buttered it. "Eh, they don't usually hang with us."

"What?" They had been there for the singing and cake. I tried to recall who'd been around when Tina had invited me along for the night. No one had said anything.

"Coach Smith always declines, saying she doesn't want us holding back on our fun because she's around giving us the side eye or something," Shae answered with a laugh. "Vickers is a newlywed so he's not about spending his free time with us. And Marni…not sure. She's only been here for a season so maybe she doesn't think she fits in."

"And most of us think Coach Adams is great at his job, but his personality sucks," Tina said, stressing the last word.

There were a few chuckles and head nods in agreement with her statement. As the waiter arrived to take our orders, I tried not to read too much into the optics of me being here. That was easier to do than my failed attempts at ignoring Shae's leg whenever we brushed against each other. I focused on keeping my hands above the table at all times even though I desperately wanted to run my fingers along her soft skin.

I had to bite down on my tongue more than once to stop myself from telling her how stunning she looked. Even worse, to keep myself from voicing my fantasies of unzipping her dress and kissing every inch of her flesh.

Shae Harris was anything but forgettable.

And under different circumstances maybe, just maybe, I could give the whole relationship thing a go again. I could attempt to take things slow and simply let them develop instead of trying to force things to fit the long-since-missed timeline for where I should be in my personal life. But she was on the other side of the line I'd drawn in the sand.

However, sticking to my guns and maintaining a strictly professional relationship was easier when we were at work. *Somewhat…*

As the night came to an end, I found myself wishing for a way to prolong it. But also, I needed to get home and spend some time with Deliah, my trusty vibrator. After hours of sitting next to Shae, listening to her voice, being warmed by her musical laugh and the accidental brushes of skin, I was frayed. Everyone said their goodbyes and peeled off to their respective vehicles, and somehow it came down to Shae and I.

"Well, I guess this is where we say good-night."

"I guess it is. Thank you again for the gift. I can't wait to try it."

"I hope you enjoy it." With nothing left to say I turned and headed to my car, with Shae falling in step beside me. "Am I getting an escort?"

"Not quite. I'm parked in this direction as well."

The short walk was spent trying to come up with something to say. Should I apologize for my terrible explanation from earlier? Should I tell her how amazing she looked? I couldn't decide on anything and all too soon we were standing at her truck.

"Looks like I'm the one who got the escort." Humor colored her tone, which managed to put me somewhat at ease. She hit the button on her fob to unlock and set the gift on the driver's seat.

"You are the birthday girl. I should have told you earlier, but you looked...look amazing tonight."

"Thank you." Her gaze roamed the length of my body. "And same to you."

Walk away. That's what I needed to do. Say good-night and get in my car and simply go home.

"You look like you want to kiss me."

"I do." The answer slipped out freely before I could stop it.

"But wouldn't that be breaking your rule?"

I nodded, my mouth dry, my attention fixated on her lips. We were partially hidden, boxed in because of the large SUV parked beside hers. The privacy and closeness... One kiss, one kiss wouldn't hurt, right?

"You're sending me mixed signals, Dijah."

The sound of my name tumbling from her lips sent a shiver down my spine. I closed my eyes for a long blink and let her statement serve as a course correction. Toying with someone's emotions was not something I did.

"I'm sorry. You're right, and I shouldn't."

An easy grin spread across her face as she reached out and ran her thumb across my lips. I held my breath, hoping, praying she'd do it anyway. That she'd be braver than I was.

Instead, she withdrew her hand and settled into the seat of her SUV. "But knowing that you want to—" The sexy smile on her face widened. "I'll see you tomorrow."

# Ten

## Shae

Pulling the laces tighter on my white skates already had the tension leaving my shoulders. No music. I needed the sound of the wheels against the wood rink to bring the calm. Standing, I stretched and took in a deep breath, letting the familiar scent fill me with peace, then pushed off. I moved with ease around the oval, picking up speed as I went.

The subtle breeze against my face as I let my momentum carry me had me closing my eyes and settling into the freeing motion of it all. This was my second love. It especially helped when I needed to think, and being a partial owner in Roll With It had its perks. Like being able to spend time mostly alone before the doors opened for the day.

It'd been an interesting few weeks. The team was coming together, and we were working out the kinks of adding the new players to the roster. We got a couple of good rookies, and picked up two new semi-seasoned players on trades. Growing pains. But we were getting a feel of their strengths and weaknesses to see how they'd best benefit our already established plans. The first game was in two days, and the nerves I usually got closer to opening day started earlier this season.

I pushed harder, moving along to the symphony of thoughts playing in my head. I'd been playing ball since rec league yet remained unable to stop the doubt. Would I bank my shots? Would I be fast enough on the rebound? Would I pull my weight?

I always did. It was rare I had an off game, but I knew the chance was always there.

Preseason had gone smoothly, but that meant nothing in the long run. Being ranked the seventh or eighth seed and getting eliminated in the first round of postseason was getting old. And that was for the seasons we hadn't been cut from playoffs completely. If we could get it together, we could be real contenders.

The flying sensation calmed my ever-raging thoughts as I picked up speed. I wasn't cocky enough to think I carried the team, but I was more than aware of how much responsibility I put on myself as I gained recognition and fame for what I did on the court. Especially with the league still not being given the same interest or respect as our male counterparts. "Breakout" stars put butts in the seats, so I had to make sure I continued to do my part not only for the Cannons, but for the WNBA overall.

And that included not being distracted.

*Khadijah.*

I spun and weaved my way around the rink backward as

thoughts of her elbowed their way to the forefront of my mind. Since my birthday she'd been trying harder to maintain a strict work-only stance. And I tried hard to respect the boundary she was attempting to erect. But damn if it wasn't difficult with the way she continued to contradict herself. Every time she had her hands on me, no matter how innocent the intention, the looks that accompanied those instances had a way of making them feel more intimate.

On my next loop, O rolled onto the floor, easily catching up to me. I smiled at the older man as we made a few rounds in silence. He had on his signature oversized white T-shirt that was stretched across his large stomach and denim shorts that were so long they could almost be pants. Square black glasses took up most of his round face. A full, bushy majority-gray beard took up the rest. He was never without a hand towel tossed over his shoulder, which he used to constantly wipe across his bald head—whether he was actually sweating or not. I had to guess it was more habit now than anything else.

When I'd first moved to Atlanta, I was more than a little unsettled. New city, far from my family and friends, trying to get the lay of the land. I'd found this place doing a Google search. I'd needed something familiar to help me feel not so alone during the first few months as I got acclimated. I'd come nearly every day, which eventually led to me striking up a conversation with Mark—though most folks called him Big O—and his wife, Sheryl.

"No music today. You must really be in your head about the season," he commented in his gruff voice.

A wry smile tugged at my lips. Coming here and doing a few spins had become my ritual, though normally I'd have my game day playlist going. The fact he'd noticed the difference and joined me twisted the knot in a different way. He and Sheryl had really become like surrogate parents over the years and were nearly as proud of my accomplishments in the league as Mom and Dad were.

"Our first game is against the defending champs," I answered without breaking a stride. "In their house." I hated starting the season with an away game. It was like starting with a disadvantage. Especially when the city meant a change of time zone.

"Now, Shae, you know that ain't nothin'."

"It is when we haven't won a game against them in three years." I sounded whiny. I hated that I sounded so damn whiny.

"Welp, with thinkin' like that, you're right, g'on and lose then. Hell, why show up at all?"

I cut him a side eye, but couldn't stop the small laugh. "You know what I mean. It's added pressures this season and I'm feeling more distracted than usual."

He nodded thoughtfully. "Yup, I can imagine, Ms. Captain. I don't know why you are so resistant to the leadership role when you're such a damn natural. You know damn well you dominate on the court and that your teammates look to you whether you hold a title or not. So, what's really goin' on?"

I let out a heavy sigh as I rolled over to the half wall and took a seat. "Damn, O, can't a woman just be in her feelings a bit?"

"Nah, you know I don't play that shit. I can get Sheryl if you wanna keep bein' all moody for no reason. I know she coddles yo ass." He flicked my arm with his towel before swiping it across his head.

I shook my head and laughed. If nothing else, Mark Owens

was good about telling me about myself. Which was exactly what I needed at times, to not be swallowed up by the what-ifs and worries.

"Now come on so I can once again school yo ass in the proper skating style so you can give up that Detroit shit. You in the South, girl, act like it." He grinned wide, showing off his gold-edged front tooth. Big O was old-school indeed.

I pushed to standing and barked a laugh. "Oh, you mean the 'style' that is basically a mash-up of everything 'cuz y'all ain't original. That 'proper skating'?"

He pulled his glasses down so they perched on the tip of his nose and peered at me over the top of them. "Disrespectful."

I parked my Wagoneer in the driveway of Courtney's three-story Johns Creek townhome. I still couldn't believe my friend had bought the place considering she'd wanted to stay in Downtown, but she said Sasha had fallen in love and she couldn't tell her no. Even though the few hours at the rink had done me some good, I'd debated on calling for a rain check on lunch with the Bradfords. It wasn't that I didn't enjoy hanging out with Courtney and Sasha—it was just always up in the air which version of them I'd be with. When they were good, they were great, but when they weren't, it could be tense for everyone around.

Sasha opened the door for me no sooner than I'd rang the bell. "Shae!" she exclaimed, juggling Vuitton, her two-year-old Yorkie, to the side and opened her other arm for a hug, careful not to spill what was probably a mimosa.

Courtney had gotten her the animal hoping he would keep her company, especially since Courtney played in the European league during our off-seasons. I recalled the fight the two of them had one night when we'd been out to dinner. Sasha had gotten a little tipsy and accused Courtney of being neglectful because she was gone all the time, and the two had gotten so loud, I'd been sure they were going to ask us to leave. To say their relationship was volatile at times would be an understatement. In fact, some of their public arguments had been talking points on ESPN a time or two.

"Hey, Sasha. Missed you at my birthday dinner."

"Yeah. Sorry 'bout that. Had to go back to Fort Valley because Big Momma was on her 'deathbed' again. But I'm convinced that woman is too mean to die." She rolled her eyes and pushed her glossy pink lips into a frown.

Her current wig was a bubblegum pink color, slicked down without a strand out of place, and tied up into a long braided ponytail. Her light brown skin tone worked well with most of the colors she chose.

"So, Court was tellin' me that ol' girl from the club works with y'all. Did y'all two hook up or what?" She glanced back over her shoulder at me, eyebrow raised. "Sorry I didn't get to talk to her much, that Henny took me the fuck out." She finished the statement then nearly drained the drink that was in her hand.

I followed her up the flight of stairs that led to the open-concept kitchen, dining, and living room. Courtney stood next to the oversized island, munching on those tiny dill pickles.

"Uh, she does," I answered, purposefully ignoring her question.

"Who does what?" Courtney inquired.

Sasha put the tiny animal down and he immediately whined

to be picked up again, which she ignored and instead went to the fridge to pull out some OJ. "Oh. I was just askin' Shae about y'all's new trainer."

Courtney nodded. "Yup, Shae has it bad for her," she said with a sly grin.

"Ooh, what? I mean I can see why. I know that night is a bit fuzzy, but if I remember right, ol' girl was pretty damn hot."

I slid onto one of the bar stools. "Let me get some."

"Just juice, or you want a mimosa?" Sasha clarified.

"Juice. And don't listen to your wife." I tried to keep my face neutral and my voice even. Courtney and Tina hadn't stopped giving me shit, not that I expected them to. I should count it as a small miracle they at least seemed to behave and not be all nosy with Dijah.

"Yeah, right. In all the years I've known you, PT time was always your least favorite. Now ya ass be practically skipping to the training room. Lurkin' about and shit, tryin' to be the last one there. What I said fucking stands." Courtney twisted her lips to the side and gave me a hard side eye.

Sasha laughed as she handed me my glass. "Damn, Shae. It's like that? We'll have to invite her over so I can get to know her better."

I took a gulp of my drink. It wasn't that I didn't like time with the trainers before. I knew it was a necessary part of my job to make sure I was ready to play. But I would be lying if I said I didn't look forward to the one-on-one time, nearly as much as I did the new yoga time she'd incorporated to both loosen the team up and strengthen the key parts of our bodies. Though that probably had more to do with her choice of outfits for those days. I had a hard time keeping my eyes off her when she walked around in yoga pants and a fitted tank top.

Finally, I lifted one shoulder. "She's a very good trainer."

"Good trainer my ass," Courtney shot back. "But seriously, I know you've been kinda tight-lipped, but what's goin' on with y'all?"

"Nothin'."

She twisted her lips to the side and tilted her head. "Look, you do you. Live and let live and all that jazz. But…"

"But what?"

"We all grown, long as it don't fuck up the team…"

I sipped on my juice and let Courtney's words—no, more like warning—rattle around in my head. It wasn't a big issue. Like she said, we were grown. If anything else happened between me and Khadijah it would be all good, and wouldn't have any impact on the team.

# Eleven

## Khadijah

I wheeled my suitcase behind me and stifled a yawn. Traveling always took a lot out of me. More because not only was our flight delayed, my shorter-than-everyone-else self was stuck with the middle seat between Jason and Marni during the five-hour flight to LA. The players were "lucky" enough to get the upgrade to the economy plus seating rather than standard, but the coaching staff, not so much.

I tried not to put any thought into the fact our first game was back in the city I'd recently moved from. All I wanted was a hot shower and to fall into bed hoping Marni wouldn't be a talker or a snorer. Having to share rooms had been a shock. I liked my privacy, and you could never know the cleanliness level of the other person. Nothing against Marni—we got along great for the most part—I'd just rather be on my own. But Coach Smith was the only one lucky enough to have that luxury.

I'd popped my melatonin gummy while we waited on luggage so I'd be primed and ready for a good night's sleep. Luckily Marni said she'd be up later; she stayed in the lobby to call her daughter. That would give me time to shower and go through my bedtime routine without feeling as if I was hogging the bathroom. Well, if she stayed down long enough.

I made my way to the bank of elevators and caught a glimpse of Shae as the silver doors started to close, but she stuck her hand out in time to force them open again. Courtney and Tina shuffled to the side to make room for me, opening a space for me to squeeze in beside Shae. She got along with everyone as far as I could tell, but it was also very clear that she, Tina, and Courtney were tight-knit. The three of them could be seen together fairly often, so much that I'd heard some of the other players refer to them as The Three Musketeers.

"Thanks for holding the door."

"No problem," she answered. "What floor?"

"Six." On instinct, my eyes went to the buttons and saw that number was already lit.

I bit my lip and kept my attention on the handle of my luggage, trying not to read too much into the silence or the way I could almost feel the two of them watching as if they expected something.

"So, are you ready?" Tina asked, thankfully breaking the awkwardness.

I turned to look at her. "For what?"

"Your first pro game."

I laughed quietly. "Um, I've already had it with the preseason games."

They each looked offended, or mildly horrified, or both.

"Those don't count," Tina said with her nose turned up. "Those are more like scrimmages, especially since the rookies tend to see more floor time to get them added experience."

"Oh, um, well in that case, I don't know. I'm not the one in the spotlight. They're there to see y'all. No one even knows who I am."

"You're kidding, right?" Courtney laughed out the question as she quickly started scrolling for something on her phone.

I met Shae's amused expression in the mirrored doors before they slid open. Shae stepped out first, onto my floor. If our rooms were next door to each other, I was for sure going to curse the universe for continuously finding new ways to test my resolve where she was concerned.

The other two followed, with Courtney handing me her phone. "Have you not checked your Insta feed?"

I stared at the image. It was the shot from outside the restaurant, and it had over thirty thousand likes plus comments. "Um, no. I haven't logged into my account in months. I'm fairly bad at social media." I handed her back the phone. "But that's still y'all. I'm behind the scenes."

Courtney smacked her lips. "Girl, please. Half those comments you didn't read was folks asking about the hot short one. I tagged you."

The four of us started walking down the hall. I didn't think much about any of the social sites despite how much Jah and my bestie Nikki tried to tell me I needed to have an online presence. Especially if I wanted to have my own business.

"When I get to my room, I'll log in and check it out."

Shae fell into step with me, readjusting the over-ear headphones around her neck. "Are you going to answer all the enquiring minds that want to know if you're seeing anyone?" She quirked her lips up into a half smile.

I swallowed, glancing ahead of us at the other two ladies before cutting my eyes in her direction. "No one wants to know that."

She let her gaze unabashedly travel down my body, her smile widening. Like every other time she aimed that bright and friendly smile in my direction, my heart skipped a beat. Not to mention my focus was once again so intent on her closeness that I hadn't noticed the other two had dipped off to their rooms until the elevator dinged, stealing my attention. *How did I keep losing myself around her?*

It was Marni—so much for claiming the bathroom before she came up. "Are we down that way or...?" She looked down at her key card then up at the direction plaque on the wall. "We're this way." She pointed to the left. "Night, Shae," she called, then headed off in the other direction.

Shae checked her own key card before glancing up to the doors we stood between. "Looks like this is me."

She slid the plastic into the slot and the light went from red to green. I should have left, headed to my room to sleep, but as usual, I lingered in her presence for a little longer.

Shae pushed her door open and wheeled her suitcase over the threshold, using it as a doorstop. "You have that look again." She leaned her beautiful body against the frame, arms crossed, face soft, and eyes sparkling with amusement.

She really was too stunning for words and her ability to temporarily short circuit my brain was not a good thing. I tightened my grip on the handle of my bag. "What look?"

Like the night of her birthday dinner, a playful smirk with a hint of smugness graced her full and all too kissable lips. "Like you want to kiss me."

I swallowed hard and pressed my lips together. I did indeed dream about kissing her and more, but the fact I was apparently failing at keeping those thoughts from showing on my face irked me. I was a professional. We were coworkers and I had rules. Nothing could happen again.

Too bad my head and body apparently failed to get that memo.

"Good night, Shae."

"Sweet dreams, Dijah."

When I got to my room, Marni was already in the bathroom and had claimed the bed closest to the door. I wheeled my suitcase to the other side of the space and took a seat before pulling out my phone. I scrolled through the apps and realized I didn't even have Instagram installed. My laziness for all things social media kicked in and I instead decided to go the simple route and google Shae's name. The flurry of articles that came up were not what I was expecting.

A small wave of nerves hit me as I took my seat on the bus. Tina's question about me being ready for my first game replayed in my mind. I would have been if I'd been able to get the good night's sleep I so desperately needed. Instead, thoughts of Shae had battled with the effects of my gummies, keeping me up.

I had to put her out of my mind. No matter how mutual the attraction between us was. Dating someone you worked with could only lead to disaster. The cons outweighed the pros. I mentally ran through them.

*Things would get awkward when the relationship inevitably fizzled.*

*I'm more replaceable than Shae, so I could be out of a job.*

*It could cause tension in the team.*

And those were only the top three. I had more—especially after the various articles on her dating exploits—which all led me to the same conclusion: entertaining any idea, any hope of potential possibility was ill-advised. And yet... I huffed out a breath then pulled out my tablet. *I'm focusing on my career. This is the last stepping stone before I can open my own facility. I can't get involved. I can't jeopardize that.* Another reason, and the one I really needed to keep in the forefront of my mind. I started scrolling through who would need what from me once we arrived at the arena. Work. That's what I was here for, not to daydream about a woman who commanded too much of my attention.

Especially after my dive down the rabbit hole led me to a picture of the two of us at Lucky Lady. I'd been so caught up, I'd never even seen anyone with a phone pointed at us. My face couldn't be seen, but I recognized my body. And the hold Shae had had on my waist. And the way her body had felt against mine. And the fucking caption. That came roaring forward like a big blinking light. *The next Harris Honey?*

Coach Smith settled beside me, her sudden appearance yanking me back to the present.

She leaned over to take a look at my tablet. "My starters all good?"

"Yeah, yes. A few stopped by my room today for some extra stretching and such, but everyone is all good and ready to go. I'll be using the kinesiology tape on Shae's knee and will get Tina's ankle all wrapped up for the extra support. Everyone else, there'll be work as needed to make sure they are taken care of for optimal performance."

She nodded and my eyes drifted up as Shae boarded. She wasn't one of the players to seek me out today. In fact, I hadn't seen her since last night. The headphones that had been around her neck when we'd talked now covered her ears and her head bobbed along to whatever song she was listening to. Despite all my earlier thoughts, a weird thread of disappointment weaved through me when she didn't even glance in my direction.

"They like you."

Coach Smith's comment stole back my attention. Had I given something away? Was my face showcasing my feelings? Last night I'd been grateful Marni had kept the conversation limited to work-related topics and figuring out the bathroom order. She'd looked as tired as I'd felt. But now I worried that maybe there had been some talk.

"What do you mean?" I asked with a twinge of caution in my tone.

She leaned to the side in her seat to look at me. "That you're fitting in well. Listening to their needs. Really working to personalize the treatments. I can tell they've gained a lot of respect for you in the short time you've been here. We need that, the cohesiveness."

Her words were unexpected, but welcomed. "Oh. Wow, thanks, Coach."

She pursed her lips and narrowed her eyes. "If you don't call me Dillyn…"

I smiled and nodded. She'd fussed at me before about using her name, but it was probably the Southerner in me that had me wanting to give her an honorific. Plus the other coaches I'd worked with had all seemed to want their titles used.

"Anyway, I have a good feeling about where we are as an

organization. Today's game is gonna be tough, but overall, I'm feeling like this year could be our year."

Again, I nodded along. Despite what Jah had fussed at me about, I still hadn't bothered to research the team stats. It had no bearing on what I did, but I knew enough to know I needed to say the right words to feign understanding. "I'm ready to do my part to make that happen."

Sports held zero interest for me. I didn't care or get the same rush of endorphins others did, which made me an anomaly given my job. However, if the Cannons had a winning season, it'd add to my job security. I pulled up the Notes app on my phone and made a memo to find out their past record.

When we arrived at the arena my nerves amplified. Thoughts of my conversation with Dillyn were fresh in my mind. Mentally I went through the checklist of items I'd packed, suddenly worried I'd forgotten something. The players all milled around waiting for their bags to be unloaded. Most talked and joked with each other, but not Shae. She stood off on her own, headphones still in place, a look of complete concentration on her face as she rocked side to side while seemingly dribbling air. It was different seeing her so focused. So serious. None of the playfulness that I'd been used to getting from her was present. And it was a change I wasn't quite sure what to make of.

Once inside, I wheeled my cart of items to the end of the locker room where two tables were placed next to the immersion tub. A quiet energy filled the room. The players rotated coming to me. Shae was the last to climb onto the table. Her headphones now hung around her neck, but she didn't say anything. She reclined back, listening to Dillyn as she and

Jason went over plays and all the stuff I typically tuned out. I kept my attention on my task, remaining as clinical as possible as I touched her.

After I finished, I finally glanced up to find her watching me. In near slow motion, the smile I'd missed seeing spread across her full lips. Shae bent and straightened her leg a few times before swinging them both to the edge to sit up. "Thanks, Dijah."

I didn't want to admit that the softening of her expression and the way my name always sounded like an intimate caress made my heart rate accelerate a little.

"Alright, huddle up, everyone," Coach Smith bellowed. I started cleaning up the bits of discarded tape until she singled me out. "Upton, you too."

I set the ball of sticky adhesive on the table, eyeing the team, who all glanced in my direction expectantly. Making my way over, I squeezed into the circle between Tyler and Marni, sliding my arms along their backs in the same fashion they'd done mine. We started rocking from side to side as Coach hyped them up, repeating the question of "Are we ready?" followed by a resounding "Yes!" Then "Who are we?" with a rumbling "Cannons!" in response.

The energy buzzed around with the rocking picking up speed the more the team collectively got into the zone. I'd always kept myself a little removed, but even I was hit with a wave of excitement during the pregame ritual. Residuals of that energy stayed with me as I took my seat courtside.

I'd always watched the games through the lens of my job, notebook at the ready. Tracking the players' movements. Noticing how they stepped and turned. Cataloging potential treatments they'd need during halftime and after the game.

However, as I watched them run up and down the court, my attention lingered mostly on Shae.

It was more than how she moved, graceful in her actions. Shae had presence on the court. She led and commanded attention from the rest of the Cannons. She played with determination and focus. The same focus she'd had pregame. She was a force. I'd never cared much for the sport—any sport—but seeing her in her element, I found myself invested in the outcome.

When the final buzzer sounded after the last shot, the disappointment on her face from the six-point loss had me wanting to go to her. To give her some words of encouragement, some comfort. Simple platitudes of "better luck next time" or whatever was said in times like these didn't seem enough. They were too generic. But, despite anything I'd been telling myself, I still wanted to make it better for her.

# Twelve

## Shae

I ran the towel down my face, keeping it in place as I took a few steadying breaths. Coach Smith gave her standard postgame talk, pointing out what went well before moving on to where we could improve. Jason and Tyler backed her up, highlighting how close the game had been despite what the commentators expected of us. But all I could think about was where we'd come up short. The rebounds we'd missed, the turnovers we'd had. The air balls, and the shots that had bounced off the rim.

I pulled in one more breath before draping the towel over my leg and glancing around the room. My team. They'd played hard. We did better than most had expected, even if it wasn't the outcome I'd hoped for. Wallowing in the loss did no good for morale. Before everyone dispersed to the showers, I stood to get their attention.

"Y'all, we played our asses off. We all knew going into tonight that everyone counted us out and expected a blowout. But like Coach said, we held our own. Losing always fucking sucks and we had way too much experience with that last season. But that's behind us now. We showed up tonight and made them work for it, and that's something we will take into the next game."

Lemonade from lemons. My team—my sisters—clapped and cheered, bringing the energy up. Not quite as high as pregame and nowhere close to the high if we'd won, but also not near as despondent as we'd been. Last season had been rough, one of the worst as a Cannon, so kicking off the year with a loss, no matter how close the margin, was a hard pill to swallow.

"Okay, get cleaned up. Shae, Courtney, and Renee, y'all are up for postgame interviews," Coach Smith said as a final directive before she, Jason, and Tyler left the locker room.

I needed a quick shower and to change, but first headed to where Khadijah stood as she finished up with Tina. Tina patted me on the shoulder as she passed me. I hopped up onto the table and Khadijah slowly removed the tape.

"That was a great speech you gave. They all hold you in such high regard. It was evident while y'all played, but even more so just now."

She looked at me with such sincerity in her eyes. Her statement was genuine, and something I needed to hear. I had to remember where we were and stop myself from pressing my lips to hers—completely forgetting about the game, the loss, and instead getting lost in the woman who was slowly torturing me.

I cleared my throat and pushed the desire away. "Thanks, Dijah. That means a lot."

She nodded and broke eye contact. "So, how are you feeling?" she asked after she finished getting all the tape off. Her fingers glided against my skin, gently massaging the area. It needed the attention because after my last rebound, I'd come down wrong, felt a twinge, but pushed through.

"A little sore, but…"

We again made eye contact and the barest hint of a smile tugged the corner of her mouth to the side. "You played the entire game, so I want you to spend a few minutes in the tank."

I sat up, leaning closer so my comment wouldn't be overheard. "You just wanna get me out of my clothes."

She sank her teeth into her bottom lip and shoved her hands into the pockets of her black pants. "It's my job to look after your body."

"So, it's for purely professional reasons then?"

"Of course. I am a professional after all." The coy smiles she gave were quickly becoming favorites of mine.

I slid off the table and she didn't step back to give me room. "That you are. But next time. I only have about fifteen minutes before I'm expected to sit and answer questions like 'Where did we go wrong'? and 'How can we improve for next game?'"

I tried to keep the annoyance out of my voice. I hated post-game interviews when the reporters wanted us to sit and dissect all the ways we'd fucked up. It was my least favorite part of the job.

"Shae, I really need you to cool down."

"That'd be easier if you weren't always getting me hot."

Her eyes went wide. "Shae!" she whisper-yelled, glancing around to see if anyone could have heard. "Two minutes, in the tub. Now."

"Oh, you can be bossy. I like that." I whipped my shirt over my head and wiggled out of my shorts, leaving me in my sports bra and compression pants.

I really didn't have time to sit, but the plunge would probably do me some good. Especially since I was still feeling slight discomfort when I bent my leg. The icy temp was a welcome shock to my body. Khadijah removed the magnetic timer from the side, the low-pitched beeps sounded out as she punched in the time.

"I'll do five."

She glanced up at me. "I thought you were under the crunch for interviews."

I carefully slid to the side of the tank and folded my arms along the edge. "I am, but, if you're so concerned about the state of my body, I should listen to you." Flirting with Dijah was a distraction and helped lift my mood.

She pushed the buttons three more times then placed the timer back on the tub. "Your body is my top priority. Professionally speaking."

I settled against the back of the tank. "Good to know."

Khadijah said nothing more as she walked off to clean up the area where she'd been working. The activity of the locker room faded away as I watched her. Even though the cleaning crew would be in once we left, Khadijah picked up the discarded bits of tape and wrap, making sure they were all thrown away instead of left lying about. She wiped down the tables, doing her part to leave the area as meticulously clean as she'd found it. All playfulness aside, Khadijah took pride in her work, and I respected that.

The postgame interviews were as I'd expected, with one

particular asshole who kept harping on our last losing season and how the loss to LA was potentially setting the tone for another. I swear some of them were like sharks who smelled blood in the water, circling in for the kill. Any change of attitude I had been feeling after my interactions with Dijah went straight out the window, which was reflected in my clipped answers. Luckily Coach wrapped things up.

By the time we made it back to the hotel, I found myself in that weird space of being tired yet worked up. Alone in my room, my mind wouldn't stop spinning. My thoughts alternated between obsessively thinking over the game and gentler interludes of my interactions with Dijah. I closed my eyes and pulled in a deep inhale trying to maintain focus on her.

The sound of her voice. The melodic tone of her laugh. Her firm yet deft touch. We continued to orbit each other with her trying much harder to fight against the gravitational pull we seemed to have. I was trying to respect the boundary she set, but part of me felt like she wanted me to push it. Though it could have been my wishful thinking.

I flopped onto my back attempting to find a comfortable position and my mind settled on one train of thought. Khadijah…

I pulled in slow, easy breaths as visions of her became more prominent. I licked my lips as I recalled the taste of her. Every time I was near Khadijah, I was reminded of our night together. When she gazed at me with her dark, mesmerizing eyes, my stomach did flips. I took deeper, even breaths as I ran my hands over my breasts, slowly letting the hardness of my nipples graze the heel of my palms.

How I wished it was her touching me. She wanted me as much as I wanted her, no matter how much she fought against it—a fact I knew wasn't just my wishful thinking. Leisurely, I continued my movements, enjoying the slow build of arousal spreading through my body. But I needed more, like I needed more with her. Shoving one hand under my shirt, I shivered at how hot my own flesh was to the touch.

I squeezed and rolled my nipple between my fingers, the sensation making my breath quicken. My other hand journeyed south beneath the waistband of my shorts until I made contact with my already damp panties. Memories of her mouth on me had me biting my lip. The attention she'd lavished on my breasts drew a soft moan as I rocked my hips. The warm, wet heat of her mouth had teased and taunted me to new heights. I pinched my nipple harder, and my pussy throbbed at the added stimulation.

Why was the one woman who'd managed to enrapture me off-limits? The universe brought her into my life, yet in a cruel twist kept her just out of reach? With light pressure, I moved my fingers in circles against my clit. Phantom traces of her intoxicating aroma teased my senses.

The need grew, and my release clawed under the surface. Frustration had me shoving my hand into my underwear, needing all barriers out of the way. The slickness of my arousal aided in the easy insertion of my fingers. I moved them in and out while rocking my hips. I pressed my palm against my sex in desperation. But it wasn't enough. I wanted the weight of her body, the warmth of her breath. I craved to hear the little hitches in her breathing and gasps she taken while I'd pleasured her.

The words of encouragement she'd spoken after the game, after the loss—sincere, comforting, they'd been exactly what

I'd not known I'd needed. I pushed the defeat from my mind, attempting to refocus. I worked my hand faster, chasing a relief that remained too far out of reach. Flipping onto my stomach, I fucked myself, pumping my hips up and down at a frenzied pace, grinding for every bit of contact I could manage. My frustration grew the longer it took to get me over the edge. I buried my face in the pillow, wetness ran down my fingers, and a dull ache started in my wrist from the way I laid on my arm.

"Fuck!" I grunted, yanking my hand free before I climbed out of bed and stalked over to the bathroom.

Angrily, I washed my hands, scrubbing them as if the somewhat rough treatment was punishment for failing to do their job. Letting the water pool in my hands, I leaned over the sink and splashed the cool liquid on my face.

"Get it together, Shae," I whispered to my reflection.

I couldn't remember the last time I'd gotten this worked up over a woman. I stared at my reflection for a few more seconds and a twinge of guilt started to creep in. I shouldn't have been using her as masturbation fodder to begin with. Served me right I couldn't get the job done. Blowing out a hard breath, I grabbed one of the white hand towels to dry off, then turned out the light in the bathroom. I climbed into bed, staring up at the ceiling in the dark, hoping sleep would come soon.

# Thirteen

## Khadijah

"Holy shit that was close," Marni said, smiling down at me.

I rose from my chair, nodded, returning her grin. "They played great. And I better go get ready." I gave a parting glance at the team still celebrating while some did courtside interviews.

I waved at Sasha as I passed by her. She was seated in her usual spot, dressed to the nines as always. We'd talked a little when she'd hung around after the games, waiting on Courtney, and she had invited me to dinner. So far, I'd been able to hold her off with the season being busy, but really, I needed the excuse not to be around Shae in a personal setting.

As I walked down the corridor and the sounds of the crowd got quieter, my thoughts went to the woman of the hour. She'd scored the winning shot, and I was already picturing her smiling face and the high energy she'd bring into the locker room.

Losses happened, I knew this, but I wanted nothing but wins if for no other reason than to see the joy and excitement that radiated from Shae when they happened.

*Shae…*

It'd been a confusing three months. While she still flirted with me from time to time, I could also tell she'd backed off. Respected the boundary I'd set, though at times I had a hard time sticking to it. Jah had no problem voicing her disappointment over my "irrational stubbornness" in regards to the whole situation. But she didn't have to understand, or even approve. I knew what was best for me…even if the looks of longing Shae occasionally gave had me questioning my life choices. When that happened, I reminded myself I'd put the rules in place for a reason. Even if my vibrator was getting one hell of a workout.

Jubilant voices pulled my thoughts back to the task at hand. Claps and laughter became the soundtrack as the team entered. I tried to force myself not to search for Shae in the crowd, but my eyes apparently had a mind of their own. My own adrenaline seemed to spike when, in the midst of the excited chaos, her attention landed on me.

Luckily Coach Smith began her postgame talk. It gave me time to reinforce my willpower, which sadly seemed to weaken a little bit every day. The more I got to know her, to see how she cared for her team, how she focused on her job, how she seemed to do what she could when she could, my respect and admiration had only grown. After all the speeches were done, the players who didn't get much playing time headed off to the showers. I offered up my congrats to them as they walked by; some held up their hands for either a high five or a fist bump.

No matter who I tended to first, Shae always ended up

being the last one on my table. Was it her doing or mine? I couldn't be sure. What I did know was I avoided staring at her directly for too long. Especially when she was resting in her sports bra with her nipples making themselves known behind the team-colored fabric.

"Good game, Shae." I tossed the tape I'd peeled off her knee into the wastebasket.

"Thanks, feels good to be racking up wins. If we keep this up, we could be real contenders for the playoffs." Hopefulness laced each of her words and I wanted that for her.

I bent her leg and straightened it out a few times. "How's your knee? I saw you massaging it during the huddles."

"It's fine."

I glared up at her. "Shae, making it to the playoffs will only happen if you and everyone else are in top condition. Be honest with me so I can do my job and keep you doing yours."

A playful grin lifted the corner of her mouth. "I really like you being all bossy." She put her hands up in surrender before I could make a comeback. "It was fine until the jump shot during the third quarter. I might have landed a little harder than I should."

I sighed and shook my head. Without a word, I moved over to the racks to retrieve a bolster pillow from the shelf and an ice compression pack from the freezer. We didn't speak, but I felt her eyes on me, watching my every movement. With gentle hands I slid the pillow under her leg to elevate it then placed the ice pack across her knee. Shae didn't even react to the coldness touching her skin.

She adjusted, resting her arm behind her head. "How long do I need to lay here?"

"Do you have to do postgame interviews?"

She shook her head. "Not this time."

"Okay. Ten minutes then."

Coach Smith walked over before Shae could respond. "We all good over here?" she asked, darting her eyes from Shae's knee to me.

"All good, Coach. Dijah likes looking at my body."

My eyes widened and embarrassment bloomed throughout me while Shae managed to keep a straight face. Coach Smith cast a glance between the two of us, and a small grin pulled on her lips.

"Well, I'll leave her to it then."

Before I could admonish Shae for what she'd said, Tricia—one of the rookies—came over to have me stretch out her ankle. I situated myself so my back was to Shae, and I did my best to laser my focus on Tricia instead of wanting to look over my shoulder to see if Shae was watching me.

I pulled into the parking lot of the Sandy Springs shopping center. I'd been looking forward to the two days off before the next away game at Indiana. A night out with Nikki was exactly what I needed. Hanging with my friend would be the perfect distraction, and it was another reason to be grateful I'd gotten the job.

Not only had I missed my family, but I'd missed my friend. Yes, I'd found other wine and paint places, but I couldn't beat the laughs I had when it was me and my girl, sometimes Jah. But as her pregnancy progressed, she was getting crankier, which meant she'd opted out of tonight.

Exiting my car, I headed toward The Painting Party with

my bottle of chardonnay. My smile got wider when I laid eyes on my friend. I'd been busier than I'd expected lately so we'd not had as much time to hang out as I'd hoped. Luckily, she'd been understanding, new job and all, but still I had inklings of guilt over being back and yet unavailable.

I leaned in for a tight hug. "Hell must be a solid block of ice if your always late ass beat me here."

She frowned while shaking her head. "Had to sneak out because Imani is too damn clingy these days. Her dad be right there doing nothin', but she needs me for every damn thing."

I laughed as she talked about my nine-year-old goddaughter. She was a sweet child who was at an age I would have thought made her more independent. And she was for the most part. However, she was very much a mommy's girl and wanted to do most things with Nikki. We hooked arms and walked toward the door.

"Hey, you better enjoy it now. Before you know it, she'll be a teenager and you'll no longer be cool to hang out with. At least that's what people say."

Nikki scrunched her face. "Please. I will always be the cool mom."

The host greeted us as we entered and instructed us to grab our canvases, paints, as well as the plastic wineglasses. We took our supplies then found a space at one of the back tables.

"You're still going to make it to Imani's birthday party, right?" she asked as she worked to set up her station.

"It's what, a month and a half away? That'll put us in playoff time if we make it, but I asked some of the players how it all would go, and luckily her party falls on an off week, depending."

"Not as good as a solid yes, but now that you're in the big leagues I'm surprised you have time for us peasants." A playful grin was on her face as she handed me one of the plastic paint trays.

I rolled my eyes. "Why are you always so damn extra? I'm not doing anything I haven't been doing for the last decade. Besides, I'm slumming here with you right now, aren't I?" I added with a slight shove to her shoulder. "But I am going to do my damnedest to be there. I can't keep disappointing my girl."

When I got the schedule, the time around her birthday was the first thing I checked. It'd been years since I was able to attend Imani's birthday parties and I didn't want to disappoint her again this year. It was unfortunate her birthday fell outside of regular season, but based on what I'd been told, chances were good I would make it.

After Nikki finished setting up her area, she opened the wine and poured us each a glass. "Good, because she's been going on and on about Auntie Dijah and whatever cool and over-the-top gift she might get this year."

I may or may not have spoiled Imani, but when you lived the family life you were desperate for vicariously through others, going overboard happened from time to time. As my romantic prospects seemed more and more like a pipe dream, I was fully settling into my role as "rich" auntie. Or trying to. Part of me still held out some hope, the part that Shae had awakened despite my best efforts otherwise. I shook my head trying to dislodge the thoughts of the woman plaguing me at every turn.

"What does miss lady want anyway? Besides world domination?"

Nikki took a sip then dramatically smacked her lips before releasing a sigh. "Well…"

Oh shit. With a start like that I knew it was something big. And something I was probably going to bend over backward trying to give my precious goddaughter.

"Omar has been attempting to get her into sports. Father-daughter bonding and all that. And because he wants her to know it's not just a 'boy thing,' they have been watching women's sports."

I narrowed my eyes as I drank the slightly sweet and buttery alcohol. She was about to hit me up for courtside tickets. I could feel it in my bones, and was already going over in my mind who I'd have to plead with to make it happen. I knew getting tickets was a job perk, but I'd not really put any thought into figuring out that aspect.

"There are a handful of games left in regular season, I'll talk to Coach Smith about tickets."

"What? Oh no… I was hoping for something a bit more special."

"More special than courtside seats? She wants a signed jersey or something?"

The sly grin on my friend's face was highly suspicious and made my stomach knot. Nikki set her glass down then whipped out her phone.

"Those are both great, as a backup option." She typed away for a little while. "But she was really hoping you could get…" She turned her phone to face me, and I nearly choked.

Shae's team picture was on the screen. I took a bigger gulp of my wine. Even on my off day, the universe wouldn't let me be free of her. Nor would my dreams at night, or wandering thoughts during the day… Again, I shook my head before I ventured too far down memory lane.

"Shae Harris. What about her?" I was thankful I managed to keep my voice even instead of it hitching up an octave over the growing distress.

Nikki darkened the screen. "Well, I was hoping that maybe, possibly, hopefully, you could get her to make an appearance."

I blinked slowly and hoped I hadn't heard her correctly. Luckily the instructor got everyone's attention and started his spiel welcoming first-timers, thanking returning patrons, and giving a general rundown of how the night would go. I tuned him out, much like when the flight attendants did the safety speech. My thoughts were occupied with my friend's ask.

I would do almost anything for Imani, and hell, maybe if it was one of the other players…but this was a lot. An over-ask. One that would further blur the line I was fighting to keep clear and distinct.

I stepped closer and kept my voice low. "I can probably swing a signed jersey or something. But it's not very professional of me to ask her to show up like that. I would be infringing on her time off. Not to mention I think they usually get paid to make appearances, so, I'd be costing her time and money."

"Oh. She stuck-up and bitchy like that?" Nikki turned her nose up in disgust.

"No. Why would you say that?" The question came out harsher than I intended. It was a flippant remark that irked me more than it should have. I knew it wasn't personal, but still, I didn't like that judgment being passed on Shae.

Nikki turned to face me, a frown pulling at her lips. "Because you are normally all 'I'll see what I can do' and shit. This time you're shutting me down quick, so I assumed it was because of Shae. You know some of those B-list celebs are the worst. A little fame goes straight to their heads," she said with a shrug before turning back to her canvas.

I took a few calming breaths and focused on my own canvas and creating a soothing mountain scene. Painting, creating, usually was the best way to bring some serenity to my life, my outlet, a way to let go. Doing it with my friend normally made for great downtime. Instead, she had my mind racing. Nothing Nikki had said was anything out of pocket. Talking shit about celebs was one of her pastimes. My thoughts went to the woman who had a smile for everyone. Shae Harris wasn't a woman full of herself, and I had to admit her zest for life was magnetic.

We sipped and painted for a few minutes before I spoke again. "She's not like that."

"Who?"

"Shae. She's the furthest thing from stuck-up."

"So, you think she'd do it?" Hopefulness colored her tone as she refilled our glasses and promptly ignored my reasonably laid out objections.

Knowing Shae, she'd probably say yes. But I'd never find out. I'd been pushing my professional, no mixing business with pleasure rule, so I could not be a hypocrite, asking her to give up her personal time to attend something for me. *With me.*

"I'm not asking. I mean really, what I look like asking a woman I barely know to attend a family function with me?"

Nikki stood back from her painting to admire her progress. It was her go-to, a large multicolored sunflower. "You say it

like you're asking her out, not… Wait. Would it be you asking her out?" Nikki's eyebrows shot up and a giant smile took
up residence on her face.

I groaned. "No. And that's the point. You know I keep
work and dating separate."

"Pish. What dating? Your ass is trying for the born-again
virgin or some shit."

"I'm not celibate."

Nikki frowned. "You ain't? Since when?" Her question
came with a heavy dose of skepticism. "Because unless you've
been holding out on me, last time you talked about anyone,
booty call or otherwise, was four years ago." She pursed her
lips before draining her glass.

Had it been that long? I had stopped sharing because I'd
jump in with both feet, get a plan in place for how things
should progress, only to do the "walk of shame" shortly after
when things went sideways. Because they always went sideways.

"Anyway. I'll get her tickets and try for a team-signed jersey." It was a fair compromise and a great gift. And it was one
that wouldn't have me singling out Shae and further blurring
the lines I'd drawn.

# Fourteen

## Shae

As soon as the wheels touched down, I pulled out my phone to power it on. If the timing was as I expected, then my parents should have already arrived at the hotel. Dad always wanted to get an early start to beat traffic. As much as I looked forward to the game against Indiana, I was equally excited about dinner with them and finally getting my cake since I'd convinced Mom to bring it.

Once signal was restored to my cell, it vibrated consistently in my hand with the flurry of messages coming through. Mom sent one for every stop they made along the way: gas, food, bathroom breaks. I got a play-by-play of the road trip. It was a bit excessive, but it was how they operated, and at least if something did happen, I'd know exactly where to look for their last location.

Courtney leaned across the aisle, stretching her neck to see the screen of my phone. "Your parents arrive?"

"Yup. Checked in maybe an hour ago. Brandy got me their tickets before we left, so they're all set."

"Cool. Cool. Glad they made it safely. And I know they'll be hype tomorrow. They always bring the energy."

I smiled, thinking about how my parents acted at the games. My mom, usually the more laid-back one, turned into Ms. Hyde when it came to sports. Especially when watching "her baby" play. Another reason this was the only away game I actually looked forward to.

The moment the plane stopped moving and the seat belt sign went off, we stood and stretched. With the curtain that separated the two areas open, I rested my hands on the back of my seat, leaning forward to see if I could get a glimpse of Dijah. The entire time we'd sat waiting to board, she'd been in what looked like a deep conversation with Marni, both of them on their tablets, scrolling, making notes, and probably discussing player needs and such. I'd tried not to give creeper vibes as I kept glancing up from my phone to sneak a peek at her, something Tina absolutely called me out for.

I rocked sideways as I was shoved lightly. "What the hell?"

"We're getting off, so move your ass," Tina said, an annoying grin on her face. "You inviting her to dinner with us?"

I reached up into the overhead bin to grab our bags. "Who?"

"Don't play, you know who."

I simply rolled my eyes and filed out to deboard. When we got on the bus, I was happy to see the seat next to Dijah empty. She startled when I plopped down beside her. I ignored the annoying, knowing grins from both Courtney and Tina as they boarded. Rain pelted the roof creating a rhythmic almost calming white noise.

"This seat taken?"

"If it was, would you move?"

"Do you really want me to?"

I held her gaze, flashing her my full grin. She tried to maintain a serious look, but broke and displayed a big smile of her own, bright enough to lighten up the dreary day.

"Not at all. We can discuss your needs before tomorrow's game."

I licked my lips, giving her an appreciative once-over. "All of my needs?"

"Shae!" She quickly glanced around.

"What?"

She shook her head, but the smile didn't leave her face. I placed my arm on the armrest next to her, and it could have been my imagination, but she seemed to inch hers closer until we touched.

Leaning in, I angled my body toward her more. "You have plans for dinner?"

She shot me a sly side glance. "Shouldn't you be getting rest for tomorrow? Not asking me out?"

"So, that's a no," I replied, undeterred by her faux rebuff.

"I didn't say that."

"But you didn't say you had plans either."

She stretched her fingers out against mine, before balling her hand into a fist and glancing up at me. "No, I didn't."

I could easily get lost in her deep brown eyes. Being around Khadijah, seeing her struggle to deny the connection we had, brought out the competitor in me. The chase wasn't something I'd had to do for a while, nor had I wanted to. But with

Khadijah, it was part of the appeal. I liked that she challenged me, even if it came across as half-hearted some of the time.

"This is a special away game for me."

"Oh, really? Why?"

"Because of my parents. They don't like to fly, but they drive down from Detroit to see me play when we come here."

Her expression softened. "Is this game the only time you get to see them?"

"Nah, in the off-season I'll go home for a week or two. Catch up with family and all that fun stuff."

She slipped her hand into mine and squeezed. "That has to be hard. It was the part I disliked the most when I worked out of state. I'm glad you have this game to look forward to seeing your folks."

We let our fingers walk in minute motions, neither of us seemingly wanting to break the connection. There was a comfort she offered that I didn't fully understand, but at the same time couldn't get enough of.

"So…dinner?" I said, lowering my voice as I let her soft strokes lull my weariness.

"You're not letting this go, are you?"

"I would if you shut me down. But you haven't, so I won't. And if you're worried about this being a date, don't."

"Oh really? Then what is it? A friendly meal between *co-workers*?"

I tried not to cringe at how she stressed the last word. But also didn't miss the hint of playfulness in her voice.

"Yes, something like that. Because we don't have any team plans, I'm doing dinner with my parents at the hotel restaurant."

Dijah pulled her hand away as she sat up in her seat, twisting to get a better look at me. "I'm sorry. Say again."

"I'm doing dinner with my parents." I spoke slowly, not sure why she had such a shocked reaction to my statement.

She again glanced around, before leaning closer to me and whispering, "You're asking me to have dinner with you and your parents?"

"And Courtney, and Tina." Again, I spoke slow, trying to figure out her quick change in demeanor. It was dinner, not a proposal.

Dijah visibly relaxed, drooping against her seat. "Oh. Um, is this a usual thing?"

"Yeah. Long as timing works out. No delayed flights messing up things, it's happened before. Downside of flying commercial."

She nodded slowly and I tried to figure out what had spooked her so much when I mentioned dinner with my parents.

"So, are you good to join us?"

Dijah sank her teeth into her full bottom lip that I desperately wanted to kiss. "I don't want to intrude on whatever preset ritual or whatever y'all have going."

"There is no intrusion. Meet me in the lobby at six thirty. That way we can keep everything on the up and up. No damage to your reputation."

"As opposed to…?"

"Me knocking on your door and telling Marni we're going to dinner." I hit her with another large smile, which got an eye roll in response.

"I suppose if this is a casual thing, like your birthday dinner, then I'm available."

I nodded. "Ah...so that's the qualifier? You'd really turn me down if it was only going to be the two of us? That hurts." I hoped the last comment sounded as playful as I tried to make it.

Part of me was joking, but the part of me that still wanted to explore what we could be wanted—no, needed—to hear her answer. I understood she had boundaries, which I worked hard not to cross, but that didn't mean I didn't remain hopeful she'd stop fighting and give in to what I knew we both felt.

Dijah turned to look out the rain-streaked window. The city was a blur of gray as the bus navigated the streets heading toward our destination for the evening. We had a push-and-pull thing going, and most times I could believe it was all part of the game, but other times, her actions, or rather reactions, could and did cast a shadow of doubt. The longer she took to answer, the more the shadow grew. I watched her chest rise, then fall with a controlled breath before she faced me again.

Dijah placed her hand on my forearm as she made direct eye contact. "No, I wouldn't have turned you down."

# Fifteen

## Khadijah

*Why didn't I pack more clothes? Better clothes?* Like the birthday dinner, this meal would also be casual, no pressure, but that didn't stop the rapid-fire worries invading my head. *Why had I said yes? What was I thinking? Why was I having such a hard time sticking to my rules?*

Because Shae…

Big grin, laid-back attitude, and soulful eyes that drew me in and made me forget all common sense. I wanted to be around her. I was drawn to her. And it seemed my heart overruled my brain each time an opportunity presented itself outside of work.

But this was work related. Somewhat.

Just a dinner with friends…coworkers. No big deal.

"Khadijah?"

The sound of my name snapped me out of my head. "Huh?"

Marni sat on her bed, phone in hand, with a confused, somewhat comical expression on her face. "I said are you okay?"

"Yeah. Why?"

"Because you are chewing the hell out of your thumbnail while staring at your suitcase so hard, like you're hoping something else suddenly appears."

I snatched my hand down and shoved both into my pockets. "Oh, no. Just a lot on my mind."

Marni set her phone on the floating nightstand between the beds then rested back on her hands. "Work related? Or...?"

In the months since I started with the Cannons, Marni and I had never had heart-to-heart talks. We got along well enough. I knew a little about her outside life, I told her the basics on mine, but we kept our conversations mostly work- and occasionally TV-show related. And not that I had anything against her attempt, but one thing I'd learned the hard way early in my career was not everybody was your friend. Not to say Marni would fall into that category, but considering the topic, keeping the issue to myself seemed wise.

I pulled my dark-wash, high-waisted jeans from my suitcase along with my oversized light blue button-down. "It's me overthinking and stressing per usual." I gathered up my toiletry bag.

Marni made a noncommittal noise. "Got plans?"

I shook my head. "Not really. Having dinner with Courtney, Tina, and Shae."

"The Three Musketeers," she said with a quiet laugh.

"Yeah."

"It's interesting, out of all the ladies on the team, those three are really tight, and they seem to be bringing you into the fold."

She arched a brow, but didn't expand on her statement since her phone rang and her mood changed. No doubt a call from her daughter. I took the opportunity to escape into the bath for a quick shower to wash off the travel and make myself somewhat presentable to meet Shae's parents.

Half an hour later, I stepped off the elevator, scanning the lobby for my would-be dinner party. It didn't take me long to spot them and Marni's comment about them "bringing me into the fold" popped into my head. I wasn't sure if that was a dig, a fishing statement, or simply an observation. I'd worry about it later.

Slowly, I approached them, already feeling a bit like an interloper since I was the last to arrive and they were involved in conversation. Bits of laughter carried my way. Shae turned and spotted me, and my breath caught at the joy radiating from her. The rest of them noticed where her attention had gone and I forced my feet to carry me the rest of the way.

"Evening, everyone."

"Doc, you joining us?" Tina asked.

"Yeah, Shae damn near insisted."

Both Tina and Courtney grinned, but said nothing. My focus shifted from them to the older members of the group.

"Mom, Dad, this is Khadijah, our new athletic director. Khadijah, these are my folks, Charles and Doreen."

I shook both their hands. Shae's height came naturally as both her parents were fairly tall, with her dad towering slightly over the rest of the ladies. He was a gruff-looking man, the kind of guy who always looked pissed off even though he wasn't. Deep frown lines marred his forehead and his mouth rested downturned surrounded by a salt-and-pepper beard. His eyes, the same ones he shared with his daughter, did turn friendly when he greeted me. Both of them were outfitted in

Cannons gear, a visual sign of support for their daughter and the team.

"Doc? Is that just something they call ya or what?"

"Um, technically I am a doctor, though I rarely introduce myself that way. Some of the players took to calling me Doc and I just rolled with it."

"How are you 'technically' a doctor?" Mrs. Harris asked.

I'd known some kids could be damn near spitting images of their parents, but I'd never run across a pairing so close before Shae and her mother, the biggest difference being Mrs. Harris had much darker eyes than her daughter. Her hair was silver and bone straight, pulled back into a ponytail. Seeing it made me curious as to what Shae's hair would look like out of the braids she'd had the whole time I'd known her.

"Well, there was a doctorate program I completed…"

"Whew, child, then claim that shit. Talking about 'technically.' You did the work, you earned the title."

Shae pinched the bridge of her nose and groaned. "Ma."

"What?"

"How you fussin' already? And at someone you just met? Come on now."

"I'm not fussin'. I'm simply telling the young lady don't be downplaying her accomplishments. Now, let's eat."

She sauntered off in the direction of the restaurant. Mr. Harris simply shrugged and followed behind his wife, leaving the four of us standing there.

Shae placed her hand on my back and stepped closer. "Sorry about that. I promise they have home training."

I suppressed the shiver that threatened to shake my entire body from her proximity, and the sparkle in her eyes from her joke did ungodly things to my good sense, because I was tempted to say fuck it, wrap my arms around her neck, and get reacquainted with her lips.

Someone clearing their throat broke the spell. "We all have rooms, y'all need to go use one?" Courtney asked, a knowing grin on her face.

I remembered where I was, and why, then stepped away while glancing around to see who else might have witnessed the encounter. It was too easy...too damn easy to let my guard down around this woman.

"We shouldn't keep your parents waiting."

A half grin kicked the corner of her mouth up before she tilted her head in the direction we needed to go. As I walked, I pulled at the front of my shirt, needing to create space, air, separation, something to cool me down and to provide camouflage for nipples I was sure were at attention, but I was too chicken to look down and check.

"Y'all get lost?" Mr. Harris asked when we joined them near the hostess station.

"Nah, I needed to apologize for you two embarrassing me so early in the evening." Shae's reply was smooth and quick, which was good because I wasn't sure I could form a coherent sentence.

My thoughts jockeyed back and forth between the exchange we'd had and how I'd wished tonight, more than ever, I had my own room because I needed relief—sweet, sweet relief I wouldn't be able to get. Wondering if any of the players milling about had seen anything. And if they did, what they thought. I did my best to shove those worries into a box for another day.

Dinner was relaxed, and like at Shae's birthday, it was fascinating to see another side to her, and her friends. It was easy to tell the women had been a part of each other's lives for several years and that Shae's parents held them in kind regard. I was only mildly distracted because I somehow ended up seated next to the woman who short-circuited my common sense.

Mr. and Mrs. Harris were down-to-earth people, friendly and warm, much like their daughter. They cracked jokes in the midst of talking stats and getting updates on the season. It very much felt like a dinner with friends and not a dinner to "meet the parents," which had been my initial worry when she'd offered the invite.

"Khadijah, do you like German chocolate cake?" Doreen asked as we were exiting the restaurant.

"Yeah, I don't mind it."

"Good, good. Be sure to have Shae give you a slice. Spoiled child had me bring a whole cake with me for her." Doreen's face softened as she set her attention on Shae. "But she is my baby and since we don't get to see her as often, I do what I can."

We stopped outside of the restaurant, moving off to the side to make sure we didn't block the entrance.

Shae wrapped her arm around her mother's shoulders for a quick side hug. "And I appreciate it, Ma."

"Yeah, Doc, you should absolutely stop by Shae's room and have cake," Courtney said, barely containing her laugh.

Tina snorted and started coughing, drawing curious glances from both of Shae's parents. I didn't dare risk a look at Shae to see her reaction to the innuendo.

"I appreciate the offer, but I wouldn't want to deprive Shae of her treat."

"She can't, and shouldn't, eat an entire cake by herself. Especially not in one day," Charles piped in. Either he didn't understand the undercurrent tones of the conversation, or he stayed willfully obtuse to them.

"It's just a couple of slices," Shae objected. "But I don't mind sharing my cake with you, Dijah."

How she managed to deliver that line with a completely straight face was masterful. Meanwhile, I was internally dying from a mix of slight embarrassment and renewed desire to take Shae up on her offer.

# Sixteen

## Shae

My parents ditched us to go to a jazz club not far from the hotel. They seemed to like Khadijah, and I knew Mom would be asking questions that I was frankly surprised she didn't bring up at dinner. Especially after Courtney's comment followed by Tina's reaction.

Once they were out of the area, Khadijah shoved Courtney. "What is wrong with you?"

Her responding bark of a laugh turned a few heads. "Sorry, Doc. Was just having a little fun."

"By making inappropriate innuendos in front of Shae's parents?"

Courtney held up her hands. "I just said you should get cake. Ms. D makes the best. If *you* took it to mean something more, well that's your mind in the gutter."

Dijah started to respond, but kept quiet.

"I'm pretty sure there are books about that sort of thing," Tina added.

"What sort of thing?" I asked.

"You two. 'Go get it out of your system.'" She made air quotes around the last part. "Then y'all will be all better." Her corresponding smile was as big and conspiratorial as Courtney's.

All three of us stared at Tina, who simply shrugged. "What? I like romance novels."

Her reading choices could work in my favor, and I had to give it to my friends for playing the roles of excellent wing-women. Though I was damn certain the only thing sleeping with Khadijah again would do would make me want her more. Which I was one hundred percent okay with.

"Okay. Well, I think that's my cue to call it a night, ladies. Shae, thanks for inviting me to dinner." There was a lingering look before she turned and walked off.

"You think she's mad?" Courtney asked.

"I… I don't know, but I'll go find out. See y'all tomorrow."

I sped up my steps to catch her as she stepped onto the elevator; I got there right before the doors shut, sticking my leg out to force them to reopen.

"Shae. If those had closed on your ankle that would have been a disaster."

"But they didn't so all good."

"How are you so cavalier about possible, avoidable injuries?"

"Because I have you."

"I'm not Mr. Miyagi, I can't rub my hands together to heal a potential broken bone."

I blinked a few times before letting loose the laugh I'd tried to hold in. "So, you are mad?"

"What? Mad? About you not waiting to catch the next one? Annoyed maybe, because you shouldn't be taking unnecessary risks like that."

I moved so I stood in front of her. Dijah crossed her arms and tilted her head up to meet my stare.

"I needed to be on this one."

The elevator stopped and a couple got on, keeping any retort she might have made to herself. I slid behind her, close enough so I could feel the heat of her body and pull in the soft floral scent of her when I inhaled. The same smell that had slowly tormented my senses during dinner. When the doors opened two floors later, she started to get off but I slipped my arm around her waist.

"This is my floor."

"I think you're mistaken."

She peered back at me at the same time the couple who'd gotten on looked at us. The doors closed again, and we moved on to the next floor.

"Hey, are you Shae Harris?" the guy asked.

"Yeah."

His eyes went wide. "Can I get a picture?"

"Sure."

The doors opened again and Dijah didn't protest when I walked us forward, with the couple following behind us. She did attempt to step out of frame as the guy got closer to take the picture with me, but I held her hand, keeping her close. They thanked us, wished me a good game, then pressed the button to call for another elevator. We waited and waved once the doors opened and they stepped back on.

"Why did you keep me in the picture?"

"Why were you trying to escape?"

"Because he wanted you, not some random chick."

"You aren't a random chick, you're a Cannon."

She shook her head and released a slow breath. "I'm not sure I should be seen on your floor, let alone going to your room."

I reached back to grab at my hamstring when the second elevator door dinged then opened. Claire and Tricia stepped off, one carrying a pizza box.

Claire's eyes went wide when she saw us. "Shae, you okay? What happened?" She hurried forward, grabbing my arm and putting it around her shoulders.

I worked hard to not laugh and put somewhat of a grimace on my face. "Think I caught a cramp. Was messing around downstairs after dinner and with traveling…"

I let the statement drop off as I fished my room key from my pocket, handing it to Dijah, who looked a little shell-shocked.

"Um, what room?" Dijah asked, finally coming out of her short stupor.

"1011," I answered, adding a bit more hobble to my steps as Claire so graciously helped me down the hall.

Tricia trailed behind us. "You need me to get anything? Some ice from the machine?"

"Nah, I'm good. Doc said she'd take care of me. It's nothing some heat and a quick massage won't work out, right, Doc?"

She shot me a side glance as she slid the key into the slot but didn't say a word. Once in my room, Claire helped me to the bed and sat me down. I felt a little bad about lying, but I figured it was for a good reason, and it was a fairly harmless lie.

"Okay, well if you're sure you don't need anything else, I guess we'll leave you in Doc's capable hands."

"Thanks, for the help."

Dijah also thanked them and they gave one last glance before exiting my room. I rested back on my elbows, large grin on my face as Dijah stared at me with narrowed eyes.

"I cannot believe you did that."

"You were worried about what someone might think, I feel like I was quick with a solution. And a near Oscar-winning performance."

She slumped back against the desk across from me. "Claire seemed genuinely concerned about you."

I sat up and inched toward the foot of the bed. "Yes, and I do feel a little bad about that. But it was a hamstring cramp, something we all get from time to time. Tomorrow, she'll likely ask me how I'm feeling, and I'll answer good as new."

"And you did all that because…"

I stood and crossed the short distance to her. "Because you are worried about your reputation, or professional outlook. Although it does hurt a little that you feel like being seen with me is a negative."

She shot up, bringing her body closer to mine. "What? No…that's not… I don't see being with you, specifically, as a negative at all. It's circumstances." She spoke the last two words softly, almost like an apology.

She reached up and lightly touched my arm, letting her fingertips trace the lines of my tattoo. The contact was soothing, wanted, needed, replenishing. It was unrestricted. Without worry. In the confines of my room, the longer we stood, the more the barrier she tried to keep up seemed to slip away. I cupped her cheek, and she looked up at me with soft eyes and lips slightly parted.

"I don't think it'll work."

"What?"

"Trying to get you out of my system."

Her comment was music to my ears. My chest expanded when I took in a satisfied deep breath and a lightness spread through me. I slipped my other hand around her waist, pulling our bodies closer, and leaned down until our lips hovered centimeters apart.

"You know the cure for that, don't you?" She shook her head. "Practice. We should practice until we get it right."

Her tongue darted out to moisten her lips before she stretched up to close the space between us. I slid my hand down to the plump curve of her ass and squeezed. Her resulting moan was like a match strike to the desire that continuously simmered under the surface whenever I was around her.

Our mouths were hungry and excited at being reacquainted. Dijah worked to unbutton my shorts, her actions hurried and heated. A desperation that mirrored my own. Months of pent-up want finally able to break free. I moaned against her lips and squeezed her ass tighter when she slipped her hand into my underwear.

She pressed her palm against me and I tilted my hips forward in response, in urgent need for more contact. A slow forward-and-back motion with her fingers sliding between my pussy, a frustratingly beautiful tease. I broke from the kiss, running my nose along her jawline, and lightly nipped her earlobe. A sigh of happiness pushed past my lips when she finally slipped her fingers inside me, followed by a soft groan of disappointment when they were withdrawn far too soon.

Dijah leaned back so we were face-to-face. With a slow

grin, she brought her hand to her mouth and licked, sucking her digits clean of my arousal. "I need to taste direct from the source."

Before I could respond, she dropped down, taking my shorts and panties with her. The moment her mouth made contact I pulled in a sharp breath, falling forward to brace myself on the desk. She ate me with precision and determination, flicking her tongue back and forth, spreading me with each pass.

Fumbling, I worked to kick my shorts loose, looking for the freedom to widen my legs, allowing her more access. My body was an inferno of need, her soft "mmm" of enjoyment heightened my own awareness. The scrape of my nipples against the fabric of my bra, a sweet torture to complement the sensations Dijah created.

My knees weakened as the effects of her attention pushed me closer and closer to the end. I hiked my leg up onto the desk, wanting her to have as much access as humanly possible. She responded by digging her fingers into my ass and pressing her tongue into me as far as it would go.

"Oh, fuck." I grabbed the back of her head, tangling my fingers in her thick hair.

I rocked against her face, fast and furious, chasing after the high of release. The coiling in my belly. I knew I was close. Bracing for the impending descent, I shifted, slapping my free palm against the wall as the welcomed convulsions cascaded through my body.

"Fuck! Yes!" Blissful euphoria had my head swimming while the aftershocks ricocheted through me.

Her licks slowed and I released the hold I had on her head. She placed a kiss to the inside of my thigh then wiggled her way from between me and the desk. Slowly I lowered my leg before collapsing into the chair. I remained there, waiting for the world to stop spinning.

"Are you good?" she asked after she returned from the bathroom.

My mouth dry, I could only nod in response. She was too far away, I needed to touch her. To hold her.

I reached out and hooked my fingers into the loops of her jeans as I stood. "You have on entirely too many clothes."

She glanced up at me, tugging the corner of her lip between her teeth. The same lips that had taken me to new planes and my limbs remained loose and relaxed as a result. The same lips I wanted to spend the rest of the night kissing.

"That's probably a good thing."

"I would disagree. I can't do all the things I'd like to with you dressed."

Dijah placed her hands on my shoulders, stretching up for a kiss. It was soft, tentative, and over before it started. "Which is precisely why I need to keep my clothes on," she whispered against my lips.

# Seventeen

## Khadijah

The joy draining from Shae's eyes twisted my gut.

"You're not staying?"

I shook my head and tried to keep the fact I was slightly appalled she'd asked me that off my face. "You know I can't."

My body protested my decisions. I was a mess of pent-up need burning to be set free, but I couldn't, or wouldn't, allow myself to give in. It was penance for not keeping the boundary clear, for crossing the lines I'd put in place.

"I'm here, literally ass out." She indicated to her bottomless half and I couldn't suppress the smile in response to her statement. "And you are gonna just dine and dash?"

I stared at her for a second before I burst out laughing. "Did you…did you just say dine and dash?"

Shae joined in on the laughter while simultaneously pulling me closer. "What else would you call it?"

Her question sobered me up. "Shae."

She stepped away, moving to retrieve her panties while I remained rooted in the same spot.

"Yeah. You're right. Doesn't mean I wasn't hopeful you'd want to all the same."

The disappointment coloring her words made the ache that much heavier. *You're sending me mixed signals.* The comment she'd made the night of her birthday dinner raced to the forefront of my mind and added to the guilt threatening to suffocate me.

I was making a serious mess of things. I had plans, goals, an outlook to attain, yet Shae managed to make it all want to take a backburner. I was honestly surprised at myself for being able to resist her for as long as I had.

But my actions weren't fair to her...to either of us. "It's not that I don't want to, Shae. I can't. I won't insult or hurt you by saying anything was a mistake because it wasn't. It's just..."

Shae half sat on the desk, crossing her arms. "It's just that we work together and it's a bigger factor for you than the fact *we* work together."

The emphasis she put on "we" made my chest squeeze. None of this was going to plan, mainly because none of this was planned. But from the moment I'd seen Shae in the locker room, and knowing how often I'd be seeing her, my world had a slight tilt to it no matter how much I tried to right it.

"I should go so you can get some rest before tomorrow. You don't want more trouble out of your hamstring."

The tease at the end had the desired effect as a slow grin spread across her face. "If it does, you'll rub it out for me, so I'm not worried."

"Good night, Shae."

"Night."

I forced myself to turn and walk out the door instead of stripping and climbing into bed with her. Luckily the hall was clear, and I could only hope Marni would be asleep when I got back to the room.

Shae's words played on repeat. "We work together." Sexually? One hundred percent. But everything else? Hard to say since I hadn't really given it a chance, but her certainty was definitely something for the pro column.

After affixing the other side of the banner above the bay window, I stepped back to survey my handiwork.

"Let me guess, it's off by a millimeter," Jah said as she came to stand beside me.

I cut my eyes over at her. "You know it's rude to be sarcastic to the person who organized all this, right?"

She rubbed her ever-growing belly and shrugged. "You organized the shower because, one: you were being OTT about everything."

"I was not being 'OTT.' I was asking logical, basic questions, like when did you want to have it. Questions you couldn't even answer. People have lives, Jah, calendars. They need to know stuff in advance."

Jah again shrugged. "'Sometime before your in-utero nephew is born' was a perfectly reasonable answer. And two: you love me." The last part of her comment was accompanied with a big smile and a hug.

I ran my hand over her stomach then leaned to talk to it. "Your momma be testing my nerves sometimes."

She shoved my shoulder. "Whatever."

"When will you two learn to behave?" Mom asked, ripping open the package for the yellow-and-green gingham tablecloth.

I walked over to help her spread it out onto the table where the gifts were to be placed. "When Jah learns to properly thank me for my services instead of poking fun at my organizational skills."

"Did you show Mom your itinerary for today?"

"We have an itinerary?"

Jah fished her phone from her pocket. "Oh, yes." She tapped the screen a few times then showed the device to our mother. "From two to two fifteen, guests arrive. Two fifteen to two thirty, mingle, have light refreshments."

Jah shot a glance at me when Mom took her cell and began scrolling. I kept smoothing the plastic tablecloth in hopes of getting out some of the creases. She'd put me in charge with the only directives being to keep the décor gender-neutral and that the shower would be held at her house. All other choices had been left to me since Vance was of the "happy wife, happy life" stance more and more these days.

"Well, your sister is nothing if not thorough," Mom finally said, handing Jah her phone back.

"Thanks, Mom. I spent a lot of time researching fun games and things for us to do. So, you should appreciate my efforts."

"I do, sis, I do. But what kind of baby sibling would I be if I didn't give you a hard time?"

"Um, a nice one."

Mom simply shook her head, laughing at both of us. "My girls."

"We got ice."

"And the cake."

Dad and Vance announced as they entered the house. Things were falling into place despite the expected snide comments from the very person all this was for. She might get on my nerves every so often, but I loved her bratty ass and wanted to make sure the shower went smoothly. While they finished the little ins and outs, I headed to my car to retrieve the gifts I'd deliberately left for as long as possible.

"Here, let me help," Vance said as I made a somewhat noisy reentry into the house. "Man, D, I knew you were excited for Little, but this is a lot."

"What's a lot?" Jah asked, rounding the corner.

"Your sister already spoiling her nephew."

"This isn't all from me," I finally got out. "Nikki had a booked and busy day at the salon so sent her gift by way of me. And…"

"And?" Jah said, crossing her arms over her belly and arching a brow. "That takes care of one of these."

I set everything onto the gift table. "Hey, Dad, there's one more in my trunk."

"Khadijah, what's all this?" Mom inquired.

I smoothed down the sides of my hair and blew out a breath before facing the family. It was only one of them I expected to make a big deal of what I was about to say, but either way I had to answer the questions, especially as Dad came in with the biggest box.

"So, some are from the team."

"The team?" Jah asked with a hitch on the last word. "Or one player in particular?"

I shot her a "don't start" look, which resulted in a grin I knew all too well. Meanwhile, my parents and brother-in-law were trying to figure out what was what.

"A *couple* of players on the team, like I said." I turned to face Mom, wanting to *not* meet Jah's scrutiny head-on. "I'd been asked to hang out but told them I couldn't because of the baby shower. So, they were kind enough to want to send some presents along."

Sasha had again asked me over after the last home game, and again I'd turned her down, but this time it wasn't because of some fabricated excuse. However, when I'd mentioned Jah's shower, she'd gotten really excited, which in turn had earned me a glower from Courtney for some reason. It had snowballed from there.

"Aww, that was nice of them," Mom said.

"Who exactly?"

I turned back to face my sister. "Does that matter? Besides, I'm sure there are cards so you can send thank-you notes later."

She rolled her eyes at the mention of the thank-you notes. I'd had to stay on her to send them out after her wedding and I could see that would be the case again.

"Why are you being so secretive, Khadijah? I mean strangers, who don't know me, sent presents along? I find that hard to believe."

"Jah." I put as much warning in her name as I could, not that it would matter.

"What's going on with you two now?" Dad asked.

Of the three, Vance was the only one who seemed to know what was up. Everything in me had said refuse the presents, but they'd wanted to be nice, and I couldn't shit on their gesture.

My sister arched her back and began rubbing at her side. "Remember when y'all fussed at me about leaving Khadijah at that club? Well, turns out the ladies were players for the Cannons. So, see, I didn't leave her with any ol' body."

I was absolutely going to kick her ass after she gave birth.

The grin on her face irked my soul as she knew exactly what that statement would do to our parents.

"You're dating someone? From work?"

I shot my sister another murderous look before forcing myself to calm down. "No, Mom, I'm not dating anyone. Let alone someone I work with. We're friendly, that's all. And since they met Jah that night, they wanted to do something nice for her because of that friendship."

"Oh, well you should have extended an invitation."

My mouth hung open and eyes widened at Dad's comment. "Wh-why would I do that? This is about Jah and Vance."

"Because I raised you to have manners," Mom lightly scolded. "They did something nice for you and your sister, it's the least you could have done as a thank-you to your new friends."

"Yeah, Dijah, I wouldn't have minded at all. In fact, you should text Shae and see if she wants to drop by," Jah commented, the grin on her face too damn smug.

I chewed on the inside of my cheek. *I love my sister. I love my sister.* I repeated the words so I wouldn't be tempted to cuss her out for instigating.

"They had plans, remember, I turned them down so I could be here for you. Let's focus on getting finished for that and not my…coworkers. Guests should start arriving in a few minutes and I want to make sure everything is perfect for my favorite sister."

I was thankful they let up, especially once the party was underway. But in the back of my mind, Shae lingered. Like always. I couldn't escape her, not that I fully wanted to. I really needed to do a deep dive into the fact I had to be some sort of undercover masochist to keep myself in this loop. Unable to fully compartmentalize and leaving enough of an opening to torture us both.

# Eighteen

## Shae

"Thanks, Tina," Dijah said.

"No problem."

They both came walking out of Dijah's office all smiles. A few other teammates were hanging around, easing in and out of her office.

Since we'd successfully made it past the first round and would be heading to the semi-finals, I stayed on the court to do a few extra reps to work off some of the nervous energy, so I'd missed out on whatever party was happening. I jutted my chin toward her office door. "Looks like I'm missing all the fun."

Dijah looked back as Tina excused herself to hit the showers. Since Indiana, Dijah had been trying more than before to keep the line clear between us. And I respected her decision… mostly. She was fighting so hard against something…some*one* she wanted, and I couldn't understand why. And although I wouldn't say it out loud to her, it hurt, her dismissal of me. Of us—over something as arbitrary as our jobs.

"It's nothing." Dijah slid her hands into her pockets and met my gaze head-on. God, her eyes. Deep, soulful, mesmerizing. "My goddaughter's birthday is coming up and some of the players are helping me with her gift."

I hopped up onto one of the tables and stretched out. "Should I be offended you didn't ask me?"

Dijah rolled her eyes. "You can be whatever you want. You stayed out on the court to push yourself, so it wasn't like I talked to everyone but you."

"All signed, Doc. Hope she likes it," Claire commented as she took a seat on the table opposite me.

I probably shouldn't have been annoyed she didn't leave, go shower, anything but settle in to stay, but I was. It had become my mission of sorts to be the last player Dijah had to work on so that I got her undivided attention. Most times it worked.

Dijah turned her focus on Claire while she continued massaging my knee. A perfect combination of gentle, yet firm pressure. "I think she'll go crazy when she opens it. And the fact that I managed to swing courtside seats."

Their conversation, along with the rotation of my teammates in and out of her office was giving me a case of FOMO. "What's the gift?"

"Huh?"

"For your goddaughter?"

"A signed jersey," Claire offered up before Dijah could answer. "Your jersey," she added with a bit of singsong in her voice.

At that news, my grin got so big my cheeks would likely

start hurting. I sat up, swinging my legs over the table, forcing Dijah to step back. "Oh really?"

Dijah whipped her head around to look at Claire. "Why would you say it like that?"

Claire shrugged. "Please, none of us are blind. You two have the hots for each other. We peeped that at Shae's birthday dinner. And if I had doubts, those were shot to hell in Indy." She leaned closer to Dijah to whisper, "My room was on the other side of the wall. And I have never sounded like that when I got my hamstring worked on."

All I could do was laugh as a look of shock, embarrassment, or something came over Dijah's face. I'd tried not to be overt, but my teammates were smart women. And maybe it being out in the open—somewhat—would be the push Dijah needed to let go of the notion she—we—were fooling anybody.

"Were you planning on asking me to sign? Especially since it's my jersey?"

I was already off the table and heading toward her office. Claire's laugh faded away as she left the training room. Again, I stamped down the twinge of rejection that came from her overlooking me, even if that wasn't her intent.

Laid out on the desk was in fact my jersey, with signatures and messages to the mystery birthday girl. There were notes of encouragement from some, and just the signatures of the others. How in the hell had she managed to get them to do this and I hadn't even heard a whisper of what was going on?

Hell, even Coach had signed it. I wasn't surprised everyone had agreed since the team all loved Dijah.

I picked up the sharpie that rested on top and uncapped it. "What's her name?"

"Imani."

Strolling around, I slid the jersey to the edge of the desk as I took a seat in Dijah's chair. The space around my last name had been left mostly bare. Dijah's request? Or had the ladies done it in anticipation of me wanting to have that top spot?

"Why'd you pick my jersey?" I asked, not glancing up at her as she stood in the doorway. Writing on fabric was much harder when I was trying to make sure it was legible, but I took my time, wanting it to be as perfect as possible.

"Because according to her mom, you're her favorite player."

Her response did make me look up as a smile once again stretched across my face. "Is that so? Which game is she coming to?"

"Why?"

"Because I love kids. And if she's interested in the sport, I am always down to do a photo op or whatever to encourage them."

Dijah's face lit up. The grin she gave jacked up my heart rate like the night we'd first met. And really anytime we were around each other. I'd always loved coming to work. I had a job that was my passion, but I found myself getting in earlier and staying later simply for the chance at more time with her.

"Wow, Shae, that's really generous, but I wouldn't want to impose. Plus, I know your mood after games—"

"Aht-aht. It's like Candyman. We're on a streak, don't you dare. Honestly, Dijah, you should know that." I tried to put some admonishment in my tone, but it came out more of a laugh.

She gnawed on her lower lip in a way that made me want to tug it free from her teeth and kiss her.

"Sorry. Anyway, it'd be great if you'd do that. Nikki, her

mom, had tried to get me to drag you along to…" She gasped and clamped her mouth shut.

"Huh? Don't stop now, sounds like something fun was about to come from those luscious lips of yours."

She quickly shook her head in denial. "It's nothing."

I finished my message and recapped the pen before giving my undivided attention back to the woman who I couldn't get out of my head. "It sure sounds like something." I spoke slowly as I pushed to my feet.

"It's not. And doesn't matter, you offered an even better compromise that will work. And I don't even have to blur the boundaries I've put in place."

I closed the small distance between us, but stopped myself from sliding my hands along her waist and pulling her to me.

"About that."

Dijah craned her neck up to look at me, those stunning dark eyes of hers masked in a mixture of resolve and wanting. "What about it?"

"I mean it's clear you've done a crap job keeping everyone from knowing how much you want me, and I'm pretty sure I can be convinced to give you a chance."

She blinked at me once, then twice before busting out laughing, stepping away in the process. "Wow. How much *I* want *you*?" She gathered herself and pulled in a deep breath.

I shrugged, crossing my arms to keep from holding her again. "Yes. I've been told I'm pretty irresistible."

"Have you now?"

I nodded. "In fact… I'm pretty sure you've told me as much." She fluttered a gaze up at me, but didn't deny the statement. However, I braced for the fact she was likely to shoot me down again. "How about this?" I said quickly, cutting off any impending rejection. "I'll play you for it."

Her entire face scrunched in confusion. "Play for...what now?"

"Hear me out. The team already knows or at least suspects something is happening between us. Players can't date coaches or any of the management."

"Shae, I'm part of the coaching staff."

"Yes, the coaching *staff*." I stressed the last word. "You *technically* aren't a coach or management. That restriction is for the head and assistants. Basically, anyone who could have some power over our playing time, yada, yada, yada. No offense, but you ain't got no control over that. Yeah, you can give a rec to Coach based on injury or possible injury, but at the end of the day, it's not your call. So, not a problem."

Dijah scrubbed her hands down her face. "Even if that's true, it doesn't change the fact I am the first obstacle, Shae. I don't date people I work with. It's easier. It's less complicated when things go sour. We don't want to have to awkwardly dance around each other and that's if we break up on good terms. If it's bad, then that's a whole lot worse. There'd be resentment, which would make it harder for either of us to do our jobs, which could ultimately affect the team."

This time I frowned as I stumbled back until I rested at the edge of her desk. I crossed my arms and regarded her for a long minute. "Well damn, we've had a whole-ass relationship and I missed it. Tell me, at the end, was the sex at least still good? Never mind, scratch that, if I don't remember I'm guessing not."

I wasn't really sure how to feel about her whole doomsday scenario because hearing it fed into the insecurities that were sprouting where she was concerned. I mean, on one hand, it was encouraging that she even considered the possibility of there being an *us* in some way. But the fact she skipped right to the end and expected it to be done, like we wouldn't be able to function as adults afterward, was perplexing.

"Which one of us would be the issue?"

"What?"

"Which one of us wouldn't be able to keep our shit together after the breakup?"

Before she could answer, some of the players popped their heads in to tell her goodbye on their way out. I waited patiently as they had quick conversations about stretching, or icing wrists or ankles.

After they left, Dijah slid her hands into her pockets as she returned her attention to me. Neither of us spoke as I waited for her to answer the question I'd posed.

Finally, she pulled in a deep breath and blew it out loudly. "I don't know, Shae. It's more hypothetical. Look, I just think it's easier for us to not get things all tangled up."

"And I think we're both mature adults who can handle it." She pressed her lips together and I kept going. "Have you considered an alternative outcome?"

"Like what, Shae?"

"Like we get along. We vibe well together on and off the court and we have no issues. That we would work, Dijah."

Her shoulders slumped, but she said nothing.

I again pushed to standing. "I mean, correct me if I'm wrong, but isn't there usually a pro column to go with the con one?"

"There is."

"Okay, so list out some pros."

Once more a frown marred her beautiful face. "Shae, why are you pushing this? From what I've read, dating hasn't been an issue for you."

I startled back. "Whoa, what?"

"I'm not passing judgment or anything...lord knows I have my own dating disasters. I read some stuff and basically, we both know you are one hell of a beautiful woman. Other women would be, and have been, thrilled to date you. Ones who wouldn't come with the complications I present."

Had she really? She had, she'd gone there. And it only served to reactivate my annoyance from last year. How I spent my time and who I spent it with off the court had no bearing on what I did on it. And in the case of Dijah, my past relationships, no matter how seemingly frequent or brief, had no bearing on the present. That's not how I operated.

"That was unexpected. I didn't think you were the type to believe the hype, or in this case the misguided gossip. There are always folks who want to come at me and spread bullshit."

Her face softened. "Shae, I didn't mean anything by it. Like I said, I have my own hiccups with past relationships."

"Right, well then, I guess that's where we really differ. For me, I view my life and relationships in seasons like with basketball. I look at what is present and in front of me instead of dwelling on the past and things I can't change. No one can predict the future. Just because we had a losing season doesn't mean the current one will be the same. You learn, you improve, you move on."

Admittedly, I didn't understand her hang-up. I mean, I'd heard what she'd said, but at the same time, pretending there wasn't something going on clearly wasn't working.

We unfortunately were at an impasse. She had her "rules" and regardless of what I thought about them, I couldn't and wouldn't force a different outcome.

"I'mma go hit the showers."

When I went to move past her, Dijah grabbed my wrist. "What are we playing?"

"What?"

She looked up at me—uncertainty was still present in her eyes, but she held my gaze. "You asked to 'play me for it,' so what are we playing?"

Oh, we were getting somewhere. "Come with me."

# Nineteen

## Khadijah

I followed behind Shae down the corridor toward the arena. She was right, pretending—well, trying and failing to pretend—the attraction wasn't there was not working. Dating someone I work with...the idea still terrified me because I continued to run through all the scenarios of what could go wrong.

Then I pondered Shae's rebuttal question: What could go right?

That was on top of her having apparently researched the rules of engagement with fraternization among the team. And the hurt expression that had darkened her features when I brought up the reports about her dating life. I hadn't meant to feed into the negative connotations, I'd just wanted to point out how our outlooks were different.

But was that a bad thing?

My way of doing things clearly hadn't been working.

"Alright, you ready?" she asked, pulling me from my thoughts.

I nodded. I still had zero clue what game she wanted to play, but I had agreed all the same. Hell, I was unclear of what we were even playing for exactly. The arena was mostly empty except for the janitor who was moving the large blue dust mop back and forth on the other half of the court. Shae jogged over to the rack, which held about eight basketballs, and picked up one. She easily dribbled it as she walked back toward me.

"A quick and simple game of Horse. You win, and I'll attend whatever event you were trying to not tell me about. If I win, you give me a date."

I tilted my head. "Um…two things. First, those both sound like a win for you. And second, explain what Horse is."

Shae caught the ball and tucked it next to her side as she frowned at me. "You're kidding, right?"

"About which part?"

"The game, because the other, well…" She shrugged and grinned, not the least bit ashamed of how either way it worked in her favor. I enjoyed this side of Shae. The fun, easygoing woman who'd had my rapt attention from the moment I'd laid eyes on her.

I had a vague idea, but wasn't a hundred percent sure. "No. I mean I think I know, but I also don't really…sport."

She blinked a few times then waved her free hand in front of her face as if to clear the air. "Wait, wait, what? You're an athletic trainer for a WNBA team. Did college ball before that. And you don't 'sport'?" She made air quotes around the last word with her free hand. "How is that possible?"

I pressed my lips together and rolled my shoulders back. This wasn't the first time someone had called me on the absurdity of what I did for a living considering my general disinterest in all sporting events. "I don't have to enjoy the game to treat the bodies that play it."

Amusement continued to color her features. "You're serious? Is it just basketball you don't enjoy?"

I shook my head. "I don't really care about any sport."

Shae mouthed a silent "wow" and nodded when she began to slowly dribble the ball again. "Okay. Okay. Well, Horse is really simple, even for someone that doesn't do sports. We each take shots at the basket until one of us sinks five, essentially spelling out the word *horse*. So, like hangman, but with baskets."

I grinned. "Not to point out the obvious, but, um, you're six-two and do this for a living. I'm about five-five and haven't picked up a ball since forced participation in high school. Feels even more rigged than the stakes if you ask me."

She laughed again and I had to admit it was quickly becoming one of my favorite sounds. Her eyes crinkled and her entire demeanor radiated the joy that bellowed out. "It might work in my favor a bit. But how 'bout this. I'll shoot strictly from the free-throw line. You can be closer. And you get two shots for my one. Fair?"

I crossed my arms and narrowed my eyes at her. Short of some miracle of coordination and talent to be descended upon me as we stood, it didn't matter if she gave me five shots for her every one, I had lost this game before it had even started. And yet, I was going to go forward anyway.

I sucked in a breath and released it in a heavy sigh. "Fine. Though I really should have a proxy player to make this even.

But I can do this. And I guess it could have been worse, you could have challenged me to a one-one thing, which would have involved a lot more running on my part."

"One...you mean one-on-one?" She again laughed.

I huffed out an indignant breath and snatched the ball before moving onto the court. I knew better than to try to dribble and walk as she had, but once I got to a space almost directly under the net, I used two hands to bounce the ball a few times and tried to ignore the snickers coming from behind me. I could do this.

Gripping the orange sphere in my hands, I bent my knees then slightly launched myself off the floor as I tossed it up. The ball barely touched the bottom of the net. *Shit*. Shae retrieved the wayward ball then tossed it lightly back in my direction. Her lips were pressed together, but the amusement was clear as day.

"You know, laughing at me isn't very nice."

"I'm sorry." A small laugh broke free again. "You're right." She cleared her throat and worked to get herself under control.

I dribbled again and tried to ignore her standing within my peripheral vision. This time I took a different approach, bending my knees and shooting it with an underhanded throw. Another miss.

"Granny style...okay," Shae commented as she once again gathered the ball.

I stepped to the side and watched as she dribbled with ease, looking very much like the professional she was. One, two more bounces before she popped it up, and with a gentle flick of her wrist the ball sailed through the air then dropped down through the net. I think I even heard the swoosh as it cleared.

She bit the corner of her lip and smiled. "H."

I simply rolled my eyes and prepared for my next shot. The scene from *Desperado* popped into my head, only instead of thinking about a dick and the glass, I was thinking about the ball and the net. Over and over I repeated those words, then granny shot again. And again, I fucking missed.

"Damn it." I didn't really care about the game, I knew I would be losing when I agreed, but my pride and ego couldn't handle total defeat. I wasn't built that way.

"Here, let me help. If you don't mind," Shae said as she handed me the ball.

She stood behind me, close, and that was enough to make me want to forfeit, but I didn't give up.

She tugged me back a little. "You're too close." She spoke low and I had to stop the shiver. "Square your hips, and loosen up. You can do this." There was no mocking in her tone. She squeezed my shoulders, providing a gentle massage and soft encouragement. "Relax and take your time. And if you're gonna granny ball again, it's not all arms, it's also in the wrist. So, when you come up, flick your wrists just a little right before you release."

She stepped back and I almost complained but held my tongue. She demonstrated the instructions she'd given, showing me the movements that matched her words.

"You got this," she said softly then moved to the side to give me more space.

*Relax and take my time.* I blew out a soft exhale, closed my eyes briefly, then got set. Another miss, but closer this time as it hit the rim instead of the net.

Shae clapped. "Better. One more shot."

I waved her off. "No, fair is fair. It's me two, you one." Though I had to admit the encouragement from her warmed me almost as much as her body being near mine had during her instruction.

Shae went back to the free-throw line and easily made her second basket. As I retrieved the ball, I noticed we had a small audience. The janitor was leaning up against the post of the other goal, arms crossed, a smile on his face. No doubt laughing at my terrible shots. But seated in the first row were a few of the players. Just what I needed, people to watch my non-existent athletic ability.

"What are y'all doin'?" Tricia asked.

"A friendly game of Horse," Shae answered.

This time it was Courtney who questioned, "Why?"

Shae looked at me, and I bounced the ball a few times. No more pretending. *What could go right?* The thought once again popped into my head. "Because, if Shae wins, she gets to take me on a date."

"And if she doesn't?" Courtney asked.

Again, I glanced at Shae. "Then I get to take her."

Her face lit up into the biggest smile. A mixture of laughs, wows, and claps sounded off. My heart rate spiked a bit, letting it be known I was crossing my own boundary. Yes, apparently, they already had their suspicions, especially Courtney and Tina, since they'd been there the night at the club, but still, it was wholly different to speak it out loud.

Shaking off the nerves, I dribbled a few times, thought about Shae's instructions, then shot. And it went in. "Yes!" I screamed, dancing around as I'd finally made a basket.

There was applause from the sideline, but more importantly,

Shae held the ball under her arm as she clapped for me. "Alright, I see you. Make this next one and we're tied."

"I think I'm hitting my stride now. You better watch out." I spoke the words with way more bravado than I should have as the next one was yet another miss.

Shae at least had the decency to try to contain her laugh and simply declared *"R"* after her third turn.

"Yo, Doc," Tina called out. "Was that your first basket?"

"Yes. Unlike Ms. Never-Miss-A-Shot, I don't do this for a living."

"Shae, you know you did her dirty," Courtney said, pushing out of her chair and walking over to us. "Not only does Doc have terrible form—"

"Hey!"

"Sorry, but you do. I'm gonna assume Shae didn't let you know."

I glanced between the two tall women flanking either side of me. "Let me know what?"

Shae lifted a shoulder. "I may or may not have the league's best free-throw average." Her statement was delivered with a teasing grin and not a lick of shame. A bigger setup than I'd originally thought.

"What? I should have been given five shots to your one." I feigned annoyance. I'd gone into this challenge knowing it was rigged, I just hadn't realized how much the odds were stacked against me. "New rules. I'm calling in that proxy player. I take a shot and my second is done by Courtney."

"You might actually want Tina. Her average is better than mine."

Tina joined us on the court, crisscrossing her arms to loosen up. I'd been working with these women for months. They'd instantly accepted me into the fold, and I'd been really made to feel like part of the team. More than I had at any of my prior jobs. I got along with the coaching staff, we worked well, but with the players it was a difference I hadn't had before. Maybe it was because I didn't keep the wall there because the players I'd worked with previously had all been students.

Whatever it was, I knew there was an easiness with being around all of them that I enjoyed and it made the working environment different. Them showing up and taking interest in this friendly game that I already knew was a goner, made me feel a happiness I couldn't quite figure out.

"Okay. Cool. I have *H-O-R*. You have *H*." Shae didn't seem the least bit bothered, and with good reason. She only needed two more baskets. I needed four and only two of them had a chance of going in.

I missed my shot, but Tina got hers. As did Shae.

I planted my hands on my hips. "Do you ever miss?"

"Not often."

To the cheers and encouragement from the other players, I took a breath and sent the ball sailing. The applause got louder as I made another basket. And they all laughed as I promptly did another victory dance. Tina made her second shot and just like that we were tied. It didn't matter who won because either way, I'd be going out with the woman who I couldn't stop thinking about no matter how hard I tried.

Shae caught the ball when Courtney passed it to her. She kept her eyes on me as she dribbled, taking her time, a beautiful smile on her face. When she took the shot, she kept her attention on me and winked as the ball cleared the net.

# Twenty

## Shae

I flipped the visor down and checked my reflection in the mirror one last time. I'd been counting down to this day since our game. Excited flutters danced around in my gut. After adjusting the wine-toned fedora, I grabbed the bouquet of roses from the passenger seat and climbed out of my truck. Jah, not her sister, opened the door a few moments after I rang the bell.

"Shae. So good to see you again." She smiled wide and stepped to the side to let me in. "Flowers. Aren't you romantic."

"Hey, Jah. How are you?" I leaned in and gave her a quick hug.

She placed her hand on her stomach. "Whew, ready to evict this one."

"How much longer?"

"Four damn weeks. And thank you for the gift."

"Hopefully, it'll fly by. And you're welcome. I had zero clue what would be the best option, but Sasha picked out every-thing and I simply paid her back."

Jah laughed at my admission before my attention went to the sound of footsteps on the stairs seconds before Dijah stepped into the foyer. The excitement turned to nerves when I laid eyes on her. She was stunning as always.

"Hey. I tried to get her to leave, but she doesn't listen very well," Dijah said, frowning at her sister.

"Oh please, you know you needed my help. Otherwise, you'd leave out of here dressed like you're going to a board meeting."

Dijah's response was to give her sister the finger. I laughed as the two of them bickered. I wasn't sure whose idea it was, the outfit Dijah wore, but I loved the finished product. The dusty rose high-waisted skirt stopped midthigh. She'd paired it with a loose-fitting floral-print blouse with an unfortunately high neck and ruffled sleeves. Tan wedge ankle boots com-pleted the look. Her beautiful hair was contained in a puffy French braid.

"These are for you." I handed her the bouquet.

Her dimples went on full display as she smiled up at me. "Thank you, they're beautiful." She turned and headed to her kitchen.

"Okay, well you kids have fun. And please do all the things I would do," Jah said, blowing her sister an air kiss and wav-ing at me before she left.

I let my eyes drift to the couch on my way to the kitchen. "Your sister is…something."

Dijah scoffed. "That's putting it mildly." She proceeded to fill a vase with water before arranging the flowers inside. "I'm older, but her spoiled ass is bossy as hell. She only came over to harass me because her husband was getting on her nerves." She leaned in and took a whiff of the flowers. "And she's nosy as hell."

"Family. What can you do?"

A half smile lifted the side of her plump lips, which were made more distracting thanks to the glossy red lipstick. "Love them despite how they work your nerves."

I laughed and nodded. "Heard. Me and my brothers are always at each other over something."

"How many do you have?"

"Three. All older. And they subscribed to the idea that they could give me hell, but be damned if anyone else did."

Her eyes went wide. "You're the baby. That explains it."

"Explains what?"

She crossed her arms, and a playful Mona Lisa smile curved her lips. "Your pursuit in getting your way. Like Jah."

I stepped closer, stopping just shy of touching her. "You wanted me to get my way."

Her brows knit together, and she rested her hip against the counter. "How so?"

"When I proposed the challenge, you could have said no, but you didn't. When you learned what the challenge would be, you could have opted for something a bit...fairer. You didn't." I finished my comment, mirroring her stance, daring her to refute my words. Her conviction against dating someone she worked with had been shaky ground since Indiana, and I wasn't ashamed to admit I did what I could to exploit that weakness.

"If I'd had all the facts in the beginning, I would have asked for different terms," she countered.

"You want a do-over?"

Slowly she shook her head. "I'm already all dressed up."

"You look beautiful as always. But…"

She frowned. "But? Why is there a but after that?"

I wanted to touch her. To kiss her. But I feared that if I did, we'd not make it out of the house, and I really wanted to take her out. "But…as much as I think seeing your legs are sexy as hell, you might want pants."

Her frown deepened. "Why?"

"Well, because it will depend on how well you are on four wheels. Because if you're no good on skates, I don't want you flashing people should you fall on your ass."

Dijah's eyes widened. "Skates? You're taking me roller-skating?" I nodded. "Wow, that's… I've not been skating since I was a kid, and certainly not what I expected for a first date."

"What were you expecting?"

She lifted a shoulder. "I don't know. The typical dinner and—" She trailed off. "But yes. I should probably put on pants. Give me a sec." She got to the bottom of the steps then turned back. "Wait. Are you supposed to be doing that? Because I think there were some restricted activities for you guys during the season."

She wasn't wrong. The GM and coaches had a "code of conduct" for our behavior, which included certain activities they wanted us to avoid because they'd deemed them high risk for injury.

"Rollerblading. That's what they would like us to avoid doing. Roller-*skating* is not Rollerblading."

"That's splitting hairs, don't ya think?"

"Maybe, but I'm technically within the guidelines."

"You and your technicalities," she said with a smirk before disappearing up the steps.

A few minutes later we were in my truck on the way to Roll With It. Dijah had changed into a pair of red jeans that hugged her ass like a second skin and while I missed the opportunity to admire her legs, I also couldn't have her out there possibly caught up in an embarrassing situation should she fall. Not that I'd let that happen. Her possibly being on the beginner end of skating meant built-in excuses to touch her. It'd be rude of me to not offer all the assistance I could.

She turned in her seat so that her back rested against the door. "So, why skating?"

"Because it's something I enjoy doing and I wanted to share that with you." I cast a glance in her direction. "But if you'd rather do something else…" I'd thought about doing the fancy dinner thing, but I always did that because I felt like that was what was expected. But for Dijah, I decided to choose a location that would be more chill. Someplace where she'd hopefully relax and enjoy herself.

And her comment about my dating still stung. Regardless of the fact she'd said she hadn't meant anything by it, I wanted to take her someplace real, that was me.

"No. It'll be fun. And I like that you're sharing something you enjoy with me." She lightly squeezed my arm before readjusting in her seat.

When we pulled into the parking lot, it was nearly packed, as usual on a Saturday night.

"Who knew this was the place to be," Dijah commented after I killed the engine.

I nodded. "Yeah. After we renovated a couple of years ago,

Saturday night was switched to adults only. It started out as a once-a-month thing, but since it was a hit, it became a permanent change."

"We?"

"Yeah. After I first moved here, I was missing my family and home, so I was on the hunt for something familiar. Skating has always been something I've enjoyed. I hadn't really gotten close with anyone on the team and was lonely. Did some googling and came across this place."

I exited then opened the back door and grabbed my bag. Dijah waited for me on the other side, and I slipped my hand into hers as we made our way toward the entry.

I appreciated her openness about the evening. There was no hesitation or her being in her head second-guessing what was happening. Hopefully, by the end of the night, she'd see how good and easy we were and this wouldn't be a one-off.

"So, how did that turn into the 'we' part of your comment?"

"Oh. I started coming here often. The owners were hella nice to me, and we struck up a friendship. They sort of acted like surrogate parents. Anyway, they mentioned maybe having to close since people weren't coming in like they used to. Them getting too old to try to keep up with everything, so I offered to help out. Becoming partial owner of this place was my first business venture."

Dijah stopped walking. "Wow. When you said you enjoyed it, I thought it was just an extracurricular type of thing. But to sink money into a business that was near failing, that is more a passion project." She looked up at me with soft eyes, her voice full of wonder, with maybe a hint of pride.

"Yeah. I guess. This place was where I found my solace as

I adjusted to being so far away from everyone and everything I'd known. The idea it could close hurt me so I did what I could to make that not happen. Now it's thriving. The team does charity events every so often, like back-to-school drives."

Not many people knew I co-owned this place, and I liked it that way. Yes, after a while I'd talked some of the team into joining me for back-to-school fundraisers and things like that. In turn, management caught wind of it and made it into a full PR thing for the franchise as a whole. Giving back to the community and all that. But as long as it helped the kids and parents who would otherwise struggle with supplies, clothes, and shoes, I didn't care that they wanted to slap the Cannon name on some things.

She placed her hand on my waist and stepped directly in front of me. "I'm glad you found a place to help with the loneliness. I remember the adjustment when I moved to LA. I wish I'd had something like that. I mean, don't get me wrong, I eventually found people through painting and cooking classes. But nothing that soothed the way this place apparently did for you."

There was a melancholy in her voice that filled me with questions. I cupped her cheek and ran my thumb back and forth across her soft skin.

"But I'm home now. Have a nephew on the way and a sister who never bothers to call before she shows up at my house. Plus, I'm back with my bestie and goddaughter." She sighed then smiled. "Now, let's go have some fun, because said sister will be all up in my business tomorrow."

"You do Sunday brunch every week?" I asked, taking her hand and continuing the short journey to the building.

"Yes. It's the day no one in the family works. Well, until the season got underway. I've missed a few because of games and whatnot, but other than that, it's when we catch up."

I opened the blackened glass door for her, a soft whoosh of air hitting us both. The muffled music got louder as we stepped inside. Colorful roving spotlights twirled in time with the beat of the music.

I led us past the small line at the counter, nodding at Kevin and Sarah, who were handling the admissions and skate rental.

"Won't I need a pair?"

"Nah, I'll get yours from the pro shop."

She tightened her grip on my hand and pressed closer to me as I weaved us through the throng of people, smiling and acknowledging a few of the regulars. The energy of the place was already seeping into me. The rink was alive with bodies flowing easily, each making room for the others and the various styles of skating. Most were doing the south "Atlanta" style, but others were sprinkled throughout.

We made our way to the newly expanded area that housed the restaurant and bar, which boasted semiprivate booths. The wall of large picture windows allowed diners to still be part of the action while enjoying their meals.

Micky straightened as she saw us approach, sliding her phone into her back pocket. "Hey, Ms. Shae. Back corner booth is open and waiting for you." She slid her eyes to Khadijah, and she grinned a little wider as she handed us two menus. "I'll be sure to send Sal over."

"Thanks."

"I know it's been a while, but damn, Shae. I think this has

got to be the nicest rink. The ones I remember had the hideously patterned carpet and those hard orange booths."

I laughed. "Told you we remodeled. Bought the building next door, knocked down the wall to add this place. I wanted to add more food options than pizza and wings at the snack bar."

No sooner did we slide into the plush black booth than a young Hispanic guy hurried to our table. Likely the Sal Micky mentioned; he had to be a new hire because I hadn't seen him before. The poor kid's hands were shaking as he sat the water on the table.

"Relax, kid. I promise we'll be your easiest table for the night."

He nodded so fast he looked like a bobble head. Khadijah hid her grin behind her menu.

"So, is it because you're the boss or because you are Shae Harris, WNBA player?"

I shrugged. "Probably more likely because they told him I'm the boss. I don't really like the other attention. I know I have to deal with it sometimes, but even after eight years, still can't say I'm used to it."

"Well, from what I've seen, you and the other players all handle it well."

"Thanks. Since the league is still growing, we do what we can to continue to build and nurture the fans that we have."

Dijah slid her hands across the table and I did the same, intertwining our fingers. "I'm glad I let you win."

I let out a hard laugh. "You *let* me? That's how you're gonna play this?"

"Yup. That's my story and I'm sticking to it."

I was maybe reading too much into a simple statement, but

damn did her words set off imaginary fireworks and cover me with a sense of validation. I hadn't been continuing to pursue things for nothing, and I wasn't off in my belief Dijah wanted this as much as I did.

# Twenty-One

## Khadijah

The two hours spent talking to Shae were chill, reminiscent of our first meeting. Being around her was easy. Too easy. Mr. and Mrs. Owens came by the table and chatted for a while. They were a sweet couple, gushing about Shae being a miracle helping to save the place. They'd opened the rink in memory of their son because despite their best efforts, they hadn't been able to keep him out of the streets and they'd wanted a place for kids to go to keep them from meeting the same fate.

As they talked, I noticed how Shae continuously tried to shift the focus and downplay the impact they said she had. She really wasn't a fan of being the center of attention. A trait I found rather endearing.

She had an easygoing nature, something I noticed in her interactions with the rest of the team. At least what I'd been witness to. Years of working in sports let me know that, no matter how close a team was, there were always ripples at one point or another. And I usually stayed out of those as best I could. Keeping a certain level of separation had served me well. And yet...

*No! Positive thoughts.* I'd promised myself an open mind and a go-with-the-flow mentality.

Shae wiped her mouth and settled back against her side of the booth. "So, I need to know."

"Know what?"

"How you ended up doing what you do, considering you don't like sports." She said the statement with a small chuckle before washing down her bite with water.

"Oh." I took a sip of my chardonnay. "Would you believe it was accidental? The sport part?"

Shae propped her elbows on the table and rested her chin on her hands, giving me her rapt attention. "How does that happen?"

I bit the inside of my cheek then took another drink, letting the buttery liquid coat my palate. I'd never shared my disinterest in sports within my work environment and it'd never come up before. As long as I showed up to do my job, whether or not I was a fan wasn't a factor.

"Well, I knew I wanted to go into physical therapy. My dad was in an accident when I was younger. He'd been in the crosswalk and some careless ass ran a red light and hit him."

"Oh, Dijah. That's terrible."

I nodded. "Happened when I was maybe fifteen. Anyway, he had a long road to recovery and his physical therapist was instrumental."

I twisted a napkin in my hands remembering the day we'd gotten that call from the ER. Dad had always been the rock of the family. The image of him in the hospital bed flashed back into my mind. I pushed it away with a little shake of my head. Shae reached across the table and placed her hands over mine, causing me to smile. The gentle stroking of her thumb calmed me and kept the old feelings of helplessness and fear from taking root.

"Anyway, after graduation, I did the typical thing of applying for jobs. First to offer was from a local private high school. It wasn't what I'd expected to be doing, but I found I enjoyed the work. Took some additional courses with more of a focus on sports medicine. I stayed there for a few years, but wanted better pay. Since I now had sport-related experience, the university in LA hired me. I was assistant for both the women's and men's basketball teams."

"So, then moving on to professional was the next logical step?"

I shrugged, keeping the other memories at bay. The politics of it all. In this day and age the university passing me over not once but twice for the lead position because the idea of a woman, especially a Black woman, being in charge wasn't something they were ready to deal with. But they didn't say that of course—it was always some other BS excuse.

"I was tired of being second fiddle you could say." A watered-down version, but the night was going so well I didn't want to bring down the vibe with my ranting. I'd done enough of that to both Jah and Nikki. Both women were instrumental in getting me to let that job go and to think bigger, because my stubborn ass was wanting to stick around out of pure spite, and that wasn't serving me or my future plans.

I glanced down at our now-intertwined fingers, then up to meet her eyes. Her gaze was lasered in on me with the same focus she had on game days. The noise and life around us didn't seem to matter to her in the moment. I was all she saw, and that fact hit me with a wave of emotion out of nowhere. *Simmer down, Khadijah.*

I blinked a few times to get my thoughts back on track. "My main dream is to open my own clinic one day, to help more people on a larger scale, to have an impact for some family like the therapist did for my dad. But for now, being an athletic trainer lets me see the results of my work in real time. I know I'm making a difference still, just in a different way."

"I get it. I still find it amazing that in all those years you haven't found any interest in the sport."

I shrugged and pulled my hand free to pick up my glass. "It wasn't what I was there to do. And my lack of interest had no bearing on how I performed my job." I drained the last of my wine.

Shae sat back against the booth. When she crossed her arms, I couldn't stop myself from dropping my gaze down to her more pronounced cleavage behind the formfitting button-down she wore. When I looked back up, the large grin on her face brought one to mine.

"And now?"

"And now, what?"

She licked her lips and leaned forward. "Has anything about the sport piqued your interest, now?"

I slid my empty glass gently back and forth on the table. "Yeah, I'm definitely taking an interest these days."

For the first time ever I was curious about basketball, if for no other reason than Shae's passion for the game. I would probably never be a hard-core fan, but I now had a vested interest in the outcomes.

She giggled low and amusement danced in her eyes. "I think

opening your own place is a great idea, even if that means we'll lose you eventually."

Her immediate support of my plans spread like wildfire through me. "Thanks, Shae. That means a lot."

"I'm being for real. I know I can't ball forever, and it's different for your job, but having an 'after' plan is the way to go. My finance guy is fucking awesome. Let me know if you want a connect, I'll give you his info. I don't know where you are in your journey, but Nick is a fucking wizard."

I stared at her for a moment trying to process her words. She was ready to jump in and offer assistance without a second thought. On top of the fact she had plans for a future after retirement. That was sexy as hell.

"Thanks. I don't have a financial advisor or anything like that, but it would be a good idea to probably talk to one, so yeah. Thanks."

She nodded and widened her smile. "I'll be sure to send you his info. You finished?"

I nodded. They hadn't brought us a bill, but that wasn't unsurprising considering she partially owned the place. She pulled out her wallet and dropped two hundred on the table and placed my wineglass on top of it.

She slid out of her side of the booth, holding her hand out to me. "I'll have to work harder to make you a fan."

The glint in her eye coupled with the curve of her mouth had me ready to follow anywhere she led. I bit my tongue to suppress the urge to blurt out I was one hundred percent a fan of Shae Harris.

The music got louder as we exited the restaurant. PYT played and the floor was alive with moving bodies. The energy in the building was infectious. People were laughing, skating, and having one hell of a time. Shae led us through the crowd and surprisingly no one stopped to bother her. Yes, some waved and spoke, but no one asked for pictures or autographs. They generally treated her like a regular person.

We made our way to the pro shop. Shae kept her hand on my hip, standing right behind me as we approached the counter.

"Hey, Ms. Harris," the young lady greeted as soon as we walked in.

"Shay, I've told you to call me Shae."

The young girl laughed. "No can do, Ms. Harris. My granny would kick my ass."

"I wouldn't want that." Shae quickly made introductions, and a weird fluttering sensation rippled through me being called her date. It wasn't some big declaration, it was the simple truth, but hearing the word made everything a bit more real.

Every interaction she'd had with people so far made it easy to tell that this place really was a refuge for her. Yes, she was more than at home on the basketball court, but here she gave off a different level of comfort and I was immensely privileged she'd wanted to share this with me.

"What's your shoe size?"

"Seven and a half."

"Ah, I guessed right. Shay, did my order come in?"

"Yes, ma'am. Let me go grab it."

I turned to face her and tilted my head to the side. "What did you do?"

"There's only one brand of skates that I like, but we don't carry them in the shop on the regular, so I ordered them."

Before I could say anything, Shay returned from the back carrying three boxes. "Here you go." She set them on the counter and smiled in my direction.

"Why are there three? And what's wrong with the ones you sell here?"

I took stock of the various skates lining the wall on display. To me any of them would have worked, or hell, even renting since I didn't need my own pair. But she was determined and excited, so I went with it.

"Okay, so I may not have completely guessed right. I did a range." Her adorable, playful grin spread across her face.

I laughed. "You could have asked me instead of wasting money."

Shae shrugged. "The others can be returned. Sit." She pointed at the chairs at the end of the counter.

I did as instructed and took off my shoes. Shae kneeled in front of me and assisted me with the skates. I started to tell her I could manage, but she worked quickly and diligently getting them on and laced up to her apparent satisfaction.

"How do these feel?"

She rested her hands on my knees and I had to work hard to not widen my legs in a silent plea for her to move them up further.

"Uh, they're good."

"You sure? Not too tight or anything?"

I shook my head. "Nope, perfect."

With athletic grace, she rose to standing then helped me do the same. After she secured my shoes in her bag, we said our goodbyes to the other Shay and I was being pushed through the crowd once more and over to the DJ booth. It was hard to focus on much of anything with Shae resting her hands on my waist while standing behind me as she propelled me forward.

"Also, real skaters know not to buy from the pro shop. It's

like getting store brand instead of name brand if that makes sense. There's always a mark-up, so you're paying higher-quality prices for lower-quality skates."

She spoke the words close to my ear so I could hear over the music. I worked not to shiver when her lips brushed against my lobe. I'd thought she'd simply ignored that part of my question, but I should have known better, because Shae always paid attention even when I might not want her to.

When we made it to the booth, she introduced me to the guy working the turntable as she dropped her bag on the bench behind him. I managed to maintain my balance when she let go to make quick work of putting on her own skates.

"Our stuff will be good here. I don't usually use the lockers because I want to save them for the patrons. And if we go back to the office, O might never let us leave."

I smiled, thinking back to the conversation with the older couple. They were both wonderful and it was easy to see how much they both cared for Shae. With her family being out of state, it genuinely made me happy to know she had people around her. Supporting her.

Shae held her hand out toward me. "Ready?"

An infectious, childlike, giddy energy radiated through her. The ever-present smile that had been on her face. The way she'd been totally relaxed from the moment we'd crossed the threshold. It was a whole world I knew nothing about, but she was happy to share, and like with basketball, her enthusiasm and dedication amped up my own interest.

"Yup."

She stopped at the entrance to the floor. "So, this is like being on the interstate, slower folks keep to the outside."

I glanced at the bodies moving, almost as if they were one with the ease of flow. No one seemed to be going slow as they all danced their way around. I had a momentary fear I was about to make a complete spectacle of myself and was glad she had suggested I change. If I was going to end up on my ass, I didn't need, nor want, to be showing it to a bunch of strangers. Especially not in this digital age. People may know Shae here, but that didn't mean a well-timed embarrassing moment wouldn't be fodder for someone.

Shae inched closer, easily pulling my body to hers. "I got you. Don't worry."

"Like riding a bike, right?"

She stepped onto the smooth wood floor first and kept a hold of my hand as I eased down, hugging close to the wall like kids did the first time they attempted skating. Shae turned so she faced me, holding both of my hands as she effortlessly skated backward while pulling me along. I felt ridiculous and my pride was taking a big hit. Not being good at something irked me, which was another reason I stayed away from all things sport. I learned early that my uncoordinated ass didn't have an athletic bone in my body.

"You're getting it," Shae encouraged.

Other skaters whizzed past us, but we maintained our own pace as I found my sea legs. The old-school R&B hits kept coming and like the night we met, Shae easily moved from one beat to the next, still moving backward. She sang along to the songs and swayed her amazing body and just vibed. All the while she kept me safe and secure in her hold.

By the time we completed a second loop I had more confidence, and we began our own dance. She whirled around so she was behind me, body pressed against mine, arm around my waist, reminding me of our dancing at Lucky Lady. We moved as one, still slower than the others, but it didn't matter.

It was us.

The electric band that had snapped around me that first night squeezed me tighter. There was something about her that pulled me into her orbit. A gravitation I was losing a battle against.

The DJ announced he was slowing it down. Some of the individuals cleared out and mostly couples were left. Shae whipped around so that she was in front of me then lifted my arms so they were around her neck. Sade's "No Ordinary Love" started playing. As I'd done for most of the night, I let her take the lead and simply focused on staying upright.

I could feel each breath. Was aware of the slightest movements of her fingers along my back, resting above my ass. When she leaned and kissed my neck, it was a jolt to my senses. When she began singing in my ear, a tsunami of need rocked my body so hard I nearly lost my footing, but Shae's quick reflexes meant we only crashed into the wall with a small thud.

"You good?" she asked.

"Yeah, sorry…you just, it was a bit harder to concentrate on staying upright with you singing in my ear. Had me thinking about getting you horizontal with a quickness."

She moved the hand resting at my waist around until she cupped my ass. "Is that your way of saying you're ready to go?"

I shook my head. "Not really. I'm having fun. But…it is my way of telling you you're totally getting lucky on the first date."

# Twenty-Two

## Shae

A sense of déjà vu hit me as I drove back to Dijah's townhouse. The night had gone smoothly, and I enjoyed every moment spent in her company. When she let us be, we were good together. I pulled into the drive, put my SUV in park, and killed the engine.

There was a nervous energy between us. An anticipation that had been simmering all night even though we'd been here before. Leaning forward, I slid my hand along the back of her neck and pulled her forward.

The kiss was soft, a quiet promise of what was to come. Dijah wrapped her fingers around my wrist and slipped her tongue past my lips. Sweet and warm, and it'd been far too long since I'd been able to experience her. Really experience her, since our time had been cut short in Indiana. As quickly as the kiss started, it ended with her pulling away.

"We should go inside before I climb over the center console."

I licked my bottom lip before giving her a quick peck. "For someone who was so resistant before, you certainly have it bad now."

She responded by lifting one shoulder before exiting the car. I laughed quietly to myself as I grabbed my overnight bag from the backseat. I didn't want to be presumptuous, but... Dijah said nothing, but I didn't miss her smirk when she saw my bag.

The anticipation of tonight was different from the last time we'd been in this moment. While our desire was mutual, the frenzied need we'd had the first time wasn't there. We had time. And I knew I'd be seeing her again. Often.

I dropped my bag at the foot of her bed as she immediately began unbuttoning my shirt. Dijah had touched me plenty because of her job, and each time, no matter how mundane, a spark of excitement always radiated through me. But now, as she explored my exposed skin with the tips of her fingers, my stomach did flips.

She stretched up on her tiptoes to press her lips to my collarbone. "You are so beautiful," she whispered between kisses.

I slipped my hands under her shirt, opening and closing my fingers against her smooth flesh. Slowly moving upward until the silky fabric of her bra caressed my palm. She felt as good as I remembered, but also, somehow better.

"Mmm," she moaned when I ghosted my thumbs across the hardened buds poking behind the satin.

I mimicked the sound when she licked down the center of my chest to the valley of my breasts. Our gazes met and she maintained the eye contact while freeing one of them from its confine. God, she was fucking sexy.

I sucked in a pleasured breath the moment she closed her

lips around my nipple. The wet heat of her mouth, the gentle flicks of her tongue. It was everything I'd been craving. Everything I'd been starved for.

"I need you naked, now," I groaned.

The smile she gave me was a lightning bolt to my pussy.

She tugged her shirt off and unclasped her bra. "Now who's eager?" She wiggled out of the ass-hugging jeans that had teased me all night.

I made quick work of shedding my remaining clothes. "Have been since day one," I answered with no shame.

She stepped closer, pushing against my waist until I complied with her silent command to sit. I inched backward on the bed with her crawling forward in a slow stalk.

"Well, I better make the wait worth it."

I cupped her face and claimed her lips again. Our tongues moved in a coordinated dance as she settled her body on top of mine. The cool wetness of her arousal was a welcome shock to my heated skin. The scrape of her hard nipples and the rock of her hips drew a moan from me.

When she pulled away, I inhaled a deep breath. The throbbing between my legs was in time with my rapidly beating heart. Dijah loomed above me, a sexy smile on her face. I easily returned it while I ran my thumb beneath her bottom lip.

Dijah leaned forward for another soft kiss. A lustful glint was in her eyes as she worked her way down my body. First my chin, then a lick to the divot at the base of my neck. She moved at a languid pace until she took one nipple into her mouth, lightly closing her teeth around it. My breath hitched when she applied pressure, and I arched into the sensation, gripping onto her hips. When she pulled and tweaked the other one, I whimpered. This woman drove me wild in the best possible ways.

"Too much?" she asked.

I shook my head. "No. Keep…keep going."

It was too much and not enough all at the same time. Each light nip or pinch made me clench my pussy. My body was in the slow climb to a free fall of bliss. Dijah's treatment was a gradual decent into the best kind of madness.

I held on to her ass, enjoying the feel of the plumpness in my hands along with the small gyrations she did with her hips. Just when I didn't think I could take it anymore, she stopped and continued her journey down my body.

I propped on my elbows, mesmerized by the sight of her. She locked her eyes on me then licked my stomach. Watching her lick her own juices from my skin had to be one of the most erotic things I'd ever witnessed.

I held my breath when she moved to the place that wanted her attention the most. My legs widened to make room for her almost of their own will with little to no input from my brain.

"Holy fuck!" I screamed out the moment she flicked her tongue across my clit.

My body was primed and ready for release so I knew it wouldn't take long. Dijah pushed my legs up, and I grabbed behind my knees, opening myself up to whatever she wanted to do to me. But that wasn't enough, as Dijah spread me wider, pulling my pussy open so she could thrust her tongue against my sensitive flesh. Quick strokes up and down, then in and out. Over and over in a sensual assault. Tighter the coil wound until the only option was to rapidly spiral free. I released my legs and gyrated against her actions. My body jerked and shuddered in a desperate need to wring out every last drop of the pleasure it was receiving.

Kadijah licked then bit the inside of my thigh while she continued to stroke me. Every little touch made me shudder.

She slowly inserted a finger inside me. "Are you good?"

Out then back in with a second. I clenched around her digits and sank my teeth into my bottom lip.

"Do you like this?"

"Mmm-hmm," I half hummed, half moaned in response.

I dug my heels into the bed and slowly rocked my hips in time with her movements. Khadijah was in no rush as she finger-fucked me.

I'd never been shy when it came to sex, I prided myself on vocalizing what I wanted, but she had me speechless.

"Christ," I groaned when she blew across my exposed flesh right before she flicked her tongue against my still-sensitive clit.

When she closed her lips around it, I damn near lost the ability to breathe. With my body still dealing with the aftershocks of the last release, I knew it wouldn't be long before the next hit. I palmed my breasts, pinching my nipples to re-create the bit of pain she'd caused with her teeth.

Faster she went, easily inserting a third finger to thrust in and out of my needy pussy.

"Fuck, yes…almost…"

Like being on a roller coaster, the drop came hard and fast, seizing my body in the grips of pleasure. Every muscle contracted, holding me temporarily hostage before the relief turned my limbs to jelly.

I was vaguely aware of her kissing her way up my body until she once again loomed above me. A slight sheen on her face and a positively smug grin on the very lips that had sent me to nirvana. Somehow, I got my arms to work and I reached up to cup her face.

"You weren't lying when you said you'd make it worth the wait."

Khadijah lowered so her heated body covered mine and I instantly adjusted so I could grab her ass. I loved the weight of her, the feel of her nipples pressed against me, the wet evidence of her arousal, the scent of me all over her, of simply being with her.

She kissed me softly with a ghost tease of her tongue running along my bottom lip. "Did you think I'd disappoint?"

I shook my head. "Not at all. But…you were a lot more take charge."

She ran her fingers along my collarbone. "It didn't seem to be a turn-off for you." She adjusted so that her thigh was wedged between my legs. "In fact, I think I could coax another free."

A low groan rumbled in the back of my throat as she ever-so-slowly moved her leg back and forth. She wasn't wrong, if I let her keep going, I'd hit number three easily enough, but I needed to have my fun too. And since the night she'd left my hotel room, I'd been wanting to get my hands on her again.

I flipped us so I was on top. "No, it's my turn."

# Twenty-Three

## Khadijah

When I exited the bathroom Shae sat on the edge of the bed and two bottles of water were on the nightstand. Her confidence and go-with-the-flow attitude that extended to the bedroom was such an added turn-on.

The sight of her in my dual harness with both dildos in place, ready to go, re-intensified the throbbing between my legs. When she'd asked what my favorite toy was, I'd hesitated on being completely honest, but there was something about her, about how I was with her—I found myself answering truthfully, and without worry.

"You gonna keep staring, or are you gonna join me?" she asked as she slid backward on my bed.

I pulled the corner of my lip between my teeth while taking another long appreciative glance. "I do like the view."

She stroked the larger of the two attachments with a wicked

grin that had me clenching my thighs together. "It's even better up close."

I flipped the light off in my bathroom then strolled toward her. "Yes, it is."

Shae rested up on her elbows to watch my approach. "What's the best way?"

I crawled over her, easing over the two protrusions to settle on her abdomen. She leisurely ran her hands along the inside of my thighs until her thumbs met in the center.

I closed my eyes briefly, enjoying the light strokes. "Me on top," I finally answered with a shudder.

A short laugh escaped her. "Why does that not surprise me, you like to top."

I inched back, grabbing a hold of the thicker shaft to rub myself along it. "You're about to fill me twice over, and I'm topping."

"Yeah, because you asked to be filled twice over." Her reply sounded matter-of-fact, but she intently watched as I rubbed myself along the silicone dick.

The ridges of the fake veins stole a moan from me as I teased my overly sensitive body. Shae watched me with hooded eyes, slowly opening and closing her fingers against my outer thighs.

The anticipation of riding her, of sharing this side of me with her...

Shae picked up the lube from the bed—we kept our eyes on each other as she poured some into my awaiting palm. Reaching behind me, I grabbed the smaller dick to coat it liberally.

"Tell me what you need," she whispered.

I lifted up on my knees. "Hold this one steady."

Shae nodded as she gripped the larger dildo. I held on to

the smaller one with one hand and leaned forward to support myself with the other then lowered down slowly.

Shae didn't move as I eased the two silicone dicks inside, groaning from the delicious stretch. With her free hand, Shae massaged my hips, gentle encouragement. Her eyes were trained on my pussy, watching with great interest as more and more of the toy was enveloped inside me until both were fully inserted.

I didn't move for a moment, giving myself the necessary time to adjust to the fullness. Shae lightly ran her fingers up and down my inner thigh, ghosting her thumbs over my clit and back again. Each pass made me shudder.

Slowly I rose up on my knees then sank down again. "Fuck," I moaned at the delicious stretching in my ass and pussy.

"That's fucking sexy," Shae groaned, her eyes focused between my legs.

My stomach responded the same way it always did when her intensity was zeroed in on me. A delightful mixture of schoolgirl giddy and unbridled lust. I closed my eyes and repeated the action, fully dialing into the yearning, the need, the desire.

Shae planted her feet on the bed, the action pushed the two dildos deeper.

"Oh god, yes."

Another slight upward thrust of her hips had me whimpering from the joy of it all. Leaning forward, I rested my hands on her stomach and started riding. The veining massaged my inner walls causing the right amount of friction. I kept my movements paced and rhythmic, fully drawing out the sensations created as the two toys easily slid in and out of my body.

Down I went, gyrating my hips in a small circle, the move

drawing simultaneous groans from both of us. My body was alive with heightened awareness.

With each rock forward my nipples rubbed against her dewy skin, which was another tease edging me closer to the end. Flesh to flesh, our mingled heavy breathing was accompanied with the light squeaking of my bed as my pace picked up.

"Come on, baby," Shae grunted, with a smack to my ass.

I pushed back against her palm. "Again," I begged.

The most delightfully sinful grin spread across her face as she happily gave me what I'd asked for. The second strike sent a rush of heat through me. I clenched around both toys as the euphoric high descended upon me like a thick fog rolling in.

Shae gripped my thighs, aiding in my movements. When she applied slight pressure to my clit it was sensory overload. My next release that had been simmering under the surface burned through me. I arched back, bracing my arms between Shae's legs, the move sent both toys deeper, both hitting me in the perfect way to set off a second shock wave before the first had time to subside.

I became an incoherent jerky mess and was vaguely aware of arms around my waist and whispers in my ear.

"Do you know how fucking beautiful you are right now?" Shae pressed her lips to the side of my neck, peppering me with light kisses.

She ran her fingers up and down my sweaty back, holding me to her until the ringing in my ears stopped and the world quit spinning. The only sound was our heavy breathing, and I wasn't sure if I was feeling the rapid thumps of my heart, or hers, or both.

Once things started to settle, I lifted my head and was met

with the sweetest grin from Shae. She said nothing but leaned forward and kissed me slowly. I slipped my arms around her neck, deepening the connection. Our tongues swirled, not in a wrestle for control, but more in a tango, moving together as one. I cupped her face, the subtle move shifting the silicone dicks still inside me, and I moaned into her mouth.

Shae pulled back. "You okay?"

I nodded then blew out a slow breath. "But it'll be easier for me to get up if you lay back."

Shae did as asked, flattening her long legs and resting her hands on my waist. She helped me as I pushed up and the smooth feel of them sliding out of me sent one last shiver through my body.

I collapsed on the bed beside her knowing I needed a minute before testing out my legs. Shae placed a kiss to my shoulder before rolling off the bed. I had enough energy to turn my head and watch her ass as she walked toward the bathroom. The straps of the harness pushed her plump cheeks together and all I could think was how biteable it looked.

I lay on my bed listening to the sounds of her moving about. The water coming on then going off. A flush. The water again. I needed to clean up myself, but I couldn't move. There remained the electric zing buzzing under my skin and a euphoric lightheadedness I wanted to bask in for as long as possible.

"You good?"

I turned to find Shae resting against the door frame, her lean form backlit from the light in the bathroom. She really was a stunning woman.

"Yeah." I pushed to a sitting position. "Want to join me for a quick shower before bed?" I was tired and sleep was calling my name, but I needed to wash the sex off me before I could rest. My thighs were wet and sticky; my skin had a clammy feel to it from the sweat.

Shae's lack of an immediate response had my palms sweaty for a whole different reason. She'd brought a bag—that was indication enough she'd planned to stay.

"Depends."

"On?"

The corner of her mouth kicked up in the playful grin I enjoyed so much. "How early do we have to be up in the morning?"

A slow smile spread across my face. "Oh, um, brunch is at eleven, so I'll get us up about nine."

She licked her lips as she strolled toward me, giving a quick glance at the clock. "How sleepy are you?"

It was a little before 1:00 a.m., and I was fairly tired, but the lust in her eyes kicked my lower half into a second wind that slowly spread through the rest of my body.

I slid back on the bed as she crawled over mine. "I feel like I downed an energy shot."

Shae leaned down to kiss my neck and I tilted my head to the side, giving her more access, while running my hands up her arms, feeling the slight twitch in her muscles as she supported her weight.

"So, what I'm hearing is we have time and can still be well rested before going to your parents in the morning."

"Mmm-hmm," I mumbled, lost in the feelings she created until there was a slight clearing of the fog and her words registered. "Wait, what?" I jerked back. "Did you say...did you just..."

Shae didn't change positions, so she loomed above me with brows drawn together. "What?"

I shoved her shoulder gently and she rolled to the side as I scrambled to sit up. "Did you invite yourself to brunch?" Maybe I'd heard her wrong. I hoped I'd heard her wrong.

"Uh, was that not the plan? We already have the birthday party tomorrow afternoon, wouldn't it make more sense?"

"In what universe does that possibly make sense?"

She shrugged. "Uhhhum, logistically. If we're going to the party together, why not make a day out of it?"

I blinked a few times then started shaking my head. "Logistics? You meeting my parents is more than logistics, Shae. That's like step ten when we are only on step two."

Shae's brows damn near touched she had them so pulled together, and her mouth hung open. "Steps? What steps?"

"The logical ones. You don't just go around meeting a person's parents after fucking them twice. There's an order to things. I can't just show up to my parents' house with you in tow. We aren't there yet."

It was all wrong. Moving too fast. She couldn't meet the family yet. Hell, I couldn't even tell them about her yet because I didn't know what to tell them. And I had adamantly said I wasn't dating anyone from work. Was I a liar, or a hypocrite, or both?

It was too soon. Telling them now would put an end to things before they even got started. That's what always happened. I needed time. A plan to ease into the admission.

Shae simply stared at me, not saying anything. A range of emotions seemed to flash across her face as she processed. I couldn't believe she actually thought...that she actually invited herself to my *family* brunch. Who even did that? Relationship guidelines aside, that was poor etiquette.

"So, let me get this straight," she finally said. "Not only did you have some pro-con list of reasons why we shouldn't go out. Now you have a list of checkpoints I'm supposed to know about and follow? Did I miss anything?" Her tone was flat, and I knew the tone. It was the same one she had in interviews when she thought the reporter had asked her a pointless question. It was the tone of annoyance and being completely over the situation.

Even if I hadn't started to recognize her moods during postgame, I knew the general attitude because I'd dealt with some version of it throughout my dating years. They would grow weary of my way of doing things. They would not understand and decide figuring it out wasn't worth the effort. I don't know why I thought it would be any different with Shae.

"Do you have these steps written down somewhere?"

Her question surprised me. Slowly, I shook my head. "No."

"Then how am I supposed to know the playbook you're operating from?"

I released an audible sigh. "I don't have a playbook, Shae."

She got off the bed and searched around until she found and put on her underwear. "I'd beg to differ, Khadijah."

Any other time she spoke to me, my name falling from her lips was a soothing caress, but this time, the way she said my name, my whole name, was like a bucket of ice water. "This is not how I planned on the night ending."

She yanked on her shirt next. "What was your plan? Because I'm learning that you always seem to have one."

I grabbed one of my pillows and hugged it to my body.

Again, she stared at me as if she were waiting for more explanation. My own annoyance grew, because what was so wrong about having a plan for how things should go? And I needed a plan. I needed the order because without it, chaos ensued. Why didn't she understand that?

"There are steps, Shae. An order to things. I have to… It's too soon." She had to understand. I needed her to understand. I wasn't saying never, just not right now. "Let's be for real here. We aren't even dating. We have fucked twice and maybe… maybe something could come from that. But how can I really know given your track record? Someone took a picture of us at the club. They called me the 'next Harris Honey' and you expect me to introduce you to my parents when we haven't even figured out what, if anything, we are."

Shae's mouth made the "wow" movement before she actually spoke the word. "Wow…okay. Heard you. That's… You know what, say less, it's all good." She pulled on her pants, keeping her back to me as she did so.

*Fuck!* I massaged my temple trying to figure out how this all went so sideways so damn fast.

"Shae, why are you so pissed? You can't honestly think meeting my parents is reasonable all things considered."

"You're right, Khadijah. It's no more reasonable than you expecting us to operate under your rigid rules of engagement. Rules, by the way, you don't give any forewarning about. You can't be running a game without having all players on the same page. But it doesn't matter, we aren't anything."

All the wind left my lungs when she said those words. She slung her bag over her shoulder, and this time when we stared at each other, the expression from that day in the locker room was all over her face again, but also somehow worse. That gut-punching mix of sadness, shock, and disappointment when I'd pretended not to know her.

"Shae…"

"No, it's good. I understand. You meeting my parents, guess that's higher up on your list. Or lower, not sure how you rank importance. But then again, I didn't worry about saying you were only a fuck buddy. My bad, but again I didn't know the fucking rules."

My stomach twisted. It was all wrong. All so very, very wrong. And I didn't know how to fix it. How to take back the words and better explain.

"You have a good night, Khadijah. I know how to show myself out. And for the record, it's been three times."

Each use of my full name made my heart squeeze and my stomach roll. She walked out without looking back, and any words I wanted to say to get her to stay were trapped in my throat. How had I fucked up this badly?

# Twenty-Four

## Khadijah

I groaned and rolled to the side when my alarm went off. The offending device continued its melodic chimes before I finally pressed the off button then moved into a seated position. A heavy sigh pushed past my lips when I glanced over my shoulder at the empty space where Shae should have been.

"No," I said, getting out of bed and stopping myself from replaying the disastrous end of last night.

Even though I wasn't rushed and running late, getting ready for Sunday family brunch held a déjà vu feeling. Only this time I knew I would in fact be seeing her again. And I had to hope things wouldn't be awkward. Unease rammed into me at the thought. Fuck! This was why I had rules and why I'd avoided getting involved with someone I worked with. The shit went sideways at my first attempt.

*At my doing.*

It was a sobering realization. I'd seen her disappointed before because of me, but last night was different. Last night, Shae hadn't simply been sad, or disappointed... she'd been hurt. I'd hurt her and I didn't know how to reconcile that. How was I going to make it through the rest of the season? How awkward would it be? Would I even be able to face her or effectively do my job? Having to touch her, be around her, care for her. My stomach ached at the uncertainty of what was ahead.

By the time I pulled up to my parents' house, I'd mostly put it out of my mind. It was a problem to deal with on Monday. But as a new worry hit me, I pulled out my phone and fired off a text to Jah: Don't mention my date or Shae! I'm serious!

The "read" indicator popped up, but no typing dots, even though they weren't here yet and I knew she wouldn't be the one driving. It would be fine. Jah could be respectful...she *would* be respectful of my request.

"Hey, Momma, Daddy."

"Happy birthday," Dad greeted, getting up from his seat at the island to give me a hug.

I returned his embrace, having completely forgotten about my own birthday. As I'd gotten older, they'd become less of a big deal, especially since I wasn't around anyone who would celebrate with me for a few years.

Mom was bent over pulling a tray from the oven. "Yes, happy birthday. How are you, honey?" she asked.

"Good."

I hung back and watched my parents in action. Dad slid on a pair of oven mitts and took the dish from Mom, but not before he planted a quick kiss on her cheek. Thirty-four years of marriage and there never was a moment they didn't seem head over heels in love. I wasn't naïve; I was sure they had their downs, but any troubles had been kept from me and Jah. My parents had what I'd wanted for so long. Something even my over-the-top sister had managed to find. At my lower moments, I would question—why not me?

Though I would never admit my hard-core case of FOMO out loud. But I was over that now, and had been for a while. Or that was the lie I'd been telling myself. Until Shae.

"Do you need me to put the plates out or anything?"

Mom shook her head. "Your dad took care of it already."

Slamming car doors got our attention. I clenched and unclenched my fingers in anxious anticipation since Jah had still failed to respond to my text. After she greeted our parents, Jah strolled over to me and pulled me into a hug.

"What did you do?" She whispered the question in my ear.

I pulled back and frowned at her. "Nothing."

She raised one brow and pursed her lips to the side but didn't say anything else. Throughout brunch, Jah kept giving me glances, and each time I thought she was about to be a pain and say something, but to my great surprise she didn't. However, her question sat in the back of my mind the whole time. Why would she even ask me that? I hadn't done anything but be honest.

After the meal, as per usual, we were on cleanup duty. It didn't take two people, let alone three, but Vance always felt like he should help in some way.

"Okay, I didn't bring it up in front of the parents, but seriously, Dijah, what the hell?"

I shot a look at Vance, then back at my sister. "It's nothing,

I just didn't want to have them asking a bunch of questions getting excited for no reason."

"So, you did do something."

I put the last dish in the dishwasher and mentally counted to ten. I wasn't going to get into this with her. "I didn't do anything. We went out, and now we can get back to how things were."

"Baby, let it go. Dijah is perfectly capable of handling her own dating affairs."

I shot Vance a grateful smile. "Thank you. Seriously, Jah, you're worse than Mom and Dad sometimes."

"Only because I know you get in your own damn way."

I pressed my lips together as I closed the short distance between us and pulled her into a hug. "I love you, sis, I really do, but let it go."

She huffed out a sigh. "Fine. Keep denying yourself a real chance at being happy because something doesn't fit in the boxes you try to force everything into."

Ouch. Direct hit and she knew it.

There was nothing wrong with having standards and wanting order in my life.

"This isn't about boxes, it's about incompatibility."

Jah took a seat on one of the stools at the island. "Incompatible how? I may have only been around you two twice, but y'all seemed pretty damn compatible to me."

"There's more to a relationship than physical attraction."

Vance finished his sweeping then dipped out, leaving me to deal with my bossy sibling alone. I rested my hip against the granite countertop because I knew she wasn't going to let this go. We may have approached life differently, but Jah and

I did have some similar tendencies, one of which was our inability to let a conversation go when we were determined to get to the bottom of something.

"I'm aware. But Shae seems like she's fun and genuinely into your uptight self."

"I'm not uptight!" *Or rigid…*

"Girl, please. I grew up with you, remember? You've been micromanaging your life for-fucking-ever. How many to-do, to-need, to-whatever lists are on the Notes app on your phone right now?"

I straightened and crossed my arms. "What does that have to do with anything?"

"Did you put Shae on a list?"

"What you two in here talking about?" Mom asked as she entered the kitchen. I could only assume they'd asked Vance where we were.

"Nothin', Momma," I answered, grateful for the interruption.

Jah simply rolled her eyes as she pushed up from the stool, kissed Mom on the cheek, and left.

"You two fighting about something?"

I shook my head. "No, not at all. I have to head out, Nikki texted and she needs me to pick up Imani's cake."

"Okay, and tell her happy birthday for me."

"I will." I said my goodbyes to Dad before heading out.

My conversation with Jah played on repeat in my head and I started to rethink the one I'd had with Shae. She was still wrong for trying to invite herself to brunch, but the rest… I couldn't give any more energy to it. My focus shifted to figuring out how to make sure my goddaughter wasn't too disappointed that I couldn't deliver on what she wanted. Especially since Shae not being there was partly my fault. I was grateful I hadn't told Nikki that Shae had agreed to come so there were no false hopes.

My saving grace.

*Shae.*

I couldn't keep her out of my mind. She hadn't called or texted since leaving and I realized that bothered me. But then I had to remind myself that I hadn't attempted to contact her either, so could I really sit around in my feelings about it? Logically, probably no, but emotions sadly didn't run on logic. And part of me had selfishly hoped that even though we'd had an issue that she would keep her word.

I arrived at Jumpin' Jack, the indoor trampoline place where the party was being held. I grabbed my beautifully wrapped gift, along with the one my parents had sent, and tried to balance the cake without crushing the bow. I mumbled a quiet "thank you" to the guy who held the door open for me to enter as he was leaving and ignored the way his grin widened and the once-over he gave me. Luckily, it stopped there because I was not in the mood to field off any poor flirting attempts.

As soon as Nikki spotted me, she rushed over to grab the cake. "Happy birthday, bestie. And thank you again for picking this up. Imani really did the whole 'it's my birthday and I can cry if I want to' thing. Hell, I don't even remember what caused the meltdown."

"Thank you, and it was no problem. Where is she anyway?"

"Everybody's in the party room. I stayed out here so I could meet you."

Nikki glanced behind me as if she were looking for someone

else and I knew who that was even though I'd told her from the beginning that getting Shae here wouldn't be possible. But my friend knew my weakness was my goddaughter and the pang of guilt for not being able to deliver ping-ponged through me.

"It's just me, Nikki."

She had the nerve to look confused as if I didn't know what she was playing at. We were in a brief staring contest before she sighed in defeat.

"We're back this way."

The party room was large, colorful, and loud. Oh, so very loud with around twenty kids all laughing, talking, and being general bundles of energy. Nikki directed me to the gift table as she raised her voice to call for her daughter. Imani's face lit up when she saw me, and I braced for impact as she barreled in my direction. Her hair was impeccable as always, considering her mother was a hairstylist. The Marley twists were cute, shoulder-length, and decorated with silver and gold braid clips.

"Auntie Dijah, you came!" she squealed, crushing me in a tight hug.

"I told you I'd be here."

"I know, but..." Sadness momentarily shadowed her face. Clearly, she'd remembered I'd missed out on her last two birthdays. But in true kid fashion, her mood shifted back to unadulterated joy. "You're gonna jump with me, right? Momma said it was your birthday when she was talking to Daddy about y'all going out for drinks later, but that you were spending the day with me at my party so we should make it a double party and you need to have fun like everyone else. So, will you?"

She spoke a mile a minute and held on to my hands, bouncing in place with hope and expectation sparkling in her dark brown eyes. A look I knew I damn well couldn't and wouldn't say no to.

"For a little while."

She squealed again before she was off to greet another friend who had arrived.

"They need to bottle whatever it is that makes them so hyper and sell it to adults," Omar, Nikki's husband, said with a laugh as he came over to greet me.

"They did, it's called caffeine," I joked in return.

"You right. You right."

The party hostess started giving instructions on how long they got to jump, safety protocols. I listened while resisting the urge to check my phone again in hopes that Shae had messaged. Once the hostess finished her spiel, the kids ran out, full of laughs and eagerness. Some of the parents also exited the room to follow behind them; others stayed seated at the long tables, looking relieved for a few minutes of blessed silence. I started arranging the various packages on the gift table into a more orderly grouping.

"I see you ain't changed one bit."

I turned to see Will, Nikki's cousin. Back in the day, we called ourselves "trying to date" until we realized our time together was mostly spent pointing out people we found attractive and we noticed the pattern was always guys for him and the ladies for me.

"Will." I opened my arms wide and engulfed him in a hug. "It's been a minute. How's Florida?"

"Fucking hot, but otherwise I'm loving it."

When we broke apart, I noticed a guy standing behind Will.

He was a shorter, dark-skinned man with a shaved head and a full, well-groomed beard.

Will reached his hand out to pull him forward. "Dijah, let me introduce you to my fiancé, Reggie."

I turned my attention to the guy who had a large smile on his face and shook his outstretched hand.

"Oh wow, congrats." I forced out the words.

Not that I wasn't genuinely happy for Will and Reggie, but that tiny portion of self-doubt that had gotten bigger after my talk with Jah now had me again wondering why I couldn't get to that point. Luckily, Will's deliberate placing of his gift in the wrong spot pulled my attention from going too far down the "why-me," or rather the "why not me," path.

I playfully rolled my eyes before moving his small gift bag to the right side of the table with him laughing. We did some quick catching up as we exited the party room in search of Nikki and the kids. Luckily Imani spotted me and insisted I join her on the trampoline right after Will hit me with the "are you dating" question.

"You not really going in there, are you?" Nikki asked, face scrunched as I took off my Chucks.

"Um, yeah. I can't let the birthday girl down." As soon as the words left my lips, a new twinge of guilt hit.

It would be fine though, I was sure, or at least I hoped. Shae would hopefully be okay with a quick photo op when they came to the game. Near courtside seats had to be as good as a visit. I was thankful those worries were kicked out of the way and replaced with new reasons to be slightly terrified. There was real levity in the free-falling sensation when I jumped, and, for a brief moment, was suspended in air, before falling again. Focusing on not making a fool of myself while being surrounded by ten ten-year-olds who were all doing their best to make me lose my balance took those straying thoughts off my mind.

I enjoyed the moment. Let their infectious and slightly villainous laughs seep in and lift my mood. Though there were stray moments of imagining how much Shae would have enjoyed this. But only in the off-season.

After about twenty minutes I had to call it quits and it wasn't long before the host was wrangling the kids back to the party room. As the pizza and drinks were being distributed, another employee popped her head into the room asking to speak with Nikki and Omar.

"Everything okay?" I asked.

She shrugged before exiting the room with the young lady. When they returned, both of them were all smiles.

She strolled over to me and bumped me with her hip. "Okay, I see how you are."

The other young lady who had come in to get them clapped her hands to get everyone's attention before I could ask Nikki what she meant.

"Imani, there is a special guest here for you," the party host said.

My goddaughter immediately snapped her head in our direction. The excitement on her face was the polar opposite to the confusion on mine.

There was no way she'd still show up. She'd only agreed to it because she'd wanted to go out with me, but I'd effectively killed that. Hadn't I? She'd left last night. No calls or texts all day. I pulled in a sharp breath.

"You okay?" Nikki whispered.

I couldn't even answer as time came to a standstill when the mystery guest walked through the door. Imani's high-pitched yell was nearly drowned out by the whooshing in my ears.

There she was, and like my first day in the locker room, my stomach plummeted to my feet. Shae Harris stepped in, oversized grin on her face, decked out in Atlanta Cannons gear and followed by Tina. Imani rushed forward and wrapped her arms around Shae's waist, jumping up and down as she held on. Most of the other kids seemed to have no idea who she was but fed off Imani's excitement, and a few of the parents had their phones out and were snapping pictures.

My attention remained glued to the woman who didn't appear to be bothered in the least by a ten-year-old hanging on to her. And like that first day our gazes met, my mouth went dry, and I had to figure out how to make it through the remaining hours of this party without things being weird. If ever there was a moment for be careful what you wished for, this was it.

# Twenty-Five

## Shae

I was going to owe Tina a nice dinner for coming with me, even though she'd offered after I'd given her a rundown of what'd happened. I'd had to talk to someone, but when I'd called Courtney, she'd been in the middle of her own thing with Sasha. In the years I'd known Tina, she'd never dated that I could recall, but I'd had to get that shit off my chest because I'd really thought I was tripping—who the hell had a relationship itinerary?

Khadijah Upton, that's who. It had to be some sort of karma from my serial dating ways that the universe put a woman who was the exact opposite in my path.

*But it was more than that.*

As Tina and I posed for another picture, her real smile was transforming into the one she always had in the team PR photo shoots. She was probably regretting life decisions. Hell, I wasn't expecting so many kids, and even though we'd done other kid events, this was way more concentrated with only two of us.

And with the way Dijah was trying to avoid looking at me, I was regretful as well. However, I'd offered to show up even though she hadn't wanted to impose on my time. I was a woman of my word—plus when she'd talked about her god-daughter I had wanted to come because it was clear how much the little girl meant to Dijah.

The parents of the birthday girl introduced themselves and thanked us for making an appearance. The party hostess gave us wristbands in case we wanted to go jump and I planned on dragging Tina out to do so. I had too much frustrated energy coursing through me, which needed a constructive outlet.

"Thank you again for coming," Nikki said for the second time after the thrill wore off and the kids settled down again.

"I was happy to be invited. Dijah was explaining how Imani was a fan, and I'm always happy to encourage that."

Nikki glanced back over her shoulder at her friend. Dijah hadn't approached to speak, and I wouldn't lie, that shit rubbed me the wrong way. It was like salt to the wound. I replayed it over and over in my head and no matter how I tried to look at it, she'd been fully appalled at the idea of me meeting her parents. *Fucked twice.* That's what she'd reduced us to.

"I don't want to take up too much of your day, but if you're free this evening, maybe you can join us for drinks to celebrate Dijah's birthday."

Just when I thought it was safe to go back in the water, I'm hit with another fucking knock. It was her birthday and she didn't say shit to me about it. "Nah, I don't want to intrude, but thank you."

I shifted my gaze to Dijah, who finally left the two men she'd been speaking with and headed my way. Nikki looked between the two of us, an inquisitive smirk on her lips—as if she was debating staying, to see what we'd say to each other—before she left to go help her daughter since she was about to start opening the gifts.

"Hey. I didn't think you would come."

"I said I would."

"I know, but since you left last night, and hadn't texted…" She lowered her voice as she glanced around the room.

I cut my eyes over at her briefly. "The phone works both ways."

I hadn't said anything out of pocket, though calling her rigid probably could have had a better delivery. But at the end of the day, I'd been confused as hell by all the steps and checklists she apparently had when approaching dating and I'd only let my feelings on the situation be known. Her dismissive attitude had me feeling like some dirty little secret. I was good enough to fuck, but nothing else.

Dijah nodded slightly before giving me her full attention. She placed her hand on my arm and I didn't want to admit how that little contact was somewhat soothing. "You're right. I just… You're right. Thank you for still showing up today, and bringing Tina. You made Imani's day."

When she graced me with a smile, it only added to the pain. I had it bad for a woman who, for the most part, didn't want me. Dijah returned her attention to the party as giggles and oohs-aahs rang out during the gift opening.

"You're welcome. I wouldn't want to disappoint her." I bit my tongue and held back the *or you*.

Standing near her was fucking with my senses. For the first time I truly was uncomfortable around her, and I didn't know what to do with that particular realization. I highly disliked the uneasy, unsure energy buzzing around like a vulture under my skin.

"I'm gonna go jump."

That got a reaction as Dijah whipped her head toward me, a frown deepening her features. "Neither of you should be jumping. The risk of injury... You aren't seriously considering..." She glanced around. "Where is Tina anyway?"

"She stepped outside. She likes kids, but in small doses. The overwhelm hit. Also, hell yeah, we're jumping. Take off the trainer hat and have some fun."

She leaned closer and spoke low. "You and I both know I know how to have fun." She let her gaze travel the length of my body, giving a small ghost of a smile before she continued, "But keeping you and the other players injury free is literally my job." She made the statement while aiming her phone toward the party to snap some shots of the birthday girl.

I wouldn't take the bait. I couldn't take the bait. Looking for any and all openings in the boundaries she'd set was what had gotten me into this situation to begin with. "Well, we're not at work. And I'm annoyed as hell currently, so it'll do me some good."

A text flashed across the screen of her cell: Oh y'all fuckin. With the raised brow emoji.

Dijah shot her attention over to her friend then to me, darkening her screen a little too late. The two of them shared some sort of silent communication across the room. It was clear I'd been the topic of conversation between them at some point.

Part of me was intrigued as to what she might have told Nikki about me…about us. Though with Khadijah's relationship checklist, and the fact she apparently didn't want to be associated with me… I scrubbed my hands down my face hoping to keep the mounting frustration at bay.

Normally, I'd cut my losses and move on. I'd take the issues between us as a sign from the universe that it was time to let it go, but I wasn't fully prepared to throw in the towel quite yet. Even though at every turn it seemed like that was the way to go. I needed to figure this shit out, but this was not the time or place.

"I'm gonna go jump for a bit."

Again, she placed her hand on my arm. "Promise me you'll be careful."

I wouldn't get pulled in by the concern in her eyes. That was work related and had nothing to do with anything personal. We had a silent staring contest until a loud, high-pitched scream jolted us. I moved quickly behind Dijah, holding her waist to keep her from being knocked over from the force of her goddaughter tackle-hugging her. There were rapid-fire "thank yous" over and over mixed in with "you're the best" and "this is the coolest gift ever."

"You're welcome, miss lady. I'm glad you like it. And I'll get it framed so you can hang it on your wall."

The little girl stepped back and yanked the signed jersey on over her clothes. "Framed? I'm never taking this off." She glanced up at me. "Ms. Harris, did you see?" She turned around, thumbing to the back of the shirt. "It's yours and it's signed." She moved back to face us. "Oh, well I guess you would know, huh?" Imani rushed forward, wrapped her tiny arms around my waist. "I'm really glad you came to my party."

I returned her embrace. "I'm really glad your godmom invited me."

She pulled back and looked between me and Dijah. "You know my Auntie?"

I nodded. "Um, yes."

"We work together," Dijah added.

The little girl processed the information frowning. "Auntie sucks at sports. I beat her all the time."

I couldn't stop the laugh that escaped even when Dijah gave me a dirty look. An expression that changed when she addressed Imani.

"Remember when you interviewed me about my job for a school assignment last year?"

The little girl tapped her chin for a moment. "Oh yeah, that's right, you look at her body."

I wasn't the only one to snicker at her comment, an action that earned me another annoyed look from Dijah. Thank goodness for the innocence of kids to break the tension.

"Not exactly. I look *after* their bodies."

Imani shrugged. "That's what I said." She whipped her head between me and Dijah, then her eyes went wide. "Wait, if Auntie invited you, then y'all are friends and I'll get to see you all the time."

"I don't know. I guess it would depend if your aunt invites me," I answered, shifting my attention from Imani to Dijah and back again.

The little girl turned her expectant expression to her godmother. "You'll invite her, right? I'd be the coolest kid in school."

I could see Dijah's internal struggle. My answer hadn't been designed to put her on the spot, but it had. I should have felt bad about it, but my own irritations meant I didn't.

She kneeled down to the little girl's level. "We'll have to see. Ms. Harris is a busy woman."

Imani's shoulders slumped and she darted her eyes back and forth. "Oh. Okay." The melancholy in her tone was damn near heartbreaking.

"I'll tell you what, once the season is over, I'll have your aunt work something out."

Imani's eyes lit up. "Really?" She gave me a quick hug then raced back to her mother. "Mom, did you hear? Ms. Harris is my friend now."

Nikki glanced over to where Dijah and I stood, with a smirk on her face. "That's great, baby. We'd love to have Ms. Harris around."

No idea where this ranked on Dijah's checkpoints, but with the way she released a low sigh and pinched the bridge of her nose, I would hazard to guess we were again skipping steps.

I leaned down to whisper near her ear, "I'm gonna go jump now."

She cut her eyes over at me, but nodded. "I'll be back," she said to her friend. "Need to supervise Shae to make sure she doesn't injure herself."

Nikki nodded and laughed. She looked as if she were about to say something, but thought better of it. Once we were outside the party room, Dijah grabbed my arm.

"Shae, seriously, thank you for still coming today. And for

softening the blow for Imani. Hopefully, there won't be any hard feelings between us that'll affect work."

"Why would there be?"

"Because things didn't work out."

Damn if she didn't know how to twist a knife. She had that same matter-of-fact tone, like when she'd talked about her "reasonable" steps for progression. And just like she had those steps that only she was aware of, she had apparently unilaterally decided that because of differing opinions, things hadn't "worked out."

I massaged my temples and took a few deep breaths, hoping to loosen the tightness in my chest. Remembering where we were, I inched closer so people passing by couldn't hear, and whispered, "What was there to work out? All we did was fuck, right?" I tried to keep my tone as even and matter-of-fact as hers, but the words came out clipped.

She sucked in a sharp breath then started to speak, but closed her mouth again. She'd been the one to reduce us to meaningless hookups and as much as I was trying to let it go because of where we were, her comment about not working out needled under my skin, picking at the scab she'd created.

"Oh, by the way, I guess happy birthday is in order."

I left her standing in the hall and made my way out. The sound of loud counting in unison got my attention. In one of the trampoline areas there was a basketball goal, and there was Tina catching air while making shots. A few people around were recording her.

"She's going to hurt herself and I'm going to have to explain it to Coach Smith." I hadn't expected her to follow me, but Dijah's tone held a real hint of stress and worry as she

watched each time Tina went up and did some silly pose before firing off the shot.

"We're professionals." No sooner than the words left my
mouth, Tina went down.

Dijah rushed by me. "Shit."

She started to toe off her shoes, standing in front of the net-
ted enclosure when Tina sat up laughing. "Are you trying to
give me a heart attack?"

Tina flipped onto her stomach and pushed up onto her
knees, all smiles. "Not at all, Doc."

She said bye to the kids, with them temporarily whining
about her exit, before they picked up the ball, trying to re-
create what she'd been doing.

"I thought that look was solely reserved for Shae," Tina said,
standing in front of us both.

I glanced down at Dijah, who had a frown of displeasure
firmly in place. "Wait, what? What are you trying to say?"

Tina lifted one shoulder. "Some of us are good patients."

"Not today," Dijah shot back, which only made Tina laugh.
Dijah looked at me. "Can you please not go in there? I'm beg-
ging you."

I saw the pleading in her eyes and despite how I felt about
us in the moment, Dijah was a woman who took her work
seriously and I didn't need to cause her any additional unnecessary stress, even though I desperately needed something to
get my mind off everything.

"Okay, and I guess we'll head out then."

"Oh. Already?" She had the nerve to look disappointed.

"Yes. There's no reason for me to keep sticking around."

We were once again in a stare-off. What the hell did she

want from me? Her signals weren't just mixed, they were downright contradictory from one moment to the next and the whiplash was killing me.

"I'm going to get a slice of cake," Tina quietly said before leaving the two of us standing there.

Slowly her eyes drifted closed in a drawn-out blink. "I'm sorry."

"For what, Khadijah? Are you sorry you reduce us to nothing more than sex? Or about throwing my past dating life in my face again? And when I mentioned us spending the day together last night, you couldn't even be bothered with telling me today was your birthday. What exactly are you apologizing for?"

She shifted from side to side, avoiding my gaze and not answering the question.

*That was it? That was all she had to offer?*

"I've never been around anyone who was so ashamed to be associated with me and I don't know what to do with that."

Her attention snapped to me. "I'm not."

"You could have fooled me." I waited a moment to see if she'd say anything else. When she didn't, I blew out a breath and nodded. "Tell Tina I'm in the car."

# Twenty-Six

## Shae

"Do you not want it taped up?"

I glanced up from sliding on my knee brace to see the woman behind the question. She chewed on the corner of her lip as she rolled the kinesiology tape between her hands. It'd been four days of waiting to see if she'd say anything. Four days of trying to pretend all was, or would be, okay and back to usual. Four days to let it sink in that she really didn't see anything past a few fun nights.

Fun was what I did. It was who I was, but to be reduced to and dismissed as only that hurt. More than hurt…it was confusing, and frustrating, and it made me second-guess everything that had transpired over the last few months. Looking at her twisted something in me. Being near her constricted my breathing. And having her touch me was damn near torture.

"Nah. I'm good." I pushed to standing, expecting her to move back.

"Shae, I'd like to…"

"I said I'm good." I glanced over her head to see a few eyes focused in our direction. "I need to get out on the floor to warm up."

I maneuvered around her to exit the locker room. I did my best to ignore the whispers behind me, but I couldn't tune out the person behind me calling my name. Turning, I saw Nina jogging to catch up to me.

"Whatcha need, Nina?"

"What's going on?"

"Nothin', why?"

"Look, your personal life is your personal life."

Warning bells went off with that statement. "Yeah, it is, so why you in my face right now?"

She stepped closer, not backing down like I needed her to. "You and Doc beefin'? Because I'm not sure this is the time for a lover's quarrel."

A few of the other players started down the tunnel; they slowed as they approached us. I glanced at them, then back at Nina.

"Ain't no beef. Or lover's quarrel. Why you all up in my business anyway?" I tried to maintain calm and keep my composure, but this was not the shit I needed to be talking about right now. And it wasn't any of her damn concern.

"Because you made it our business when you decided to let your dating life cross with the team."

"Excuse me?"

Anger prickled under my skin. Being near Khadijah and trying to figure out where the fuck we went from here was distracting enough. I didn't need this shit on top of it. Nina had been here for five years and we got along well enough, like that one coworker you were cordial with because your working relationship synced, but on a personal level…not so much.

"Don't act brand-new, Shae. Last year was bad enough with you and Courtney vying for who could have their business in the streets the most."

I advanced so we were near face-to-face. "The fuck you say?"

"Is there a problem here?"

We both turned to see Jason. He stayed pretty removed from anything off the court, but he'd walked by at the right moment. His attention darted between me and Nina. The other players in the tunnel watched with nervous curiosity.

Nina put her hands up and moved back. "I was just making sure Shae had her head in the game."

"Worry about your own head, and get out there for warm-ups."

I let out another slow breath and tried to remain calm even though I really didn't want to deal with her shit. As team captain I had to remember myself and not dropkick her ass, even though the smug look on her face made me want to.

Who I did or didn't date ain't never fucked with my game and she knew that. That shit never made it onto the court so I didn't know why she was trippin', but what we didn't need right now before game one of the semis was the team divide she was trying to sow. She gave me one parting glance before continuing on out to the arena.

"You good, Shae?" Jason asked.

"Always."

★ ★ ★

I plopped down into a seat near the back of the bus and rested my head against the window. The game had been an absolute shit show. Turnovers, missed shots that should have been easy for us. And I'd thrown up more bricks from the free-throw line than I had in a long while.

Despite what I'd told myself before the game, my head was in fact not in it. And the team as a whole played as the most noncohesive unit. We only lucked out that Seattle played a bit worse so we came away with the win. Barely.

All I wanted was to go back to my hotel and sleep. I put my headphones on and cranked up my music. I needed to tune out the world. When someone settled into the seat beside me, I kept my eyes closed, hoping whoever it was wouldn't try to speak to me. That lasted until the bus got rolling, then they moved one of the cups off my ear. I was prepared to cuss out whoever, until I saw Courtney's cheesing ass.

"I knew your ass wasn't asleep."

"You were 'bout to get cussed out."

"Whatever. I'm not worried about your moody ass."

I hit pause on my phone to stop the music. "I'm not moody, I'm tired."

"Uh-huh, right. That's why you and Nina were about to go to blows in the tunnel?"

Courtney hadn't even been there, but it was no surprise there had already been talk. I'd mostly ignored the whispers and side glances in the locker room.

I sat up and stretched my neck. "We were not about to come to blows. She was, however, talking out her ass about shit that don't concern her."

"I heard. But also, look, I'm the last person to be giving relationship advice, because…" She huffed a sardonic laugh. "Me and Sasha. I love her ass, but damn she can work my nerves."

I shook my head, wanting this conversation to stop before it really got started. "Nah. We not going to discuss this right now." I put the cup back on my ear only to have her remove it again.

"You need to do something, because while Nina might have been out of pocket, especially bringing that shit up before the game, if she's seeing the same thing the rest of us are, then it is a concern. 'Cuz you thought we wouldn't notice you and Doc going from always making eyes and shit at each other to the two of y'all barely looking in the other's direction?"

I rested against my seat, turning my head to watch the city pass by. We were in too close of quarters for this topic. Not that it mattered, what Courtney spoke was the truth. Maybe Khadijah had been onto something with her rule of not dating someone she worked with because the current situation was fucking with my head. And the team.

I glanced at my friend, who stared back at me in turn. "What do you want me to say? That I'll get it together? I will. I can't be letting my personal shit fuck up the team."

She nodded. "There is that. But also, I'm worried about *you*. I've seen you date, break up, date again. Everything sort of rolled off. But how you've been the last couple of days…"

I let out a long sigh. "Again, what do you want me to say?"

Courtney wasn't the most nurturing woman, so for her to be sitting next to me, expressing that level of concern, must have meant I was coming off worse than I'd thought.

Tina pressed her face between the crack of the seats. "She's right. We're worried."

"Don't you start too."

"Just sayin', Shae."

"And we weren't going to get to blows."

I leaned forward to see Nina across the aisle, one row up, scrolling through her phone, but apparently tuned into my conversation. For fuck sakes. I rested back and closed my eyes. Why was the bus moving so damn slow? All I wanted was to get to the hotel and sleep this whole thing away.

"You like her," Courtney said, clearly not letting this go. "You two need to work out whatever and get back to how it was."

"If only it were that easy."

"Hey, if anyone gets it, I do. Shit with Sasha has thrown me off a game or two. But we eventually work it out."

It was hard to work out something with someone who didn't want you, but I wasn't ready to voice those thoughts. However, wallowing in my quiet rejection wasn't doing anyone any favors. I wasn't sure if it was disappointment, sadness, or what, but I was saddled with some heavy emotions I couldn't shake. If I could articulate what was going on in my head, I could combat it, get my shit together. Not being able to put it into words added to my frustration.

But I had twenty-four hours before the next game to work it out.

# Twenty-Seven

## Khadijah

Over the last few months I'd watched Shae on the court. In that time I'd known her to be focused, sure-footed, and level-headed. She was the one normally rushing to break up shouting matches before they turned into altercations between her teammates and other players. But I sat with my heart in my throat as Nina and Courtney did their best to get between Shae and number 20 on the Seattle team. Those two had been exchanging words most of the game and I watched in horror as they got into a shoving match. More of the Cannons rushed the floor, as did the Seattle players.

Marni grabbed my arm, her eyes wide. "Holy shit. What is happening? This isn't her. She doesn't act like this."

Marni shot me a look, and it felt like a silent accusation. I couldn't swallow, or shake the anvil in my stomach, as things went from bad to worse. Whistles were blown and I couldn't get a clear view, but I did manage to see Courtney holding

Shae while she argued with the other player, or the refs, or whoever. What I did know was she was pissed and not backing down. Commotion and flailing arms as the ref repeatedly pointed toward the tunnel.

Shae had been ejected from the game.

Coach Smith got in Shae's face, walking her backward while furiously talking into her ear. She gripped her by the shoulders and continued talking, but everything was too loud, and the whooshing in my ears only made it worse. Eventually Coach turned Shae toward the tunnel and gave her a little push. She stalked past the seats, still cussing, and ignoring the taunts of some of the attendees as she went.

"I should go check to make sure she's okay."

"No," Coach Smith barked. "You, you stay here. Marni can go, because right now…you…no."

I swallowed and sank down into my seat trying not to give in to the "all eyes on me" feeling. Marni took off down the tunnel, leaving me sitting there staring but not seeing the remainder of the half, fighting back tears. It was a mess that needed fixing, but I didn't know how. I feared anything I tried to say would make it worse, and that was if she gave me the chance to say anything at all.

She wouldn't even let me do my job. I'd been walking around nauseous since Imani's party. The bite in Shae's tone when she'd commented on how all we'd done was fuck played on repeat. In my panic, I'd been needlessly crass, and that had been the moment the lightness drained from Shae and the hard edges were erected. I needed to fix it. To make a plan to lay out the perfect apology.

When the buzzer sounded, I couldn't even get up from my

seat and head toward the locker room like usual. I was scared to go there and face Shae, especially since Marni hadn't returned. The loss was bad, by forty points. It was the worst one we'd had all season. Shae being gone had a ripple effect on the team and the guilt that rested on my shoulders made me slump in my seat. But I couldn't stay there and sulk; I had a job to do. Though I feared the reactions that could come from the other players.

The mood was somber to say the least. Coach gave her talk, though it was shorter than normal and her tone sounded as if she were holding back her own frustration. Those who needed me interacted, but there was no joking around to be had. It was exactly as I'd feared: if shit went sideways and a choice had to be made, I was the replaceable one. Notably absent was Shae. She hadn't been waiting in the locker room as I'd expected, but I dared not ask about her whereabouts.

By the time we made it back to the hotel, all I wanted was to go to my room and have a good cry in the shower. One word stopped me in my tracks on the way to the elevator.

"Upton."

I turned to face Coach Smith, who looked slightly less pissed, but clearly not pleased.

"Yes, ma'am?"

"We need to chat."

Oh fuck. This was it; she was about to fire me. I pressed my lips together and nodded, not that she could see since she'd already turned and started walking to the seating area in the lobby. I wasn't even going to get a private dressing-down. I parked my bag and sat facing her, shoving my hands between my thighs to hide the shaking.

"Look, what happens between two consenting adults is none of my business. And honestly as long as it wasn't affecting the team, I really didn't give a shit."

I worked to keep my breathing steady and maintain calm despite the fact that bile burned the back of my throat. It was these types of conversations that I had wanted to avoid.

"I've never done anything like this before," I blurted out. "Being professional and focused on my job has always been top priority for me."

"And yet…here we are."

"Here we are," I parroted, working to keep the despondent tone at bay.

Like a balloon with a slow leak, the direction of the conversation was slowly deflating into the area I feared.

"No blowing smoke, I've liked how you've fit into the organization. There is a harmony happening after a few stormy seasons. The players seem to respect and like you. Apparently one in particular more than others." The half smile that lifted the corner of her mouth lessened the weight a smidge. But it quickly disappeared when she spoke again. "However, whatever is or isn't happening right now needs to stop. For the last two games, one of my best players has not been herself. Now, I get it, we're human, we go through shit, it happens. But whatever *it* is, needs to be fixed."

She maintained eye contact as if to really drive home her point and I heard her loud and clear. *I shouldn't have broken my rule. The course of action was ill-advised and I needed to course correct. If I couldn't get the harmony back, I was out of a job.* I wanted the harmony back. Yes, I was enjoying my job, but more importantly I missed Shae. The old, fun, flirty Shae who'd simply loved life until I crapped all over it.

"I understand, Coach. I like being part of all of this. And I never meant to disrespect you, or the team."

She nodded as she pushed to standing. "There's no disrespect, but I appreciate the sentiment. This is the second time the Cannons have made it to the playoffs. This is the first season we've advanced past round one. We are not ready for our run to end and especially not under these circumstances."

As she walked by me, she gave me a pat on the shoulder and left me sitting in the lobby to digest her words. If I didn't feel like shit before, I certainly did after basically being told the team's playoff success rested on my shoulders. I'd broken Shae, and I had to fix her. But how? The tears from earlier threatened to fall, but I fought to keep them back.

I took a few steadying breaths before pulling out my phone.

"You better be dead, dying, or something," Jah answered after the third ring.

"I wouldn't be in this mess if not for you, so you have to help me."

There was grunting and mutters under her breath for a moment. "Dijah, it's two-fucking-a.m. I just got your in-utero nephew to stop treating my bladder like a soccer ball and you're calling me with some random bs. What are you even talking about?"

"Shit. Sorry. Forgot about the time difference. But I fucked up and I need your particular brand of 'I told you so' to help fix it."

More grunting and she told Vance it was nothing. When

she spoke again, she sounded more awake and less pissed that I'd called. "This is about Shae? I knew you did something."

I gave her a quick rundown. Repeating what I'd said made me cringe to the point I wanted the floor to open and swallow me whole. An errant tear rolled down my cheek that I quickly swiped away.

"What the fuck, Dijah? Brunch is not some sacred thing."

"It wasn't brunch, it was what introducing her to Mom and Dad meant. And it didn't follow the timeline."

"Are you shitting me with that mess? Timeline, Dijah, really? People, feelings, aren't something you can check off. How are you the oldest and don't know this?"

"You're not helping."

"It's two-fucking-o'clock in the morning. I barely sugarcoat during regular business hours."

She wasn't lying. Jah typically spoke what was on her mind and I loved her for it. But I also wished she'd soften the blow a little even if I didn't deserve it.

"I know. But now I need you to help me with a plan to make it better. She got into a fight, Jah. Was ejected from the game because of me."

"No. Did your overthinking ass fuck up? Yes. But Shae is a grown-ass woman who is responsible for her own actions."

Logically, she was right, but it didn't change the fact Shae's mood was a direct reaction to what went down between us. And that was my fault.

"There is no planning this, Dijah. You gotta let those pesky emotions you be tryin' to dictate take the lead on this one. Now, I have to pee again and go back to bed. It's going to work out. Love you."

"Love you too."

Let my emotions take the lead. That was not something I'd ever done, and I wasn't sure I knew how. No—scratch that—I did know how. Those pesky emotions were usually in the driver's seat when I dealt with Shae. I was at ease around her because I didn't overthink it and just let things happen.

Grabbing my case, I headed to the elevators. My heart raced and the bricks piled up in my stomach, but I needed to do this tonight. I hesitated outside of Shae's door then knocked. No answer, but I heard the TV.

I knocked again. "Shae, it's Khadijah."

I waited. Again, no answer, but the volume on the TV went up. I took the hint and headed to my room.

# Twenty-Eight

## Shae

Courtney passed the ball to me. I dribbled left, then right, trying to get a clear shot around the player guarding me. Seattle had traded out Lisa Martin for this new guard since our scuffle last game. Martin had run her mouth one too many times and caught me on the wrong day. Not something I was proud of, but if she was going to talk trash, now she knew she had to back that shit up.

I personally was ready for the rematch, but instead, I had this new annoying little shit, also acting like she had something to prove. She made a move for the ball, but I was quicker, and kept it out of range before passing it to Claire, who was open.

Claire moved up the court as I tried to shake my guard, but she was on me even though I didn't have the ball. I cut right in time to see Claire attempt to pass, but Martin was on her and grabbed her arm, sending the ball flying. There was a mad dash to gain control. I heard the whistle from the refs as a Seattle player came up with control. My heart raced. We were down by four. I ran over to my teammates who were in the faces of Martin, who'd blatantly fouled Claire. We did not need a repeat of last game even if she apparently had a hard-on for it. But the smirk she shot me had me advancing until Nina grabbed my arm.

The aching dread tightened my chest as Claire took the free-throw line. She had been practicing her shots, but wasn't the best. We had fifteen seconds left in the game…if she made both and we got the ball back we could tie.

She dribbled twice, set, then took the shot. When it cleared, we all moved forward to give her a quick "good job, congrats" before we set again for the next shot. When it hit the rim and bounced back we all rushed forward. Courtney was first off the line, but a Seattle player got control. There was a single thought I'm sure we all shared: *Get possession.*

Down the court we ran with Seattle passing, doing too good a job of playing keep-away to run out the clock. As soon as Martin got the ball, Nina bodychecked her, getting an immediate whistle. We had a chance because Martin was usually shit with free throws. The sequence played out in my head. She missed, we get the ball, and hit a three to tie. We could do this.

First shot, a miss. The possibility grew. Second shot… another miss.

Claire was first off the line, got the ball, passed to Nina, who shot as the buzzer sounded and missed.

Fuck!

I hated a loss anytime, but they always stung more on our home court. It was like someone walking into your house and taking a shit on the floor. It doubly hurt knowing we'd now lost twice. One more and we'd be out. I had to keep my attitude in check. I'd already let my personal shit get the better of me and steal my focus, which had gotten us into this predicament.

Apologizing to the team for that failure was probably one of the hardest things I'd had to do, but it needed to be done. And I had to keep my promise to have my head on straight, but that was easier said than done.

I pushed through the bodies, stopping to snatch my towel off my chair, then headed toward the tunnel to the locker room. Someone else could do press.

"Shae."

I kept walking. I was not in the headspace for her.

"Shae, wait up."

She grabbed my arm and I snatched it away. As much as I wanted her to touch me, at the same time I couldn't stand it. Every time I looked at her, or was near her, was a reminder I didn't want to have.

Khadijah stopped cold to stare at me wide-eyed. "Sorry," she said, taking a step back.

"I'm good, don't need any after-game checks."

"I would disagree. You played most of the game. But that's not…" She paused as more of the team came down the tunnel.

She waited through the murmurs of "good game" and other platitudes.

I turned my attention back to Khadijah. "You should get to work." I turned to walk off when she grabbed my arm again.

"Shae, seriously, you need to at least let me ice your knee."

"She's right, Harris, get in there," Coach Smith said as she walked by us.

She kept her fingers secured around my wrist. "Let me take care of you. Please."

I could not and would not get pulled in by the pleading in her eyes or the softness of her voice. Instead, I gently slid free, and I walked off leaving her there, heading toward the training room, because regardless of my mood, Coach would have my ass if I brushed off the postgame talk.

Coach kept it simple and matter-of-fact, smoothly pointing out where we—I—could have been better, even if she didn't call out any names. But there was no denying the comments about making sure our heads are in the game and leaving issues off the court were a hundred percent her getting on my ass again without being direct.

After Coach dismissed us, I pushed off the bench.

"Yo, Shae, you good?" Courtney called out before I could make my exit.

I lifted my chin in her direction then dipped out. Voices carried into the locker room as I stripped to take a quick shower and leave. Most of them gave me a wide berth, except Claire.

"Hey, Shae."

"What's up?"

She glanced down, shuffling from side to side while holding the blue ice pack. I did my best to keep a lid on my annoyance.

"Uh, Coach said we're supposed to do postgame."

"Shit, seriously? I don't want to deal with them tonight."

She lifted a shoulder, both of us knowing I wouldn't ignore the directive from Coach.

"Oh, and Doc said to give you this." She thrust the ice pack toward me.

I stared at it for a moment before taking it and tossing it on the shelf in my locker. After a shorter-than-I-wanted shower, I dressed and begrudgingly headed to the pressroom. Both Claire and Coach were waiting right outside the doors, and the displeased expression Coach gave me let me know she'd be on my ass again at the next practice. She'd already laid into me after game two and had threatened to bench me if I couldn't get it together. I was skating on thin ice.

Things got underway and I let Claire and Coach field most of the questions, because in my head I was channeling Marshawn Lynch. Claire elbowed me and I had to stop myself from saying *what the hell*. She looked at me, then jutted her head in the direction of the reporters, who were all waiting for me to respond to something.

"Oh, sorry. Can you repeat the question?"

I recognized the guy—he was the one from last season who was always on some bullshit and the slick grin that hit his face had me bracing.

"The latest Harris Honey got you off your game like last season, huh? You were missing easy shots and had, what, three or four turnovers? On top of the fight you had in game two. Now y'all are down two-to-one. Do you plan on showing up next game or what?"

"Excuse me?" The end of my career and possible criminal charges flashed through my head. I pulled in a breath then looked to my left at Coach. She pushed back from the table and stood, with Claire and I following her lead.

"All of my players show up and leave it all on the court. To imply otherwise means you aren't watching the same game they're playing. It's been a long night, a hard loss, and we need our rest for Thursday's game."

Yeah, Coach would be on me, but never in front of the cameras. She was big on us being a united front, and even she thought them bringing up my dating last year was bullshit. Though none of the women I'd dated had ever affected my game.

Dijah was different.

"Harris," Coach called, stopping my hurried strides.

My knee was hurting, but I wouldn't dare rub it in her presence, especially since I skipped seeing Khadijah despite her instruction to do so. I'd ice it when I got home.

"Thanks for sticking up for me back there."

"I'll always have your back until you give me a reason not to. You know that."

"I do. And again, I'm sorry for, well, my lack of focus."

"I'm gonna tell you like I told Upton, get whatever this is worked the fuck out sooner rather than later. When I see you back here tomorrow, I expect *Thee* Shae Harris to show up, you hear me?"

I nodded. "Yeah, Coach, I got you."

Once in the sanctuary of my SUV, I massaged my knee, groaning from the temporary relief. It was a constant dull ache, much like the one in my chest. I sat there for a moment and let the first part of what Coach said sink in—what she told Upton? Fuck. So she'd only come by my room because of Coach? Made sense, because what was there to discuss otherwise? "We didn't work out."

Khadijah…nah. I had to get her out of my head and figure out how to turn it off as effectively as she seemingly had.

I kicked off my slides and dropped my bag at the door as soon as I crossed the threshold.

An unwind night was in order. A nice cup of tea, some popcorn, and my favorite movie. The low throbbing in my knee reminded me an ice pack would be added to the mix.

I'd just gotten settled on my couch, *V for Vendetta* cued up, leg propped up, and a nice cup of my favorite turmeric-and-mint tea when my phone started ringing. I glanced at the screen, prepared to send whoever to voicemail, until I saw the concierge's number.

"Hey, Willie, what's up?"

"Sorry to bother you, Ms. Harris, but there is a woman here to see you, but you don't have anyone on your guest list for today."

"That's because I'm not expecting anyone. Who is it?"

"She said her name is Khadijah Upton."

I sat up and pulled my phone away from my ear, not sure I'd heard him right. Then I had the momentary thought of sending her away, but remembered Coach's words.

"Ms. Harris?"

"Um, yeah, you can let her up."

"Yes, ma'am."

I stayed put with a multitude of questions running through my head. The loudest being, how the hell did she know where I lived? But I'd get answers soon enough. Pushing off the couch, I eased my way to my door, opening it and leaning against the frame to wait. She stepped off the elevator with a few bags in her hands and paused when she spotted me.

I moved to the side. "Come on in."

"Do all your visitors have to go through that?" Dijah asked after she entered.

"Not the ones I'm expecting to see. Makes it easier to send

folks away if I don't want to be bothered. Speaking of, how exactly did you know where I live?"

"Courtney told me."

"She volunteered my address?"

Dijah frowned. "Is there some reason you wouldn't want me to have it? You know where I live."

"Nah, just trying to figure out why."

She glanced around, the subtle movement making the bags she carried rustle. We didn't need to have the full conversation in my entry area.

I eased past her. "This way."

She toed off her flats at the entry before following me then offloaded the packages onto my oversized ottoman that doubled as a coffee table. "Thank you for not sending me away."

I returned to my spot on my sofa then took a sip from my cup. "So, why exactly did you drop by?"

The annoyance I'd been hoping to rid myself of lingered under the surface. Though the optimist side of me wanted to give leeway since she had sought me out again.

*Remain calm. Don't get excited.*

"I wanted to check on you."

"My knee is fine. I've been icing it since I got home."

"Not your knee. Though, good, since you didn't come see me after the game. But I came to check on *you*."

She hadn't even gone home to change first. She'd left the game and then came here.

"Why?"

"Because I care about you, Shae."

It wasn't in my nature to hold grudges, but I couldn't get her words out of my head. "Do you? Because I don't know about you, but when I care about a person, I don't put up roadblocks to prevent being around them."

Dijah pressed her lips together and shifted her attention to the stuff she'd brought. "I didn't know what your comfort foods were, so I picked up mine—and yes, I know this isn't about me—but I got ice cream, chips, chocolate, and wine. Though, shit, sorry. I forgot you said you don't drink during the season."

My attention went to the other bag she carried; it was from a restaurant I'd not heard of. Dinner and dessert, but I needed to not read too much into the gesture. I grabbed the cold stuff to put in the freezer. When I returned, Dijah remained in the same place I'd left her.

"You're trying to comfort me over the loss of the game?"

She pulled the corner of her lip between her teeth and sighed. "I miss you, Shae, and I want to make things, us, right."

# Twenty-Nine

## Khadijah

Shae didn't say anything immediately. Reserved, somewhat distanced Shae was unnerving. I missed the easygoing, full-of-smiles-and-flirty-innuendo Shae.

"So, what did you bring?" she finally asked.

"Olé Olé has the best nachos I've ever tasted, they're perfect for stress eating."

The corner of Shae's mouth lifted in a half smile. "That sounds like these are definitely more for you." Even as she said the words, she was lifting the lid to take a look. "I'll get us plates. What would you like to drink?"

"Water or whatever is fine."

She hadn't denied my visit and seemed receptive; that fact calmed some of the bees buzzing in my stomach. While I waited for her to return, I took in the space. I hadn't known what to expect from Shae's house, but somehow it fit. The building was older with lots of architectural detail, but her unit was updated.

However, the ornate crown molding and chair rails retained some of the charm.

Her sofa was an oversized U-shape in a soft green color, comfy and casual.

"I like your place," I said to her when she returned.

Shae set the plates down on the ottoman and handed me a bottle of Arizona green tea. "Thanks, my hideaway in the city. Only a select few have ever been here."

She held my gaze and I had to work to not fidget under the weight of it. Shae was friendly, warm, and welcoming, but she also deeply regarded her privacy. And I'd invaded that by showing up without an invitation.

"I'm sorry for popping up. I really needed to talk to you, and since you've understandably avoided me, I wasn't sure you'd take my calls, not that I wanted to do this over the phone, so Courtney told me where to find you because in her words 'we need to get our shit worked out.' And although no one else said anything, I got the feeling the consensus was the same."

Again, she simply stared for a moment then released a long exhale. "If I didn't want to talk, I would have told Willie to send you away."

There was a heavy truth to that statement, and I latched onto the unspoken meaning attached to her allowing me in. Maybe, just maybe, I could salvage what I'd wrecked.

"Your knee is hurting you, isn't it?" I noticed how she had a slight limp and the way she eased down, trying not to bend it too much.

"It's fine. I was icing it and had it elevated."

I spotted the ice pack lying on a pillow and grabbed both. "Here, let me." I moved to prop her leg up again and did a quick cursory check, watching to see if she winced at any point. "Look, I realize that you're pissed with me, but you really shouldn't let it dictate whether you get proper care or not."

"I wasn't sure I could handle you touching me."

I glanced up at her—she didn't need to elaborate. I'd had the same thoughts.

"Do you want me to stop?"

She shook her head and I continued with my exam while she adjusted so she could reach the food and scoop some onto the plates.

Satisfied there wasn't any swelling, I placed the ice pack then settled beside her.

"So, what are we watching?" The large-screen TV was frozen at what looked like the beginning—or maybe the ending—of a movie.

"I'll tell you after you explain your plan to fix things," she replied around a mouthful of nachos.

It was that word: *plan*, four letters that had sent everything sideways. I loaded up a chip of my own, delighting in the gooey, spicy bite. After washing it down, I wiped my mouth. I'd come this far. No point in trying to back out now.

"I went by your room when we were in Seattle, after the fight, but you didn't answer."

"I know. But letting you into my hotel room… I wasn't in the right headspace for that."

I was aware she'd ignored me that night, but hearing her admit it stung, though all things considered, I understood.

"Everything I imagined would happen if I dated a coworker has come to fruition." Shae started to speak, but I held up a hand to stop her. "Mostly of my own making."

Shae simply nodded and kept eating.

"I got scared, when you brought up brunch, meeting my parents. I reacted out of panic, and…I'm sorry."

"Scared of what exactly?"

I shoved another chip into my mouth to buy some time. I'd had days to think everything over and no matter how I tried to spin it, the answer remained the same. "Failure."

Shae rested against the arm of the sofa, her brows drew together. "Failure at what?"

*Let the emotions take the lead.*

"Us. When we first met, I honestly thought I could pull off the one-night stand, until work. Then I thought I could keep it strictly professional, but…you. You made that damn near impossible."

"You never told me to truly back off," she defended.

"I didn't mean it like that. It was me. I wanted to be around you no matter how much I tried to resist."

"So…what I'm hearing is, I'm irresistible?"

I rolled my eyes, but her flirty comment was welcomed. I'd missed that, missed her. "Something like that."

Just as quickly as fun Shae appeared, the more reserved one slipped back in. "And you bringing up my dating history. Again."

The guilt and shame hit me once more. I knew that was a sore spot for Shae, yet I'd still taken the low blow.

I set my plate down and placed my hands on her arm. "It wasn't about how often you dated. It was about how easily you seemed to move on. You asked me once if you were forgettable, I guess I feared that I was or could be."

She went back to eating. The thought of food made my stomach lurch while I waited for her to respond. She wiped her hands before setting her own plate down next to her mug. "Do you know how many women I dated last season when the assholes were making such a big deal about it?"

I thought back on some of the articles I'd seen and couldn't come up with an actual number. They'd mostly been vague "Shae Harris at it again" type of pieces. "No."

"Four. And those four weren't all during the actual season, before you get to thinking I was really busy in a matter of months. But it didn't matter. It took one not-so-smooth parting of ways and suddenly it was 'Shae Harris has as many turnovers off court as she had on it.' Which, by the way, is bullshit, because I hardly ever have turnovers."

I smiled despite myself, but quickly sobered. "I'm sorry for feeding into the stories."

She shrugged. "It's all good. I do my best to let most things slide off, but it hit differently from you. You're not forgettable in any sense. Far from it. There's been nobody, and I mean no-bod-dee, who has had the ability to throw me off my game. But the truth of the matter is, you bringing it up again wasn't nearly as painful as you seeming damn near ashamed of me. To be with me."

"I told you at Imani's party that wasn't the case."

"Then explain, because you went into full panic mode when I mentioned brunch, which would mean me meeting your parents. I thought all this time you were just trying to keep things professional and such, but after that…after that, it came across to me as something more. I went over in my head—every time you would jump away when you got too close, and people were around. Or how you tried to keep your distance. And your whole birthday situation."

The melancholy in her voice ripped through me, driving home how much I'd fucked up…how much I'd hurt her. "Shae. It was never that."

"Really, Dijah? Because replaying the last few months, I'm second-guessing everything. Yes, I get it, boundaries and whatnot, but I questioned if you ever saw me as anything more than the one-night stand I was supposed to be."

I slumped back, digesting her words. Shae had always been confident, from the first night we'd met, so hearing doubt coming from her…

"First, the birthday thing. For me, birthdays aren't a big deal. I honestly forget mine most times. That really wasn't about not wanting to spend it with you. As for the rest, Shae, I'm here because of you. Because I miss you and I got scared of what I hoped things could be, but wasn't sure would happen." I stood to walk around. "I don't think I'm making sense. I like a plan. I need a plan. And with you, whatever plan I tried to have flew out the window, no matter how hard I tried. With you I just want to *do*, and that worries me."

"What's wrong with just 'doing'?"

"Nothing and everything." I huffed. "I like things a certain way. I thrive on routine and order. But I thought about what you said, that we… Well, I was approaching things with a set of rules that only I knew and you're right."

At that, Shae cracked a grin. The wide, full one that lit up her face and made my stomach do flips.

"I was right? I like the sound of that."

She was infectious, and momentarily lightened the mood despite my lingering nerves.

"Anyway, we should be on even playing ground so…" I

pulled out my phone and hit send on the email I'd drafted earlier. "Now you have the list."

Shae's phone vibrated from the side table. She looked at the device but made no move to retrieve it. And the grin that had been there slowly melted away.

"So, we're still supposed to be playing by rules? That you decided? Do I get any sort of say or I'm supposed to simply go along with your twelve-step plan?" She took on that same deadpan tone.

This was not going as I'd plotted out. "You haven't even looked at it."

Shae shrugged. "Don't need to."

Her refusal deflated and frustrated me. I sat, annoyed she wasn't even willing. "Shae, that's not fair. You wanted to know how I functioned. I'm giving you that, and you're going to disregard it?"

She stared at me for a moment. "You're right. Okay. Though my agent is usually present for all contract negotiations."

I rolled my eyes. "It's not that serious."

"Sure feels serious." As she spoke, her eyes bugged as she looked the screen and then up at me, then back down at her phone.

"Kha…wha…wow…this is…" She scrolled, and scrolled, and scrolled. "This is a lot. And you just had this sitting around in a PDF?"

I picked up my bottle of tea and shook my head. "I told you, your comment got me thinking. I've never actually written them down before, but after you didn't answer the door in Seattle I had anxious energy I needed to channel. Making lists calms me and once I got started, it grew and grew."

She blinked once, twice, and a third time, but said nothing as she continued to scroll.

She was at least considering what I'd laid out. And despite her frustration, annoyance, her hurt…we were still getting somewhere simply because she called me Dijah.

However, I needed to fill the silence. "My panic about you meeting my parents was a me thing. In the past, I've talked to my parents about someone I was dating, having had all these grand ideas for how our relationship would go, only to have it fizzle out. So, you bringing it up, to me, signaled the beginning of the end, before we even got started. I… I didn't want that, I… I just handled the panic horribly."

She arched a brow, but said nothing as she returned her attention to her phone.

"It looks like a lot because it's a smaller screen."

The corner of her mouth lifted. "It looks like a lot because it's a lot. Your bullet points have subpoints, Dijah. You have things broken out in levels. What part of this is not a lot?" Her voice went up in inflection toward the end.

Was it really that much?

Once I'd started, more points had come to mind. I wanted to be thorough since her complaint had been that she didn't know the "rules."

"I wanted to make sure everything was laid out."

"Uh-huh. I don't think the contracts I've signed have been this detailed. Damn, woman."

I drained the rest of my tea, already starting to second-guess if I'd gone overboard or not. But for the long term, there were lots of things that needed to be considered. How could she not see that?

"Having a plan, or rather an understanding, of what each person expects in a relationship is a good thing."

Shae darkened the screen of her phone. "But these are your expectations that you want me to agree with, no questions asked."

I shrugged, feeling a bit sheepish. "If I'm being honest, yes, but...since I've been told that idea is a bit 'rigid'..." I let the word hang for a few seconds, waiting to see if she'd back track that comment. When she didn't, I continued, "It was also pointed out to me that there are in fact two people in a relationship so compromise could be necessary."

"Could be?" Shae laughed out the comment. "Okay. Okay. You wanna do this, let's do it." Shae eased off the couch and walked off to her kitchen, returning a few moments later with a small notepad and pen. I was glad that the limp was less pronounced.

I inched closer to her. "What are you doing?"

"Are we or are we not negotiating the terms? I'm gonna need counterpoints."

"You're telling me you have never, not once, considered next steps for your relationships? Outside of those others," I quickly added.

"No. I functioned on the 'where are we now' and 'how is that going.' Simply let things take a more organic course."

"And how's that worked out for you?" I didn't mean to sound as pissy as the question came out as, but the fact she kept low-key dismissing my process—even if it wasn't intentional—was needling at me.

"How's *this* worked out for you?" she shot back.

# Thirty

## Shae

She didn't answer right away, and she looked a little shell-shocked that I'd asked. But seriously, she'd written out a five-page breakdown. This was micromanaging at a whole new level. But she was trying and had given me what I'd asked for. So, while the PDF was hella over-the-top, I couldn't be too put off by it.

And she'd come. This wasn't as one-sided as I'd been fearing over the last few days, and that gave me hope.

"What would be your first counterpoint?"

My first would be to not do this at all, but I'd been intrigued by Khadijah from the moment I'd laid eyes on her. And there were in fact two people in this relationship...she'd called it a relationship—a relationship she was worried about ending before it really got started, given her own history—which meant compromise went both ways.

I quickly scanned over the list again and smiled at point

three. "You know the 'no sex on the first date' is already null and void, right?"

She returned my smile. "I'm aware."

"So, then how is that supposed to work moving forward? Are we not supposed to have sex again until after your six-date minimum requirement?"

Dijah pulled the bottle of wine from the bag. "Do you mind if I…?"

"Nope. Wine opener is in the drawer next to the fridge, and you'll see the glasses hanging from the rack beneath the cabinet."

The more I scrolled, the more overwhelming it became. Honestly, the idea of operating like this took some of the joy and excitement out of the dating experience. But I was a competitor, and no damn checklist was going to get the better of me. Time to play defense to her offense.

"Are you okay?" she asked as she returned with her drink.

"Yeah, just absorbing it all."

She took a generous sip before she settled back, tucking her feet under her ass. She was making herself quite comfortable as an uninvited guest, and I couldn't even say I was annoyed. In fact, I liked her being here. I was opening up another aspect of myself to her that I didn't share with many people.

"Shae, can I ask you a question?"

"Yeah," I answered, not looking up from my phone.

"If all of this seems so unfathomable to you, why are you entertaining it?"

I glanced at her. Dijah returned my gaze with an intense one of her own, almost as if she had a lot riding on my answer.

I put down my phone and notepad then slid closer to her.

"Look, we both know I think this is a little extreme." I laced my fingers with her free hand. "But from day one I had this desire to see how things would go with us. There is something here, between us, and now I know you feel it too. I'm willing to do what I can because I fully believe you're worth it."

Dijah made circles in my palm with her thumb. "Thank you. And I have to admit the out-of-control feeling is terrifying, but also a little exciting. I do want this though, Shae. And I'm sorry for making you doubt that."

She cupped my cheek when I inched closer. I leaned into the warmth and softness of her touch I'd missed. "You know not everything can be a checklist item, Khadijah."

"I do."

I rested my forehead against hers. "But if you need this, to help you, then we negotiate to find a way forward that works for us."

She slowly licked her lips then tilted her head up to kiss me. Any last remaining tensions drained out of me at the connection. Being close to her, tasting her, all was right with the world again. I'd missed the feel of her in my arms, the comfort she brought with her presence.

She pulled back and ran her thumb across my mouth. "So, what are we watching?"

"Huh?"

"You said you'd tell me what movie that was after I told you why I was here."

It was a whiplash-inducing change of topic. However, the smile on her face told me she knew exactly what she was doing.

"Um, *V for Vendetta*. It's my comfort movie."

"I think I've heard of it before, but never actually watched it."

One of the exchanges from the movie popped into my head. "Would you like to?"

"Yeah."

I settled back against the sofa after grabbing the remote to hit play. "Yeah." I worked to ignore the way my body craved more contact from her. But she was here, and this thing between us was something. Something she wanted as much as I did. She curled up beside me, sipping on her wine as the opening scene played out.

"You need a refill?"

A coy smile spread across her face. "Are you trying to get me drunk?"

I returned the expression. "You brought the wine. You opened the bottle. I'm just trying to be a good hostess."

She uncurled and leaned closer. "Seems like an awful convenient explanation."

I laughed. "You mean the truth."

"Toe-may-toe, toe-mah-toe. But I'll get it, you need to keep resting your knee."

I closed my fingers around her wrist as she moved past me, running my thumb back and forth across her soft skin, taking in her every feature.

Dijah bit the corner of her lip. "Everything okay? You need me to bring you something?"

"You."

She leaned down and pressed her mouth to mine. A soft, gentle connection that ended all too quickly. I released her and she continued to the kitchen. When she returned, she settled right beside me, again tucking her feet under her ass as she laid her head on my shoulder.

I rested my hand on her thigh and squeezed lightly. Concentrating on the movie wasn't easy. My mind wandered to how natural it felt to have her in my home. How easily she seemed comfortable here, not like a first-time guest, but as someone who belonged.

"I get to kick you out in the morning." I spoke the lighthearted words into her hair.

"Who says I'm staying?"

I tapped her glass. "I am."

She sat up to look at me. "Two glasses of chardonnay get my keys taken?"

I nodded. "You nearly popped a blood vessel because of a trampoline. What I look like letting you drive inebriated? In fact, keys please."

I held my hand out, palm up, doing a "give me" motion. In the grand scheme of things, she'd probably be fine—depending on how long she stayed after the movie was done, and if she properly hydrated. But how could I pass up a perfectly good excuse that kept her here?

"It's my job to look after you and make sure you aren't injured." Even as she protested, she moved from the couch over to the entry where she'd left her purse, returning shortly to drop her keys into my awaiting hand.

"Happy now?"

"Yes. You can even consider this a selfish ask if it makes you feel better."

"How so?"

"How can you look after me if you're injured or worse?"

"Ah, so not really concerned about my safety."

Taking her by the waist, I pulled her forward until she clumsily straddled me. Face-to-face, I welcomed the weight of her body. Her dark, expressive eyes bore into mine, pupils dilated. The slight parting of her lips, the gentle strokes of her fingers, all micro actions that I cataloged, and each one let me know her feelings for me were as real as mine for her. The dull ache that had been with me since our failed date was replaced with peace and lightheartedness.

I fisted her shirt, pulling her closer to me. "I'm extremely concerned about every millimeter of you."

Dijah placed her hands on my face and rocked her hips forward. She'd been a distraction over the past week, and I knew if we had any chance of trying to make it work, I'd need to get a better handle on my irritation in the long run. This was new territory for me. However, I truly felt like we'd reached an understanding tonight that would make moving forward much easier.

"Since I'm unable to leave, whatever will we do all night?"

Slowly I slid my hands from her waist down to her ass. "I thought we were watching a movie."

Dijah placed a quick kiss to my lips. "Oh, right."

She gave me another quick kiss before she shifted to settle beside me again, curled up. Our hands seemed to find their way to the other. Our fingers danced and played with gentle squeezes, light strokes, tiny ways to be connected as we watched the movie.

When it got to the scene where Evey catches V watching *The Count of Monte Cristo*, I waited to see if Dijah would pick up on the fact our conversation had been similar, but the scene passed with no recognition from her.

As the credits started rolling, Dijah sat up. "That's your comfort movie?"

I couldn't tell if the disbelief in her voice was a good or a negative.

"Yeah, why?"

She shrugged. "It's just, it was kinda heavy, the commentary. With your personality, I figured you'd like something lighter. More fun-hearted."

"I don't think *fun-hearted* is a word," I replied with a slight laugh. "But I'm more an action movie woman. That ending fight scene is my shit."

She nodded. "Yeah…yeah, that was pretty badass. And I enjoyed the film."

"Okay, good. I can keep you around then."

She frowned. "Oh, I didn't realize that was some sort of test."

"Nah, not a test, but it would make me side eye your bad taste in movies if you didn't like it."

"Is that so?"

I stood and stretched. "One hundred percent."

Dijah slid from the couch to start cleaning up. "Is there a list of your own I need to know about?" She glanced back over her shoulder at me.

"Nah. I'm making it up as I go. Keeping you on your toes and such."

I picked up the plastic bag and stray utensil wrappers. Dijah held the leftovers and our plates.

"Well, it's a good thing that I'm a woman who likes surprises."

Slowly, I tilted my head to the side. "You are a walking contradiction."

She followed me to the kitchen. "How so?"

Turning back, I narrowed my eyes at her. A playful grin graced her full, kissable lips.

"Just because I like a good outline doesn't mean I can't also enjoy a surprise."

"Like I said, a walking contradiction."

She made a noncommittal noise as she finished scraping the uneaten food into the trash. Together we made quick work of cleaning up. I dug into my pocket to pull out her keys.

I tossed them in my hand a few times. "You can have these back."

I held them out to her, and she stared at them for a few seconds before making eye contact with me.

"It's a little after midnight, but when you said you'd kick me out in the morning, I thought the sun would at least be up."

She reached out to take her keys, pulling her upper lip between her teeth. The disappointment crystal clear. Slowly, I inched forward, closing the small space between us, and slid my hands around her waist.

"I'm not kicking you out, Dijah. I'm giving you the option."

I slipped my hands under her shirt to let my fingers glide across her warm skin. She shuddered under my touch.

"If you want to stay, I'll happily kick you out when the sun comes up. If you want to leave, I'll walk you down to your car."

Dijah craned her neck back to look up at me, the keys still jingling in her hand. With eyes locked on mine, she slowly slid them back into my pocket.

She stretched up onto her tiptoes and pressed her lips to my neck. The slight contact sent a shiver down my spine. "I'll take option one please."

The lustful sparkle in her eye was a teasing promise to pick up where we left off earlier.

"Option one it is."

I linked our fingers, turning off the lights as I led us down the hallway toward my bedroom. *My bedroom...* I was taking her to my bedroom. Protecting my space, my home, and privacy as much as I could was important to me. Yet I'd allowed her in, hadn't sent her away, and was excited to share my bed with her.

# Thirty-One

## Khadijah

We'd been here before, but something about this time was different. Gone were those worries, those fears of what could go wrong. Instead, I was basking in the warmth of everything being right. Shae paused after we crossed the threshold. Before I could ask her anything, she cupped my face and pressed her mouth to mine. Her kisses were seared into my brain. Tiny tethers to my soul, each one left a lingering effect that made me crave more. Crave her. I had an unexplained urge to chase after the freedom…the possibilities of being with Shae. Her belief in me…in us, made the rules not so important.

As our tongues did the familiar dance, I gripped the sides of her shirt, needing an anchor because I was certain I'd float away. The low moans mingling in the air left me unsure if the sounds came from me or her. She was the yin to my yang. The chaos to my order. And that fact had me in a tailspin, unsure of what was what, or if I really wanted to figure it out.

When Shae pulled away, the soft glimmer in her eyes made it hard to take in a full breath. Was my heart running full steam ahead with emotions my brain refused to process? In the moment, with the erratic beating in my chest, it certainly seemed that way.

She hadn't written me off despite my inconsistent and stand-offish behaviors. She'd been honest in her wants, never wavering, and she'd woken up the part of me that longed for the type of relationships I was surrounded by. The figurative duct tape I'd used to keep those dreams locked down had been ripped away.

"You good?" Shae asked, rubbing her thumb side to side on my chin.

I wrapped my fingers around her wrist and nodded. Diverting my attention from her intense stare, I glanced around her room. The walls were a soft sage green, which made the space feel calm. A large king-sized bed was the focal point. The cream-toned upholstered headboard reminded me of a Queen Anne chair. It, like the living room, was welcoming, comforting, relaxed, like her.

Shae's movement pulled my attention. I refrained from trying to peek into the drawer she'd opened to see how organized it was. I knew both Jah and Nikki would roll their eyes that I'd even had the thought.

"I'm going to need clothes?" I asked, gently taking the T-shirt she held out toward me.

"Need? Not really, but again, options."

I bit the inside of my cheek and let my gaze travel the length of her body. I knew she was braless beneath her formfitting cami. And I'd spent the last few hours trying not to focus too much on how short her shorts were, leaving much of her long legs exposed. Shae commanded my attention no matter what, but the memories of being skin-to-skin with her...

"Is sex on or off the table tonight?"

"I don't know. You're the one with the checklist." There was a trace of humor in her tone.

We'd not finalized anything and a real discussion about it needed to be had, but later.

I tossed the shirt she'd given me onto the bed. "Would you like the amended timeline in writing?" I asked the question while unbuttoning my blouse.

Shae took a seat on the bed, resting back on her elbows. "Verbal is good for tonight, but feel free to send the update later."

Her legs hung over the edge as she nonchalantly watched me undress.

"You're sitting there as if you're expecting some sort of show."

Her signature lazy, lopsided grin kicked up the side of her mouth. "I mean, I'm not going to turn one down."

She'd seen me naked, but something about stripping in front of her—for her—set off a thrill in me. As eager as I was to have sex with her, I now wanted to take my time. To entice her.

I kept my eyes on her, slowing my actions. Shae tilted her head, but didn't break eye contact. The top three buttons of my shirt were undone, allowing a peek of my light pink bra. Music would have been nice, but I focused on the rhythmic pulse of my breathing to set a beat. Up and down, I stroked my skin, opening the flaps of my shirt wider, but not too much, just enough to tease her. The responding groan emboldened me.

Another button released. Shae sat up from her relaxed position, giving me her full attention. Her nipples were pressed against the thin fabric of her cami. I felt my own restrained behind the lace of my bra. Closing my eyes, I rocked my hips side to side, remembering how Shae's body had moved with mine the night at the club. Perfectly in sync, as if we'd danced together hundreds of times before.

The final two buttons undone, and I imagined it was her hands sliding up my body to cup my breasts instead of my own. My skin was heated, and my breathing changed the beat in my head. Moans accompanied the tune when I pinched my nipples. The slight pressure added to the heaviness between my legs.

I rolled my tongue along my bottom lip, pulling forth the tingling feelings from when she'd kissed me. God, her mouth was magic, even when it wasn't on me. She was magic. Shae got me out of my head and forced me to act on my wants, my feelings, instead of the logic that ruled me. I leaned into those feelings and gave them free rein as I eased my shirt off, letting it drop silently to the floor.

"The bra." Her soft command sounded strange, like her voice was strained.

My eyes fluttered open to find Shae with her legs wide, hand in her shorts, her intense gaze fixated on me. There was something about her touching herself while watching me strip. An erotic intimacy. The awareness of what my actions were doing to her encouraged me. I removed my bra, baring my chest to her.

"Mmm, yes," she murmured.

The dance forgotten, I desired to reveal all to Shae and witness her coming apart because of it. I clenched my pussy in a vain attempt to alleviate the growing tingling between my legs.

Maintaining eye contact, I squeezed my breasts together, lifting them to my mouth. Shae groaned when I flicked my tongue across one of my hard nipples and then the other. I repeated the action, this time drawing one into my mouth and sucking.

"Fuck, yes, do that again." Shae fell back, propping herself up on one elbow, legs spread wider, and the hand in her underwear moved faster.

Her voice was husky, causing me to shift side to side against the new wave of need pulsing between my legs. Slower this time, I circled my tongue around my nipple, remembering her treatment, then groaning around it when I pulled it into my mouth. The sensations pushed at my steadily building desire.

"Pants. I need to see the rest of you."

Her voice, a little breathless, and heavy with lust, eyes darkened with desire. I wanted to give her everything she asked for and more. Somehow, I managed to make my legs work and I moved closer to the bed, to her, unbuttoning my slacks as I went. With each step, the wetness in my panties made itself known.

I stopped in front of her and hooked my thumbs into my waistband, inching down the remaining barriers shielding me from her view. Shae licked her lips, her eyes focused on the apex of my legs as I revealed my pussy to her. I feared touching her, because I wasn't sure that once I made contact I'd be able to stop.

Reaching forward, I gingerly wrapped my fingers around the top of her shorts—electric shocks buzzed as I made the lightest contact with her skin.

"You aren't the only one who wants a show."

Shae nodded as she lifted her hips, aiding in the removal of her bottoms. I licked my lips at the sight of her wet and glistening.

She made a V with her fingers, spreading herself wider for my viewing pleasure. "See something you like?"

I nodded, crawling onto the bed. "Do you?"

She slid back, making room for me. "Hell yeah."

Lowering on top of her, I slowly traced my fingertips along her collarbone, then followed the path with my mouth. I shivered from the soft up and down motions of Shae's fingers. Her touch awakened the hope of possibilities and I'd been a fool to try to run from it...from her.

Shae wedged her thigh between my legs, gripping my ass to pull me closer. I mimicked her action, pulling a moan from her lips. The movement started easy, an unhurried back-and-forth of our hips. I continued kissing her neck as I inched my hand down to squeeze her firm breast, rolling her nipple between my thumb and forefinger. Her wetness coated my leg and I wanted more.

"Kiss me."

Without hesitation, I complied with her request. I wanted to drown in the ocean of pleasure that was Shae Harris. My body yearned to be connected to her in every way. We moaned in unison, our mouths and tongues moving at the same frenzied pace as our bodies.

Faster we moved until we both cried out in breathy grunts and groans. Her fingers dug into my flesh, holding me to her while I enjoyed the feel of her body shaking against me as my own twitched with satisfaction. I rested my head on her shoulder, both of us breathing heavily before I finally rolled to the side. I was spent, yet complete. The hole that had been in the center of my life, the missing puzzle piece, had been found.

# Thirty-Two

## Shae

"What are you doing?" Courtney asked, craning her neck to see what I was writing.

"Contract negotiations."

She snatched up the notepad before I finished writing my sentence. "What? Where the hell you going?"

I grabbed for it, but she kept it out of reach. "Bitch, give that back."

The flight attendant looked at us both, as did Renee and Tina, who were in the seats across the aisle.

"What in the hell?" Courtney said as she continued to be nosy as fuck and read through what I had. "What is all this?"

It was my fault for doing the shit on the plane, but since I had five hours to kill, it seemed like a good idea.

"None of your damn business," I said, finally getting my notepad back.

"That about you and Doc?"

"What part of nun-ya didn't you get?" I shot her a side glance knowing damn well she wouldn't be deterred.

Khadijah hadn't brought it back up, saying she wanted me to focus on the games, but it had been in the back of my mind since she'd shown up at my house. For someone who didn't know shit about sports, she suddenly became an expert, fussing at me about keeping my head clear since we were down two games to one and we needed a win to force game five. I had to admit it was rather sexy as she worked to hit all the right buzzwords for her pep talk.

We'd gotten it together and squeaked out a win. The team was back to playing like we were a unit even if I harbored a tiny bit of guilt for throwing us out of sync. It'd also helped my mood that I'd convinced Khadijah to stay with me the last few nights. Having her at my house made home so much better even with her clingy ways while sleeping. It was a minor sacrifice I was willing to make.

Courtney leaned toward me and lowered her voice. "Seriously, Shae, what is that all about?"

I rested back against my seat. "Told you."

"Yeah, but what the hell does that mean? I thought you and Doc were all good."

I rolled my head to the side to look at her. "We are. I promise. This..." I waved my hand over the now-closed notepad. "Is just a thing. Nothing major. We're ironing out some details."

"Uh-huh. You know what, whatever works for y'all. I'm just glad your ass ain't mopey no more. Now we can kick Seattle's ass in this final game then move on to the championship and take that too."

We did a couple of hand claps. "Aye, that's the shit, for real."

I wasn't normally one to count my chickens before they hatched per se, but it was a damn good feeling to be in contention for the title after the last few rough seasons.

"But seriously, I'm glad to see you back to you, only upgraded."

"The fuck you mean upgraded?"

She again leaned closer, but this time sniffed dramatically. "That's that new love smell. I remember those days."

I shoved her, but couldn't deny it. I'd let Khadijah get to know me, let her in. I'd wanted her to see me and she had. Even if the season didn't end as I held out hope it would, being with Khadijah still made it a major win in my book.

"It might be a good thing," Courtney said after a moment.

"What?"

"Whatever contract negotiations you two are doing. Talking shit out and all. Beforehand."

"This is all Dijah. You know me, I would deal with shit as it came or would move on. But, I mean, some of her points do make me think."

"I probably should have done that." There was something in her tone that drew my attention. My friend rested back against her seat as she let out a heavy sigh.

"You good?" It wasn't a conversation to have in such tight quarters, but the mood shift had me concerned.

She nodded and scrubbed her hands down her face, figuratively wiping away whatever it was.

As I'd spent real time looking over the PDF Dijah had sent, some of it was still too rigid and over-the-top, but other stuff she had listed made sense. Especially knowing the fights Courtney and Sasha had about kids of late. That was a topic

I honestly had not given any thought to. Same with views on how to handle finances. Both could be sticking points in a relationship, and knowing that made me appreciate Dijah's overly logical checklist.

Once at the hotel, I was ready for a hot shower, food, then sleep. Travel days sucked, but I was thankful each away trip this season had a built-in rest day before we played. It was a vast improvement over past seasons when we'd arrived in the morning and been scheduled to play that same evening. I debated waiting in the lobby for Khadijah to finish talking with the coaches, but opted to text her instead.

We're in room 1204

"I'm starving," Tina said as we waited for the elevator.

"When are you not starving?" I laughed in response.

"After I've eaten."

Her answer only made me laugh harder. "I hear you. Thirty, forty minutes back in the lobby?"

"Sounds good," Courtney answered for them both.

My phone chimed: We?

Yes, we as in you + me = we. Problem?

The typing dots showed, stopped, then showed again.

"You let Doc know?" Tina asked.

I nodded, still waiting on a reply that never happened. When I got to my room, I dropped my bag onto the bed. I decided I wouldn't stress even if her lack of response bugged me. Like before, no one made any real comment about me and Khadijah even though I was sure they were all aware whatever issue we had was now worked out. Most acknowledgments were vague "glad to have you back" type of statements.

A knock at my door sounded as I set things up in the bathroom. I took a quick look out the peephole before opening to a frowning Khadijah.

"So, you just decided I was sharing a room with you?"

"Sure did. Like I said, is that a problem?"

She wheeled her suitcase across the threshold, and I shut the door behind her. "Maybe. You need to rest before tomorrow night." A slow, sexy grin spread across her face.

I slid my arms around her waist, bringing her body flush with mine. "You're saying you can't keep your hands off me?"

She glanced down at where I held her, then back up at me. "Who can't keep their hands off who?" She arched a brow and twisted her delectable lips into a smirk, but even as she spoke, she worked her hands under my shirt, pressing her warm palms against my back.

"Coach said I'm supposed to keep doing what's working since my mojo is back. And since I've been doing you…you don't want to be responsible for throwing my game off again, right?"

"Oh, is that a guilt trip, or blackmail?"

I leaned down to kiss her. "Definitely a guilt trip. Is it working?"

She planted another quick kiss to my lips and nodded. "And I'm sorry—"

"We're good. Really, I was joking because I would like for you to stay with me. No other reason."

Falling asleep next to her, even with her need to cuddle, was the best feeling. I didn't even bother to tell her I wasn't a fan of the close contact while sleeping. Honestly, I was starting to get used to it. She released an audible sigh and nodded again.

"Besides, we have negotiations to discuss. I made a list of things on the plane."

Dijah furrowed her brow. "I told you we could deal with that after the season was over."

I reluctantly pulled from our embrace to get my notepad. "I know. But I had time."

She sat on the edge of the bed and I joined her. "I meant it when I said I would take your need to plan seriously." I handed her the notepad. "Honestly, Dijah, my biggest issue is the timelines."

"How so?"

"Having to do certain things by some arbitrary date kills the spontaneity for me. Especially the fact you want to wait six months before your parents know of my existence."

That one had been a major shocker and fed into the previous feelings I'd had about being some sort of dirty secret.

She ran her fingers over the circles I'd made about that point. "I can tell. Some of these were general points, not personalized for you, or us. Since my past relationships seemed to fall apart before the six-month mark, I made that the number that meant it was real."

I digested her explanation and from that viewpoint I could see why she'd have that rule. "Well, then question. When would our clock have started?"

"What do you mean?"

"We've known each other for nearly six months. But if we're only considering the dating aspect then we're not even at a week? So, which is it? Because honestly, you basically hiding me, us, even for the reason you explained, it is a sore spot. I know I don't like bringing up my own dating past, but when others couldn't wait to name-drop me when we were together, it bugs me that I want to shout from the rooftops about the woman I'm with, and she wants to stay mum. Not to mention I've introduced you to everyone that matters to me except my brothers, but they know about you."

She put the pad down then took my hands into hers. "Depending on tomorrow's game outcome, our schedule is going to be packed for the next week. But as soon as we have proper downtime, I will happily introduce you to my parents. Like I said, it wasn't about you, directly. It was one hundred percent a me thing." She placed her hands on either side of my face before she spoke her next words. "I'm in this, and I don't want you doubting that."

The conviction in her delivery soothed the lingering worries. "I don't need a full introduction, just for them to know I exist." I figured that was a fair compromise so we were still within her comfort zone.

Khadijah gave me another quick kiss. "Deal. Look at you, negotiating without your agent." The playful grin on her face made me want to skip dinner and feast on her instead.

"I'm pretty sure she would appreciate me not bringing her in on this. Though she'd probably get a kick out of it." I stood and held my hand out for her. "We have dinner plans or Tina might hulk out if she goes too long without food."

"Then us showering together is probably not advisable."

"Eh… I wouldn't say that. Oh, one other thing about your checklist."

"What?"

"There was no set date on when I'm allowed to say I love you."

It was a realization I'd come to when I'd tried to truly understand why she'd affected me so much. Why her pseudo-rejection of me had stung so deeply.

Dijah widened her eyes and pulled in a quick breath. "Um... I'm not sure I included that. Should I do another amendment?"

I shook my head. "Nope, I think that falls under one of those things that can't be a checklist item. It has to be solely when the moment is right."

"And is it? The moment, being right?" Her tone was soft as she stared at me with those dark, mesmerizing eyes that had drawn me in the first night.

"Yeah, it is."

She slipped her arms around my neck and stretched up on her toes. "I think I'd have to agree. No lists, no planning." She kissed my neck, then my chin, and finally my lips. "You have turned me into a Shae Harris fan, and I love you."

I walked us backward toward the shower, our mouths tangled in a passionate kiss as we became a mess of limbs and desperation to get our clothes off. Being able to call Khadijah Upton mine was the win of a lifetime.

# Thirty-Three

## Khadijah

The ringing of my phone broke through the sleep. I disentangled myself from Shae to quiet the offending device. "'Ello."

"It's happening. Vance called, they are at the hospital. Your sister's in labor." Mom's voice was an odd mix of frantic yet calm.

Her words made me shoot up and the heavy sleep fog cleared. "Oh, shit. Now. Um, okay." I glanced at the clock. "I can be there in like thirty, thirty-five minutes."

"No, you shouldn't come, you have to travel tomorrow, but I knew you would want to know. Your dad and I are leaving the house now."

"It'll be fine, Mom. I'll come and if things take too long then I'll leave, but I have to at least be there for support."

"What's happening? Is everything okay?" Shae's groggy voice got my attention.

I pressed my phone to my shoulder. "It's Jah, she's in labor."

Shae nodded while rubbing her hands down her face before she climbed out of bed. In the low light streaming in from the cracks of her curtains, I watched as she looked around for a bit before picking up her clothes and started to get dressed.

"What are you doing?"

"I'm assuming you're heading to the hospital."

"Khadijah? Khadijah, you there?"

The muffled sound of my mother pulled me from my daze. "Um, yeah. Sorry. I'll be there soon."

I'd told Shae I'd let my parents know of her existence at the very least, but with everything going on since we'd moved on to the finals, I hadn't had a chance to talk to them. I'd wanted it to be an in-person conversation, so showing up with Shae in tow at three in the morning would raise some questions. Lots of questions, at not the best time.

But I was all in with her and us. It still haunted me I'd made her feel as if I was ashamed of her or being with her. Proving I wasn't meant my actions needed to match my words now more than ever.

"You leavin'?" she asked.

I nodded. "Yeah. You don't have to get up."

"Do you want me to stay?"

I quickly shook my head. "No. I want you to get your rest because we fly out tomorrow, or, well, later today, and then *the* final game. I don't want you tired."

She strolled over to me, tugging me gently into her arms. "I get it, me popping up at the hospital is probably more intrusive than inviting myself to family brunch. I'll hang back. I just want to support you."

This beautiful, loving woman had nothing but truth and

sincerity in her eyes and my heart ached with happiness. It'd been a roller coaster of emotions and adjustments, but I'd come out a lucky woman at the end. Mutual respect and learning to understand each other's needs made a major difference.

"I appreciate that. And no, I don't want you to stay here. But when we get to Phoenix it will be only sleeping or I'm rooming with Marni."

Shae narrowed her eyes at me. "That's fine. I'll room with Marni too, it'll be a slumber party."

"You wouldn't dare."

"Try me."

We had a brief stare down and I knew the competitive side of her would absolutely try to pull some nonsense like bunking in the same room. I wouldn't admit that sleeping without her wasn't something I wanted either. We hadn't spent the night apart since I'd shown up at her place.

Being at her condo had become our preferred location, especially for me, knowing how fiercely she protected her personal space. The fact she not only allowed me but wanted me at her sanctum meant the world. And I was starting to have an equal preference for her king over my queen.

When we arrived at the hospital, I found both my parents sitting in the waiting room on the labor and delivery floor. My heart rate spiked when Mom's eyes shifted from me, over to Shae, and back to me again.

"I told you, you didn't have to come." Mom again shifted her eyes to Shae, as did Dad when he stepped behind Mom, resting his hands on her shoulders.

"I know, but our flight isn't until one and we don't have to be at the arena 'til ten thirty."

"We?"

"Yes. Mom, Dad, meet Shae. She's a player for the Cannons and my girlfriend."

Saying that last word felt foreign on my tongue, yet rolled off easily. Too easily. Like with most things concerning Shae.

Mom gave me her all-knowing "mom smile" before extending a hand toward Shae. "Nice to meet you."

Dad also greeted Shae. I was an adult, but something about my parents getting unrefuted evidence I'd been in bed with someone had me feeling like a teenager getting caught. But considering the fact we were at the hospital because my sister was about to give birth, it probably wasn't as embarrassing as it seemed.

"How is she?"

"Good. She was getting the epidural when we left. Should be able to go see her in a few minutes. Vance will come out to let us know."

We sat to wait for Vance and I braced for any incoming questions my parents might have about Shae and I. However, to my surprise, the only inquiries were from Dad about the season, a season he had apparently been watching and keeping up with without saying a word to me.

"Dad, I had no idea you even watched WNBA games."

He shrugged. "I hadn't until you got the job and I decided to check it out, but then I got hooked."

"If you had said something, I would have gotten you tickets."

"Next season." He cut his gaze to Shae. "And I guess I know whose jersey to wear."

Before either Shae or I could comment, Vance entered.

"She's all set." He shifted his attention to me and Shae. "Hey, Dijah. And you're Shae Harris. I've been watching your games with Ben. And, well, my wife has mentioned you a time or two." He cut his eyes back over at me.

I never doubted my family would be welcoming to Shae, but it remained surreal to witness the laidback interaction after I showed up at three in the morning with a woman they hadn't met in tow. A woman they—or at least my father and brother-in-law—knew, since they were apparently undercover Cannons fans.

My hang-ups had almost cost me one of the most amazing women I'd ever crossed paths with. Every moment I'd spent with her solidified the fact, and reminded me of what I could have lost, and of how happy and calm I'd been ever since I'd apologized. She'd been right—some things can't be controlled by a checklist, matters of the heart being one of them.

Sadly, Jah's labor was slower going than she would have liked, which unfortunately gave her plenty of time for a well-placed "I told you so" when she saw Shae had joined me at the hospital. But it also meant I wouldn't be there for my nephew's birth since we had a plane to catch for game five of the finals. However, by the time we landed, I had a flurry of messages and pictures. Ones I couldn't wait to show to Shae. She truly was part of my life, and I wouldn't have it any other way.

My leg bounced uncontrollably, and my heart was in my throat. The weight of tonight's game had my stomach churning all day. Was this what it meant to be a fan? To be invested in a sport? Because if so, I wasn't sure I liked the feeling. The stress and worry of it all. Being scared of a possible disappointing loss after watching the team work so hard all season.

The entire game…hell, the entire day, had me feeling like I was on a roller coaster, frozen in time at that half-second pause before the first drop hit. How did people live like this? But I cared, I cared a hell of a lot about the outcome. About what it meant to the Cannons as a whole and how much Shae wanted this win. To finally achieve the status that all professional players chase during their careers. To be called champion.

"I think I'm going to puke," I yelled to Marni, who simply smiled and nodded.

Everyone was on their feet. Phoenix was the fourth-ranked team this season and the Cannons were the underdogs, ranked seventh. They'd barely made the cutoff for the playoffs in general and everyone had counted them out, an easy one-two-three loss, yet like with the semis they'd fought hard and forced a full five games.

Nina sank a three and the Cannons on the sidelines erupted in cheers, swinging their towels over their heads. Their lead was up by five; they really had a chance to win. I shot to my feet and grabbed Marni's hand. My mouth went dry as the Phoenix player tried to answer Nina's three with one of her own. My heart rate spiked when it hit the rim but didn't go in. However, one of the other ladies tipped it in for two.

*Please, oh, please let them win. They have to win.*

There was a minor scuffle for the ball, with Shae hitting the floor but maintaining control. The refs blew the whistle and gave possession to the Cannons. I couldn't hear anything over the whooshing in my ears and the pounding of my heart. It was a few seconds before I became aware of the sound of the buzzer going off and the cheers ringing out around me. Marni wrapped her arms around me jumping.

*They'd won.*

*They'd won!*

There was pandemonium on the court as the players and other coaches rushed forward, including Marni, who left me standing in front of my seat stunned. I knew I needed to head to the locker room to prepare, but I stayed, mesmerized by the scene playing out. So much excitement. I'd always wondered where the T-shirts and hats came from at the end of these sort of events, and even being part of it, I still wasn't sure where they'd materialized from, but the team was already decked out in them.

I made my way toward the court instead of the locker room, scanning the crowd looking for Shae. She stood, all smiles, talking with a reporter. I laughed as some of the players photo-bombed whatever interview she was doing. A hat was placed on my head, and I was being pushed forward. I looked back to see Courtney.

"What are you doing?"

"We're celebrating, Doc, and you are part of this."

"But she's talking." I desperately wanted to congratulate Shae, but I didn't want to intrude.

She saw us approach and her smile got bigger. She was stunning in her joy, which made my stomach do flips. Courtney practically jumped on Shae with the two of them laughing. Courtney took over the interview, which gave me the opportunity to approach.

Enthusiasm and delight radiated off Shae and I'd never been so proud for someone as I was for her in this moment. I threw my arms around her neck. "Congrats! I'm so happy for you."

She hugged me tight, and being in her embrace quieted the chaos going on around us.

"That was intense, and all I did was watch. Sporting is stressful."

Her entire body shook when she laughed. "I know the perfect way to work off all that stressful energy."

"This is your big moment, and that's what you're thinking about?"

"My big moment happened the day you showed up at my house. This is a bonus."

Her words squeezed my heart. I placed my hands on her heated face and kissed her quickly, getting lost in the moment until we were both doused with something, making us jump apart. Champagne, and Tina and Sonya were laughing their asses off as they continued to point the bottles at us.

"You know, we might have been caught on camera," Shae said, after stealing another kiss.

The clicking around us finally registered with me as I remembered what was going on. I smiled up at her before again wrapping my arms around her neck.

"Well, you said you wanted me to shout it from the rooftops, so better make sure they get a good shot." I stretched up to kiss her again.

★ ★ ★ ★ ★

# Acknowledgments

When I started writing, I never imagined I'd be a Harlequin author. I am thankful to everyone that helped me get to this place. My editor, John Jacobson, for seeing the potential in this story and supporting it from day one. I appreciate the transparency and willingness to answer all my random questions as I navigate the waters of traditional publishing.

My leveling up as an author would not have been possible without Tasha L. Harrison and the Wordmaker group she created. Having that space to grow and receive constant encouragement and support has been a real game changer! Thank you to all of the Wordmakers!!

Rae Shawn, Karmen Lee, D. Ann Williams… y'all know. When I don't think I can, y'all stay ready with the "bitch please" to remind me I indeed can and will. The tough love is needed and always gets me through.

This is a sports romance and I'm not sporty, so big shout out to Jessica Terry for giving me the insights needed to make sure that those aspects of the story did what they needed to do.

Major appreciation and thanks to my family for all the love and support of this dream. Additional shoutout to my adorable "writing assistant" Agent Chaos, your baby cuddles are always a great pick-me-up.

Shoutout to my OG emotional support writers Coralie Moss and Lily Michaels, glad we can still share the highs and lows of this job we voluntarily decided to do. A thank you to all the hardworking people at Afterglow Books that worked to get Love & Sportsball into the readers' hands.

And lastly, Bob Ross and his Joy Of Painting series. For background noise, the gentle nature of the show was calming and as a pantser I related because it starts with a blank 'canvas,' and a vague idea and then let the creativity take over. It's all "happy accidents."